The Vatican Betrayal

NICHOLAS SPRATT

spratt.n.e@gmail.com

ISBN: 978-988-16709-2-2

Physical Edition: August 2012

To Miji and Mekon with love, and to the Meldorian Six, without whom my imagination would never have got the exercise it needed.

PROLOGUE

The scruffy, gray haired cartographer looked up from the mural he was examining and checked his watch. It was about ten o'clock at night. The curator of the Doge's Palace had kindly given him permission to work at night, so as to minimize the impact on the museum's tourists. But despite how late it was, the cartographer could hear footsteps climbing the stairs leading up to the map room door. *Who on earth was climbing the golden staircase at this time of night?*

For over three hundred years, the Doge of Venice had granted audiences and received guests in the Palace's map room. It was one of the Palace's largest rooms, stretching the entire width of the east wing. The room was decorated with fine wood panelling up to the height of an adult. Above the panelling, large maps were painted directly on to the walls. The maps illustrated all of the lands and seas known to the Venetians of the fifteenth century. They showed Venice's foreign colonies and the trading routes used by Venetian merchants - the source of the city's power and wealth.

The cartographer returned his attention to the map he was studying. He stood on a temporary scaffold that had been assembled to raise him and his equipment to the height of the murals. Satisfied that he knew what needed to be photographed next, he pressed his trembling hand into a sore knee and knelt down behind the tripod.

"The cold is playing havoc with my arthritis," he grumbled. But to heat the room was strictly forbidden because it would endanger the priceless paintings. He refocused the camera, squeezed the trigger, and then squinted at the small screen on the back of the camera showing the picture he had just taken. It should have been a detailed photo of the map of the Americas. But cursing his poor eyesight, he instead detached the camera from its tripod, and struggled to his feet. The scaffolding groaned under his weight as he began descending the steps, heading back toward his desk to analyze the image on his laptop.

The footsteps on the staircase grew steadily louder. From behind his desk, the cartographer stopped typing and peered at the map room door over the rim of his glasses, his face bathed in the anemic blue light of the laptop's monitor. The footsteps approached the door and stopped. The cartographer sighed irritably. There was still a lot of work to get through, in only the short amount of time that the curator had given him access to the map room. *And another interruption from the security guard was only going to make matters worse.*

There was a sharp knock on the door.

"Doctor Chan?" inquired a deep, deliberate voice. "May we come in?"

But before Doctor Chan could answer, the door was pushed open. A slightly built man, perhaps fifty years old, entered the map room. The visitor wore a smart white suit, a black shirt, and a well groomed gray beard outlining a weathered, angular face. On the lapel of his suit he wore a small silver pin – a crucifix bordered by a branch on one side and a sword on the other.

A moment later, an identically dressed, but younger and

much larger man lumbered into the room. The younger of the two visitors walked awkwardly, as though he was self-conscious of his enormous bulk. He wore a shaved head and was far taller than his older companion, even despite a pronounced stoop that looked to Doctor Chan to be caused by the weight of his muscular shoulders and his thick trunk of a neck.

The elder of the two visitors approached the desk at which Doctor Chan was working. He walked with a faint suggestion of a limp and the aid of a brushed aluminum cane. It was as though the cane was no longer necessary, but it was either an acquired habit or a reminder of an injury he had once suffered. The younger of the two visitors followed at a respectful distance.

"Can I help you?" asked Doctor Chan, struggling to remember his Italian.

The visitor smiled wanly. "I do hope so Doctor Chan, for all our sakes."

"Excuse me," stuttered Doctor Chan, furrowing his brow and confused that the visitor knew his name. "Have we met before?"

"No, but you have made yourself known to my superiors." The visitor paused, staring expectantly at Doctor Chan. "Your demands of our archivist were indelicate…" He paused again, studying Doctor Chan intently, "…and most provocative."

"Are you with the university's research council?" asked Doctor Chan, searching for an explanation for the intrusion. "Did we meet at the Chancellor's fund raising dinner?"

The visitor exhaled impatiently. "My superiors do not take kindly to blackmail Doctor Chan. But…" The visitor switched to a more conciliatory tone of voice. "I have assured them that there has been a misunderstanding. A miscommunication perhaps?" The visitor raised an eyebrow and forced an awkward, questioning smile. "A miscommunication, that you Doctor Chan, can easily resolve."

Doctor Chan rubbed his tired eyes, wishing that this latest interruption would go away. "Sorry I didn't catch your name?" Doctor Chan asked more gruffly than he had intended.

But the visitor ignored Doctor Chan's question and demanded in a harder tone, "So I ask you Doctor Chan, where is the *Proditio*?" The visitor waited.

"The what?" blurted Doctor Chan losing patience and shifting irritably in his chair. "I'm sorry. My Italian is passable. But Latin?... I've never studied Latin."

"Doctor Chan, I can understand that you're confused," said the visitor calmly. "Before this evening you had never met Brother Michael." He gestured to his younger colleague, "Nor have we ever met. You can't imagine how I could possibly know of your secret... or of your thinly veiled threats." The visitor smiled evilly. "You may even believe that we will be deceived by your feigned ignorance." The visitor's smile faded leaving only gritted teeth. "But know this Doctor Chan," he snarled, leaning menacingly over Doctor Chan's desk. "I have dealt with the godless before…"

Instinctively, Doctor Chan leant back in his chair and away from the visitor.

"…Heathen!" spat the visitor, with venomous distaste.

Doctor Chan sat motionless, his mouth half open, staring bewilderedly at the two visitors.

"Our Holy Father received, through the apostolic succession from Christ, supreme power over the Church. Not just in matters of faith and morals, but in matters of government... and discipline. It is divine revelation," shrugged the visitor, resigned to what he must do. "So while Doctor Chan, you might not let your soul be saved in the next world." A smile flickered across the visitor's face. "Rest assured that the Church will save itself in this one."

Doctor Chan could see red rising in the visitor's cheeks, his fist squeezing the cane tightly, as though struggling for control.

"So again I ask you, Doctor Chan, where is the *Proditio*?" But this time, as the visitor spoke, he retrieved a large, black leather wallet from his jacket pocket. The wallet was embossed with the same symbol that the visitor wore on his lapel pin - a crucifix surrounded by a branch and a sword. He slowly laid the wallet on the desk in front of Doctor Chan and unfolded it to reveal its contents.

Doctor Chan's eyes widened and flicked feverishly from the wallet to the now impassive visitor. Sweat broke out on his forehead.

"It is my experience Doctor Chan," continued the visitor in an increasingly detached voice, "that most people won't accept the seriousness of their situation... they can't comprehend the urgency with which their cooperation is required." As he spoke, the visitor removed a ten inch long, highly polished, steel cylinder from the wallet. It had a well-crafted, knurled handle about one inch in diameter at one end, which gradually tapered down to a two inch wide, finely chiselled blade at the other end. "Until that is," the visitor tested the blade with his thumb, "they lose the first digit." The visitor stared straight into Doctor Chan's terrified eyes. "Brother Michael," he ordered. "Hold his arm!"

CHAPTER 1

After leaving his hotel, San Lee paused for a moment to remove the lid from his coffee. He had grabbed some filter coffee to go, not having the appetite for a full breakfast. His gloved fingers fumbled with the lid in the bitter cold. The coffee was pleasantly warm and San sipped it greedily. It tasted awful. For coffee in Italy, it was criminally awful, thought San. But he drank it anyway. I haven't drunk this much coffee in years, San chided himself, but neither have I slept this badly. San was worried. *The negotiations last night had not gone well.*

San looked past the black lacquered gondolas moored along the edge of the Grand Canal. The gondolas bobbed slowly as the surf gently lapped the harbor wall. The blue tarpaulins covering the decks of the gondolas would not be removed until warmer weather ushered in another tourist season. Across the lagoon, San could see the brilliant white façade of the Church of San Giorgio Maggiore, shining in what little of the morning sun punctured the overcast skies. But he was too preoccupied to admire the view. *The client was probably very upset right now.*

San had been commissioned by his client to identify the

seller of a sculpture and negotiate its purchase before the piece was auctioned publicly. That was San's business - provenance research, and the location, care and purchase of high-end Asian art. Using his contacts at the British Museum, it had only taken a couple of weeks for him to identify the owner of the sculpture that his client was interested in buying. But the owner had been reluctant to meet, let alone negotiate a sale of the sculpture. *Still, one out of two, wasn't too bad.*

San drained the coffee and tossed the empty cup into a trash can. He drew his full length, leather jacket up around his neck to shield himself from the cold wind that whipped across the lagoon. At least the client has the resources to pay the additional costs of purchasing the piece at a public auction, he thought.

At auction San estimated that the sculpture would fetch ten million dollars at most. Any more than that and it would start eating into his buyer's commission. I desperately need to collect the commission from this job, thought San. *It's the only way that I will be able to pay off my father's debts.*

San didn't expect much competition for the piece from collectors or museums. After all, the bronze rat's head sculpture was incomplete and only two hundred and sixty years old. Neither was the sculpture of any significant artistic value, reasoned San.

Thrusting his hands deep into his warm pockets, San headed westward along the Riva degli Schiavoni toward the auction venue. The Riva degli Schiavoni was a broad promenade and had been Venice's main waterfront for centuries. Initially serving Slavic merchants arriving in Venice from the Adriatic Sea, it was now a favorite destination for tourists. As San passed, restaurateurs were setting up tables and chairs, and welcoming the day's first tourists with a suitably overpriced breakfast. Apprehensive ahead of the auction, San still didn't feel like eating. *Although a real macchiato would be nice.*

A few of the locals looked up as San passed. They didn't look because he was unusually handsome, although San was certainly presentable. He was well dressed, in tailored black pants and leather boots, and perhaps a little taller than average for an Asian man. The furrows in San's forehead and the slightest hint of white hair suggested seriousness rare of a man in his late thirties. His complexion was darker than average and easily confused for a heavy tan. But in Venice San was noticed because, although clearly a foreigner, he walked with a confident sense of purpose that was rare among what the locals expected to see - a camera-wielding tourist struggling to read a map.

His client's aversion to the publicity of a formal auction puzzled San. *Whoever the client might be?* He was accustomed to being commissioned by impersonal multinational corporations or the foundations supporting public galleries. But privacy was usually less of a priority for investors or art collectors. In fact, public exposure and the visitors it might attract to a gallery, was often precisely the reason why a gallery would purchase a high profile piece of art. But not for this client, thought San. His client's instructions were clear. Publicity was to be strictly avoided.

Purchasing art on behalf of a Chinese shell company that was averse to publicity, suggested to San an entirely different range of possibilities. The artwork might end up adorning a mistress's apartment in Hong Kong. It might be sold for cash to avoid China's tight currency controls. Or it could be used to bribe a local Communist Party secretary in return for a business favor. *Or it might be used for good old-fashioned money laundering.*

It wasn't long before San saw the auction venue appearing on the right, just one block closer to him than the entrance to St. Mark's Square. The auction was to be held in a fourteenth century palace which had been lovingly restored as the Hotel Danieli. Although one of the most famously opulent hotels in Venice, the five storey Hotel

Danieli had a modest red ochre façade. The only conspicuous details on the outside of the hotel were finely carved stone decorations around the windows. "And the mandatory green wooden shutters," grunted San, which seemed to decorate every building in Venice.

San trotted up to the entrance of the hotel, passed the two doormen, and into the revolving door. Very glad to be out of the cold, San passed the reception desk to a chorus of obligatory, "Buon giorno!" from the hotel staff. He crossed the atrium-lit lobby, looking up to admire the narrow, pink marble staircase twisting upwards toward the guest rooms. The staircase looked like one of Escher's lithographs, San mused.

On the left side of the lobby, a desk had been set up in the hotel's café area to welcome the auction participants. But San was early and there was not yet a queue at the registration desk. From his jacket pocket, he pulled out the invitation to the auction. After presenting his invitation and some photo ID, San collected his bidder's paddle and a copy of the catalog.

It was the political sensitivity of this auction that bothered San the most. The bronze rat's head sculpture that San had been commissioned to buy for his client had been part of the Haiyantang. More precisely, the sculpture had been the head of one of the twelve sculptures that had adorned the Haiyantang - one sculpture for each year of the Chinese zodiac. Built in 1759, the Haiyantang had been a large, water clock fountain in the gardens of the Qing Dynasty's Summer Palace, just outside Beijing. But the Summer Palace had been burnt down by British and French troops during the second opium war. The sculptures, or at least their heads, were seized as loot and taken back to Europe. There, over the centuries, the sculptures eventually passed into private collections. The Haiyantang bronze sculptures rarely came on to the market for sale. *It's not even certain where all of the other Haiyantang bronze sculptures are.*

But occasionally, when rich men died and their estates were auctioned, or when art collectors faced financial difficulty, the Haiyantang bronzes would be offered for sale. But those auctions would be frequently disrupted by angry protesters demanding the return of China's national treasures, San thought. *It's like China's equivalent of the Elgin marbles.*

In the past, prominent Chinese businessmen had purchased some of the Haiyantang bronze sculptures on the rare occasion that they became available. Once purchased, the businessmen would then, with great fanfare and publicity, donate them to China. Most likely they were hoping to win the favor of the Chinese political elite. *Or have past sins forgiven.*

San concluded that these political interests and sensitivities would deter as many bidders as they attract. But it was the increased unpredictability that worried him the most. The last thing San needed was to end up bidding against a corrupt billionaire who cared nothing for the artistic or historical value, but rather the political currency of the bronze rat's head sculpture.

CHAPTER 2

Agent Tao Ma paced the canal edge, searching for some reception on his cellphone. He looked underdressed for winter, wearing only a dark olive, trench coat over a simple gray suit and dusty black loafers. But he set his strong square jaw against the wind, unbothered by the cold, a permanent redness seemingly weather beaten into his cheeks. He ran a hand through his militarily close cut hair and scratched at the back of his neck, before lighting another cigarette, frustrated with his own inactivity.

It was humiliating to have to beg foreigners to sell back to China its own cultural heritage, Tao bristled. *Especially since the foreign vandals had stolen it in the first place.* Tao had suffered this humiliation personally. Every day for four years, he had walked past the ruins of the Old Summer Palace on his way to Beijing's prestigious University of International Relations. Built in the eighteenth century, the Old Summer Palace was once a residence of the Qing Dynasty Emperors, an immense garden filled with pavilions and artwork. Now, it was little more than faded stone rubble. So little of it remains, thought Tao. *Most tourists don't even bother to visit it.*

Having to use a half Taiwanese buyer was even less palatable, growled Tao, as he took another deep drag on his cigarette. French and British terrorists had burnt and looted the summer palace over two hundred years ago, well beyond the memory of anyone alive. But, the Taiwanese had stolen the contents of the Palace Museum in Beijing's Forbidden City only sixty years ago when the Kuomintang fled to Taiwan. So while the Forbidden City in Beijing stood embarrassingly empty, the National Palace Museum in Taiwan, just outside Taipei, was renowned for having the world's best collection of Chinese artifacts with over 700,000 pieces. *Where few patriots will ever see them.*

However, there were some very good reasons for choosing the Taiwanese buyer San Lee, thought Tao. He was well qualified, being a student of economics and history, and he had made the study of Asian art his career. He also had excellent references from satisfied customers in Japan, Korea, and China. But most importantly, San's family was deeply in debt and he needed to get this job done. *And that means our interests and incentives are aligned.*

Tao flicked the cigarette butt into the canal, before he sat down at one of the cafes along the canal edge and waved impatiently toward the waiter. After graduating from university, Tao had been recruited into the Ministry of State Security - China's secret service. Because he had studied international relations and languages at university, he had been fast tracked into field work. His first overseas posting was as an attaché to the Chinese embassy in Rome. This proximity to Venice had meant that Tao had been assigned the task of supervising the purchase of the Haiyantang bronze rat's head sculpture and ensuring its safe return to China. A chance to bring a part of the Old Summer Palace home, thought Tao wistfully. *Back to where it belongs.*

The complication that Tao had to manage was that China could not set a precedent of dealing with the owners of stolen Chinese art or antiques. *Quite apart from doubling the humiliation, it would triple the price!* But on the other hand, China valued the sculpture, and could not miss the opportunity to repurchase it. The sculpture's value lay neither in its historical significance, nor in its artistic merit. It was designed by Jesuits, thought Tao. *Foreigners of all people!* After centuries of humiliation at the hands of foreign aggressors, the Chinese leadership prized the propaganda value and the symbolic restoration of national pride that the return of such an artwork would embody. On a practical level, this meant that the sculpture had to be bought through an intermediary, with no obvious connection to mainland China. It was for this reason that he had hired San Lee to do the buying for them.

It was Tao's job to ensure this messy process went as smoothly as possible. Tao had been ordered to ensure that the bronze rat's head sculpture was returned to China without the Taiwanese buyer, let alone the foreign media, knowing of the Chinese government's involvement. To this end, Tao had set up a company registered in the British Virgin Islands with anonymous directors, through an off-shoring firm in Hong Kong. More than one of the banks in Macau had been happy to offer Tao an account in the company's name without having ever met the signatory. Tao would use this account to pay for the sculpture. A dummy website and its associated email addresses were used to communicate with the Taiwanese buyer. Money was no object, his superiors had told him. A little luxury of the Chinese economic miracle, smiled Tao. *And if we can avoid paying the Taiwanese buyer his commission, the Minister would be amused.*

But, Tao wished that the same economic miracle could have afforded his team slightly better accommodation. "Or at least closer to the auction," he grumbled. The academic advisors to China's National Treasure Fund, who Tao had to babysit, were all based in Murano, one of Venice's outer islands. Murano was at least fifteen minutes away from the auction venue by boat, a distance that compounded Tao's anxiety. It had been explained to Tao that having so many Chinese nationals located near the auction venue would risk drawing the attention of the media. The possibility that Tao might be identified as a government employee was a risk that his superiors were apparently not willing to take. But it was just as likely to be the mean spirited miserliness of a rigid hierarchy, he thought. *And not wanting to pay three hundred euro for a junior agent to spend a night at a hotel in the heart of Venice.*

CHAPTER 3

Inquisitor Jerome sat quietly by the open fireplace and massaged his tired fingers. After the evening's exertions, he had returned to the room that the senior Dominican bishop in Venice had arranged for him. It was a small, but comfortable apartment behind the Basilica di San Giovanni e Paolo, a short walk from St. Mark's Square. Like the Basilica to which it was joined, the apartment was an austere pink brick building. Utterly forgettable, thought Jerome, especially when compared to Venice's more famous landmarks. The room was furnished modestly with a small bed in the corner and a worn but comfortable grandfather chair facing the fireplace.

Jerome had initially felt pleased with himself. America's recent misadventures in the Middle East had diminished the respectability of enhanced interrogation techniques to some. And any fool can beat a confession out of someone, sneered Jerome disapprovingly. But the skill, no thought Jerome, the inquirer's art was the ability, amidst the blood, sweat and screaming, to separate the begrudgingly revealed slivers of truth from the incoherent babbling and desperate confession, of… *well just about anything.*

But, Jerome could not sleep. Instead, he sat motionless in the armchair and stared into the dying embers of the once warm fire.

"Toscanelli in St. Peter's," Jerome whispered to himself, mulling over what Doctor Chan had whimpered to him earlier. *What did it mean?* St. Peter's seemed a plausible location for the *Proditio,* he thought, and Doctor Chan had certainly not parted with the information easily. Jerome permitted himself a narrow smile. *Or willingly.* But he was still worried that he did not fully understand what Doctor Chan had meant. And until he did, Jerome was reluctant to report the information to the Prefect.

Some among the Roman Curia continued to make moral arguments against the Holy Office and their inquisitorial methods, grimaced Jerome, his back stiffening. *But there is no redemption without suffering.*

"Christ through his suffering and death reconciled us with God," quoted Jerome, nodding firmly. It is Di Fide - divinely infallible revelation. *To reject that, is the mortal sin of heresy.*

To Jerome, it was doctrinally obvious. "Did not Saint Augustine write that the responsible and just should not shrink from the necessities of torture and punishment?" He shrugged, before adding rhetorically. "Did not Aquinas write that the heretic deserves to be severed from the world by death?" *Our Holy Father taught us that God is always on the side of suffering?*

"Through your suffering, you will take part in Christ's salvation," Jerome whispered quietly to himself. I should know, he thought. *That's how I was saved.*

But while confident of his methods, Jerome was no closer to understanding his results. "Enough!" he snapped, losing patience with his inability to make sense of Doctor Chan's message. He picked up his phone from the small coffee table next to his chair. Jerome took a deep breath to compose himself, resigned to the call he had avoided for far too long.

Jerome did not resent the rigid hierarchy of which he was a part. Far from it, he thought. *Disciplined institutions persist.* He knew exactly where a lack of discipline could lead. His father had been a musician, wandering from gig to gig, never knowing where the next payday would come from, and never letting Jerome settle into the same school for more than six months. His mother had lost patience with that kind of lifestyle after only a couple years. After his mother had left, Jerome's father filled the loneliness with alcohol, and then later with drugs. The young Jerome was almost relieved when finally his father's excesses had taken his life, and he was free to embrace the rigor and orderliness of the priesthood. *Disciplined institutions achieve.*

Jerome tapped on his cellphone's touch screen for the first contact that he had stored in the quick dial memory. The phone rang.

"Yes?" a dry elderly voice answered testily, clearly irritated by the interruption.

"Your Eminence, I hope I have not disturbed you," began Jerome reverently.

"Jerome?" The pitch of the Prefect's voice rose expectantly. He had clearly been waiting for Jerome to call. "Do we have it?" asked the Prefect eagerly. "Is the *Proditio* secure?"

"I am afraid not, Your Eminence." Jerome closed his eyes regretfully and shrank from the phone. "The investigation proved inconclusive."

"What?" the Prefect gasped, followed by an awkward silence. "I trust you showed him the instruments?"

"Of course, Your Eminence," whined Jerome, feeling more than a little insulted. "But a man of his age..." Jerome fumbled for the best way of explaining. "Their stamina is less... less easily determinable. And consequently their testimony is less reliable… and unfortunately incomplete."

"I hope for your sake Inquisitor that you are not losing

your touch," barked the Prefect, as his surprise gave way to anger. "Because woe betides you Jerome if I discover that you underestimate this threat."

Jerome could almost hear the Prefect waving his finger at him.

"This mistake has haunted the church for over five hundred years!" the Prefect shouted. "And it falls to us, the Holy Office, a responsibility given first to us by His Holiness Pope Innocent IV, to defend, not just the integrity of the Catholic Church, but to defend the integrity of faith itself."

Jerome knew better than to say anything. He clenched his jaw and kneaded his furrowed brow between his thumb and forefinger.

"We have worked so hard Jerome." The Prefect continued in a more pleading tone. "After all these years, we finally have had one of our own elected Holy Father." His voice hardened again. "Someone with the vigilance and discipline to reverse the recent…" The Prefect was for a moment lost for words, "…accommodations."

Jerome could feel the Prefect's disgust.

"If the existence of the *Proditio* was to become public knowledge, it would be a disaster. It would erode the people's faith in the Church, it would undermine the Church from beneath our Holy Father. From beneath us Jerome! It cannot be allowed," the Prefect said resolutely, "We must have the *Proditio*!"

Jerome waited a moment, in case the Prefect had not yet finished. "Doctor Chan did indicate a location. But…"

"What did he say Jerome?" interrupted the Prefect. "What did Doctor Chan say?"

"He said, 'Toscanelli in St. Peter's,' Your Eminence."

The Prefect inhaled sharply, surprised by the revelation. "The Papal Basilica of St. Peter's in Rome? Excellent work Jerome!" The Prefect's anger seemed to have dissipated in a moment. "We would be lucky indeed if the *Proditio* was hidden right under our noses."

"Yes, Your Eminence," agreed Jerome. "But, '*Toscanelli* in St. Peter's,' Your Eminence, what does it mean? And who is Toscanelli?" Doubt crept into Jerome's voice. "I think it warrants further investigation."

"Leave that with me Inquisitor," concluded the Prefect confidently. "Your first priority is finding the *Proditio.* And our best clue yet as to the *Proditio's* whereabouts is now St. Peter's Basilica. So when I hear from you again tomorrow, I expect you to be calling me from Rome."

Jerome rubbed his eyes wearily. "Yes, Your Eminence." He had barely finished, before the Prefect abruptly slammed down the receiver on the other end of the phone line.

CHAPTER 4

After collecting his bidder's paddle and catalog, San Lee climbed the Hotel Danieli's marble staircase to the first floor. From there, San followed the signs to the main ballroom. For the auction, the Marco Polo ballroom had been laid out like a lecture theatre. Row after row of elegant blue cushioned, oval backed chairs faced a stage at the west end of the room. On the left side of the stage was a lectern, from where the auctioneer could look out over the bidders. On the right side of the stage was a cloth covered plinth on which the objects to be auctioned could be displayed. There must be room for about a hundred and fifty people in here, thought San.

San was the first bidder to arrive. What at the beginning of his career had been a nervousness that meant San arrived compulsively early to every auction, eventually became what he regarded as a good habit. If he arrived early, San would have his choice of where to sit. He chose a seat two thirds of the way to the back of the ball room, and off to one side. This should provide a good view of the other bidders and their behavior, thought San. *Whoever they might be.*

San sat and watched the auction room slowly fill up. He

recognized some of the other bidders. There was a buyer from the New York Metropolitan Museum, a Saudi princeling and dilettante, and some second tier European socialites. Most likely here for the after party, smiled San. As they took their seats, San thumbed through the catalogue. It was titled Qing Dynasty Art and Ceramics. San checked to see if there had been any last minute changes. But no, as he had expected, the Haiyantang bronze rat's head sculpture was listed as lot forty three and described innocuously as, "a Qing Dynasty bronze sculpture."

The catalog included a full size photo of the bronze rat's head sculpture. It was about the size of a football, with large rodent ears high on the head and a pronounced snout in the front. The eyes were made of a bright, yellow stone that contrasted sharply with the bronze that had dulled with age. It was a simple sculpture with no surviving details to indicate a rat's fur or whiskers. It struck San as odd that instead of the rat's neck extending horizontally from the head to what should have been the rat's body, the sculpture's neck dropped vertically from the rat's head as a human's does. *It doesn't really look much like a rat at all.*

Being lot forty three suggested that the auctioneer didn't expect the bronze rat's head sculpture to be the most expensive item among the hundred piece collection to be auctioned. That honor probably went to the pair of eighteenth century, famille rose bowls from the court of Emperor Qianlong, thought San admiringly. Being lot forty three also meant that the sculpture wouldn't be sold until toward the end of the morning session. That would be ample time to get a reading on the other more active bidders. *To assess what types of pieces they were interested in and where they seemed to set their price limits.*

San had inherited his mother's love of art and antiques. She had been a curator at Taiwan's National Palace Museum. Up until her accident that is, thought San wistfully. He had fond memories of visiting his mother after school, and being left to wander the museum's cavernous interior by himself. But, much to his mother's disappointment, San never inherited her most academic inclinations. It wasn't that he'd been a bad student at school. San had graduated with solid degrees in history and economics. But, it was what his father described as an Asian mercantilist instinct that led him to appreciate art for its financial rewards as much as appreciating it for its aesthetic qualities.

After finishing the compulsory year of military service, San went to live with his father in Osaka, Japan. San's father was Korean by descent, but had been born in Japan after his father's parents were forced to immigrate to Japan during the Japanese occupation of Korea. San's parents had met after his father had been sent to Taiwan by the Japanese trading company for which he worked. Taiwan too had been a Japanese colony until 1945 and San's mother had also been taught some Japanese at school when she was very young. So while San had done most of his primary school in Taiwan and had naturally been educated in Mandarin Chinese, it was Japanese that was spoken at home.

In Osaka, during the day, San had worked at his father's pachinko arcades in the Nanba district. But in his spare time, he established a small gallery selling Chinese art to the wealthy founding families of Japan's Kyoto and Osaka-based technology industries. The business was successful enough to eventually occupy San full-time and led to him being regularly commissioned by the Nagamori and Yamauchi families to buy art on their behalf.

But as the gallery business grew he had less and less time to help with his father's business. *And so when the Japanese economy stalled, dad's debts rose.* It was hard enough for a small entrepreneur in any industry to borrow money in Japan. But in the pachinko industry, and with dad being ethnically Korean, it was almost impossible, San thought glumly. *No wonder he had turned to less ethical lenders.*

"And next ladies and gentlemen," announced the auctioneer, dragging San from his thoughts and back into the present, "we have lot forty three."

Although San maintained a calm exterior, his stomach tensed and his pulse quickened.

The auctioneer was a tall gangly man, dressed in a blue, pinstriped, three piece suit and a bow tie. He sounded like a caricature of the English public school system smiled San, as he enunciated with excessive precision.

"An exquisite Qing Dynasty bronze sculpture of the Chinese zodiacal symbol for the year of the rat," continued the auctioneer, reading from his notes. "Designed by Jesuit missionaries, it was originally part of the Summer Palace in Beijing. A piece I believe, whose provenance needs no introduction." The auctioneer looked up hungrily. "Can we begin the bidding at..."

But, the auctioneer was interrupted mid-sentence by one of his assistants. The tall, well dressed auctioneer had to bend awkwardly low from behind his lectern in order to hear the assistant whispering in his ear. The auctioneer looked surprised by what he was being told, and he was clearly flustered when he returned to the microphone.

The auctioneer ummed nervously, flicking the fringe of his hair away from his eyes. "I am afraid ladies and gentlemen that there has been a slight change to today's program. We must apologize, but in accordance with the owner's instructions, the Qing Dynasty bronze sculpture has been withdrawn from today's auction."

"What?!" screamed San silently. He jumped to his feet. *Why would he do that?*

The room bubbled with whispers. Some of the audience were as surprised by San's reaction as they were by the announcement itself.

"This brings us to lot forty four…," called the auctioneer, trying to regain control of the room.

San stumbled awkwardly along the aisle in which he was seated, heading toward the exit. He apologized profusely as he tripped over the feet of the other bidders.

What on earth had happened? wondered San. *I have to speak to Doctor Chan immediately.*

CHAPTER 5

Agent Tao Ma sat at a small, cast iron table in a quiet cafe next to his hotel. He impatiently tapped his foot on the leg of the table, waiting for his cellphone to ring. Tao went to light another cigarette. But he had run out, and so angrily screwed up the empty cigarette packet and tossed it into the canal.

The canal that passed in front of the cafe was about the width of a two lane road. It emptied into the Venetian Lagoon, not far from where Tao sat. The canal was lined with small motor boats tied to red and white striped mooring posts. The air was clean and there wasn't a sound except for the odd footstep on the cobbled waterfront, or the lazy squawk of a seagull.

Tao watched one of Murano’s many glassmakers going about his work at one of the brightly painted factories whose showrooms opened out on to the waterfront. Clad in a protective leather apron, the glassmaker's hands were blackened and his face ruddy from the heat of the forge. It's like living in the past, thought Tao. Murano’s glass industry had changed little in the seven hundred years since Venice's glassmakers were first moved to the island of Murano because of the fire risk that the glass furnaces posed in the heart of Venice. Ever since, Murano had been synonymous with the highest quality glassware.

China is not like this, thought Tao. Beijing's geometric, gray-stone Hutong had been inexorably replaced with towering apartment blocks and an Olympic village. The Chinese people worked assembling high tech consumer electronics for export. It is progress, nodded Tao. *It is good for the state.*

Tao looked out anxiously across the lagoon to the main island of Venice, drumming his fingers on the table. Venice was about half a mile from Murano, and although Tao had to squint looking into the morning sun, he could make out many of Venice's landmarks in the city's skyline. The lagoon was calm, protected from the Adriatic Sea by the long thin sand bar of Lido. But the waters looked cold, almost as dark and gray as the sky.

Midway between the island of Murano and Venice lay San Michelle, also known as the Isle of the Dead - Venice's cemetery. Surrounded by a high, red brick wall, the island of San Michelle was the complete opposite of Venice - green with trees and devoid of people. As peaceful and quiet as those entombed within, thought Tao. *And that's exactly where I'll end up, if this auction doesn't go as planned.*

Tao's plan was to bring the bronze rat's head sculpture back to the relative quiet of Murano after the auction. Then after the academics had tested the sculpture and confirmed its authenticity, Tao was to travel the three miles to Marco Polo Airport by motor boat. At the airport there was a private jet waiting to return the bronze sculpture to China. But, the auction should have been finished by now, snarled Tao nervously. *And yet there was still no word from the Taiwanese buyer.*

Tired of waiting, Tao pulled out his cellphone and called Agent Mei-Li, the colleague he had placed in direct contact with the auction room. Tao had assigned Mei-Li the task of posing as a telephone bidder. As a phone bidder, she would be in constant contact with the auction room floor, where she could monitor the bidding activity, and most importantly, keep tabs on the Taiwanese buyer San Lee.

The phone rang only once.

"Wei?" snapped a quick tempered young lady, in her Beijing accented Mandarin.

"Mei-Li?" asked Tao, equally brisk. "It's Tao."

"Sir."

Tao ignored the formalities. "Is the bronze rat's head sculpture secure?"

There was a disconcerting pause. "No Sir, it's not."

"What?" Tao was worried, but he naturally defaulted to anger when dealing with subordinates. "What's causing the delay?"

"Sir, it's unclear. We're still not entirely sure," Mei-Li hesitated, nervously. "It appears that the auction of the bronze rat's head sculpture was not held. I repeat, the auction was not held."

Tao froze and his eyes widened, staring across the lagoon toward Venice.

"I'm waiting for a response from the auctioneers as to whether the auction was cancelled or just delayed," continued Agent Mei-Li. "But we have to consider the possibility that the bronze sculpture may have been withdrawn from sale, or worse still, it may have already been sold."

The color drained from Tao's face. Panic mixed with anger. "Where is the Taiwanese buyer?" Tao demanded. "Where is San Lee?"

There was a moment's silence. "He's gone Sir," she admitted, reluctantly.

"Gone?" Tao's heart started pounding and he involuntarily stood up, spilling what was left of his coffee. Gone where?

"The auction house confirmed that he registered for a

bidder's paddle," explained Mei-Li. "We've also checked with some of the other bidders and he was definitely in the auction room." Mei-Li swallowed, fearing Tao's anger. "But he's not there now."

"Well find him, damn it!" yelled Tao, cursing the fact he was marooned on Murano. Tao allowed himself only a few moments to consider his predicament. There were few practical alternatives, thought Tao. *I can't just let the bronze sculpture disappear.*

"Mei-Li, I'll be there in fifteen minutes," barked Tao before hanging up.

Tao dropped a few euro on the table and ran. He headed back along the waterfront, past his hotel, to where he had left the boat hired to transport the bronze rat's head sculpture to the airport. Tao unravelled the mooring line securing the four seat, wood-paneled motor boat to the pier and jumped into the cockpit. The small boat rocked precariously as Tao landed and slid into the pilot's cream leather seat. It seemed almost dangerously small for an ocean going craft. But this isn't really the open ocean, Tao told himself. *Just a very large pond.*

The deep gurgle of the idling motor steadily increased in pitch as Tao accelerated away from the dock. Tao steered the boat so as to pass the island of San Michelle on his right, and toward the eastern end of Venice. His plan was to cut through the thinner and less crowded end of Venice before turning westward toward the Hotel Danieli near the mouth of the Grand Canal. Tao estimated it would take about fifteen minutes to get to the auction venue.

As Murano shrank into the distance, Tao pulled out his cellphone again. "Agent Mei-Li?"

"Sir?" she responded immediately.

"Contact Interpol," said Tao firmly. "I want you to give them a description of San Lee and Doctor Chan. Tell them that they are wanted for questioning in regards to theft, money laundering, and the sale of counterfeit art," he ordered. "And do it through our Police channels. I don't want this being traced back to the Ministry."

"But sir, what evidence can I share with Interpol?" asked Mei-Li.

"Forget the evidence!" screamed Tao. He had to shout to make himself heard above the noise of the motor boat anyway, but he certainly didn't like to have his instructions questioned. "It's imperative that we find out where they are and secure the bronze sculpture. We have to assume that Doctor Chan, San Lee, or both of them working together; have cheated us out of the bronze sculpture."

"Yes sir!"

"If we're wrong, we can apologize later," grunted Tao, hanging up.

The motorboat skipped across the light, wind-driven chop of the lagoon.

This plan was fast moving from simply disorderly to career shortening, thought Tao. *But damn it if I'll let it become a national humiliation.*

CHAPTER 6

San Lee hurried from the auction room. He grabbed the polished wooden banister as he scurried down the Hotel Danieli's main staircase, two steps at a time. Landing loudly in the lobby, San almost tripped over a suitcase laden bellboy, as he rushed toward the entrance. Pushing back through the revolving door, San broke in to a run as he turned right onto the promenade and headed toward St. Mark's Square. It was a little warmer than it had been earlier in the day, but San was too intent on getting to Doctor Chan to notice.

The streets were now also much busier than when San had arrived and he had to slow down to negotiate the tourists crowding the Ponte della Paglia. It was one of hundreds of small bridges crossing the canals in Venice. But it was swarming with people because it was also the best place from which to get a photo of the Bridge of Sighs. The elegantly carved Bridge of Sighs linked the administrative buildings of the Doge's Palace with Venice's prison on the other side of the canal. It was the bridge across which the famous womanizer Casanova had been led to imprisonment three centuries earlier.

Only fifty yards further down the waterfront from the bridge, the Piazzetta opened up on San's right. Piazzetta literally meant little Piazza and was so called because it was an extension of Venice's most famous public space, the much larger Piazza San Marco, known as St. Mark's Square to its English speaking visitors. But instead of turning right between the Doge's Palace and the bell tower into St. Mark's Square, San headed directly across the Piazzetta to the Biblioteca Marciano – the National Library of St. Mark's.

Last night, San had met Doctor Chan at one of the many cafes lining St. Mark's Square. Doctor Chan had initially seemed wary. This was to be expected, San conceded, because it had been only the first time they had met. But it was strange, thought San, that a pleasant dinner and several glasses of wine did nothing to allay Doctor Chan's nervousness. Doctor Chan had insisted on returning to his office in order to handle the delicate negotiations for the bronze rat's head sculpture behind closed doors. As a visiting professor, Doctor Chan had been assigned an office in the library in which to base himself while conducting his research in Venice. And while the negotiations last night had ultimately proved unsuccessful, San reasoned it was probably the best place to start looking for Doctor Chan.

The National Library of St. Mark's was one of the world's first public libraries. It had begun with a gift of seven hundred and fifty books from the Patriarch of Constantinople, Cardinal Bessarion, even before the construction of the library building was completed in the sixteenth century. It had a two-storey, arcaded facade that complemented the similarly arcaded Doge's Palace that faced the library across the Piazzetta.

After crossing the Piazzetta, San turned right under the arcade that lined the ground floor of the library and followed the outside of the building until he reached the entrance. If he had not been here the night before, the library's entrance would have been hard to find. A dimly lit and dank smelling passage linked the Piazzetta and the garden behind the library. To enter the library San walked down this passageway, past two dust covered statues. But instead of emerging into the garden there was a doorway in the right hand wall of the tunnel which led into the library's lobby. San hesitated in the lobby to get his bearings, trying to remember the direction in which Doctor Chan had led him the previous evening.

Passing through the lobby, San slowed his pace in deference to the scholarly silence of the library's reading room. Row upon row of desks were lit by a large skylight two storeys above San's head. The only sound in the room was the squeaking wheels of a librarian's trolley, as she collected the books left behind in the reading room. On the far side of the reading room was a row of meeting rooms, one of which had been lent by the library to Doctor Chan to serve as his office while he was working in Venice. It was here that San had discussed purchasing the bronze rat's head sculpture from Doctor Chan the previous evening.

San knocked urgently on the research room door. "Doctor Chan?" he called out, trying to suppress the anxiety in his voice. "Doctor Chan, it's..."

But before San could finish his sentence, the door opened.

"Can I help you?" asked a slender young lady wearing a white lab coat over a smart gray skirt and a black, fitted, turtle neck top. She had long black hair pulled back in a ponytail, porcelain pale skin, and her tasteful makeup had been impeccably applied. From the style of her clothes and make up, San guessed that she was Japanese. *And very pretty.* But she was unusually tall for a Japanese lady. *Perhaps she's Korean?* Her eyes were larger than normal, and San would have suspected plastic surgery if they weren't also green brown in color. *Eurasian?* She spoke English with an Italian accent. *Maybe half Italian?*

"Yes. I'm from the auction today, at the Danieli." Not knowing where to begin, the words were tumbling out of San in an unintelligible order. "There was a problem with Doctor Chan's piece and I am trying to figure it out."

"And you are?" she asked softly, both trying to steer San gently in the direction of a more coherent explanation, and wondering whether they had a language more in common than the English they spoke.

"Sorry. I'm San Lee. I'm a colleague..." San halted, correcting himself. "No. I'm an acquaintance of Doctor Chan."

"I seem to remember your name from Doctor Chan's appointment book," she said smiling. "Please come in." She stepped backwards holding the research room door open for San to enter.

Doctor Chan's research room was a rectangular shape with a light table and map drawers on the right hand side of the room, and two desks on the left. The desk farthest from the door was buried under a mountain of books and papers. The desk closest to San was conversely neat and orderly, except for a collection of electronic components that looked as though someone was assembling a large camera from scratch. On the walls of the room were pinned large, poster-sized photos of old hand drawn maps. The air smelt unusually dry. Climate control to take care of the manuscripts, thought San.

"I'm Su-Lin by the way," the lady said, holding a clipboard to her chest with one hand and shaking San's hand with the other. "Doctor Chan is my PhD supervisor."

"San Lee," San nodded awkwardly in the shallowest of bows.

"Now, I'm sorry, but can you go through that again," Su-Lin asked, perching on the edge of a desk. "And perhaps a little slower," she added with a self-deprecating smile.

"OK, from the beginning," said San, gathering himself. "I met Doctor Chan last night. And at the time, Doctor

Chan had said that he would be selling his Qing Dynasty bronze rat's head sculpture at the auction today. So this morning when I got to the auction, I was naturally surprised to find that he had changed his mind." San studied Su-Lin's expression, hoping that what he was saying, was all making sense. "As you've probably guessed, I had hoped to bid for Doctor Chan's bronze sculpture. So I am looking for Doctor Chan to understand why exactly he withdrew the piece from the auction." San thought there was no need to share the fact that Doctor Chan had refused to sell him the bronze sculpture. "Do you know where he is?"

"Oh I see," said Su-Lin, nodding. But her furrowed brow suggested that this came as something of a surprise to her too. "As far as I knew, Doctor Chan had been planning to sell the bronze sculpture today." As she spoke Su-Lin rolled up some of the poster sized photographs from the light table and placed them in a gray plastic storage tube. "Given its value, I'm surprised that he hung on to it as long as he did. It's got quite a history you know."

San nodded. *Of this I am painfully aware.*

Su-Lin slung the gray plastic map storage tube over her shoulder and picked up a stainless steel thermos from her desk. "So I suggest you ask him yourself," she said brightly. "He's been working overnight in the Doge's Palace. I was about to take him a coffee and some of the test results from the latest scans he's taken. Care to walk with me?"

CHAPTER 7

Brother Michael had squeezed himself on to a chair at one of the desks in the National Library of St. Mark's reading room. The room was a large open space filled by rows of long desks and surrounded by high shelves, containing intimidatingly old books. Studious readers were scattered about the room, scowling disapprovingly at the slightest noise.

Michael sat, hunched over the book that the previous student had left behind. He stared at the page, pretending to read. With his head in his hands, he tried to make sense of the dense type. His brow creased with the effort. He scratched at his bald head in consternation and a deeply buried embarrassment. But the words on the page swam in front of his eyes making him feel slightly nauseous. *Never much liked books anyway.*

Michael gave up on the book and went back to surreptitiously glancing at the research room door. He had been told by Jerome to wait for a chance to search Doctor Chan's office. But so far this morning he had been prevented from doing so by the constant presence of a young lady with long black hair, wearing a lab coat and a short skirt.

"Filthy whore," muttered Michael. He hurriedly crossed himself; not knowing where the sense of guilt he felt was coming from.

And now he had another problem. A tanned Asian man, in his thirties Michael guessed, had arrived at Doctor Chan's research room. He wore a long black leather coat, tailored black pants and boots. *Another heathen by the looks of him.*

The Asian man looked like he was in quite a hurry, because Michael wasn't the only one in the library to turn around, when the Asian man began banging aggressively on Doctor Chan's research room door. After a brief conversation, that Michael was too far away to overhear, the Asian man disappeared into Doctor Chan's office.

"Damn it," muttered Michael. "How long is this going to take?" Michael's outburst drew a stern look of disapproval from the reader sitting on the opposite side of the desk. In a dark mood, Michael responded to the weedy academic by staring straight back at him with a hollow expression and flexing the muscles in his neck and shoulders. It had the intended effect and the academic looked hurriedly away. Bloody readers, Michael sneered. *Jerome has read me the only book I'd ever needed to read.*

For three months in a filthy cave in Afghanistan, reading the Bible to Michael was the only thing that Jerome had done. It was the only thing that there had been to do, thought Michael. *And it was the only thing that kept me going.* Like most of the men in his battalion, Michael had made fun of Jerome. He had been the seemingly ineffectual, slightly built, and conspicuously unarmed chaplain. It wasn't until their column was ambushed outside of Herat, and Jerome and Michael were captured, that Michael learnt just how strong Jerome really was. Half-starved, wallowing in our own filth and periodically tortured for information we didn't have, it was my faith in God that got me through, remembered Michael. *A faith I learned from Jerome.* So after

Michael's honorable discharge from the army, it had been an easy choice for him to make, and join Jerome in the service of God.

As Michael's concentration lapsed into memories, he almost missed the young lady and the Asian man leaving Doctor Chan's office. They headed toward the library's main entrance. Michael stood up quickly and grabbed his duffel bag. He crossed the reading room to the lobby and peered around the door way to ensure that they had both left the building. When Michael was satisfied that they had gone, he returned to the research room from which they had left.

He approached Doctor Chan's research room door and tried the handle. It was locked. Michael ran his hand along the white, wood door frame adjacent to the lock. He tapped the wall by the door with his knuckles. Unfortunately, this was an older building and the door had a solid timber frame over a thick brick wall. The door frame would therefore not be easily deformed. But the handle maybe, wondered Michael. *The tricky bit would be doing it quietly.*

Michael gripped the door handle tightly with his meaty fingers and tested it, to gauge its range of motion. Once understood, Michael abruptly wrenched the handle past its normal limits. The handle was cast aluminum and held firm. But the door was made of cheap plywood. It made a splintering sound as the handle and lock came loose. Only as strong as the door it's mounted to, grinned Michael. He slipped inside and closed the door behind him.

Michael found the light switches by the door, and after a bank of fluorescent tubes flickered into life, he looked around the research room. There were a lot of large photos of maps pinned to the right hand wall. Next to the maps were equally large posters that looked like medical x-rays. *But x-rays of what?* Michael was puzzled. Two desks on the left faced a table and a chest of very wide, but thin drawers on the right. Where should I start? he wondered.

Jerome had said that he would have to be quick, because there was no telling when they would return.

"Take any old codices, papers or contracts," Michael repeated Jerome's instructions. Jerome had told him that, "the *Proditio* will be a large document, and likely to have a lead papal seal, in the shape of two crossed keys below a triple crown. It is also likely to be countersigned with a chop – a square, red stamp of Chinese characters."

By the chest of drawers on the right, there were a few old maps on a table that seemed to be lit from beneath. Some of the maps were European and some were covered in a text that Michael recognized from his favorite Chinese restaurant. *But there were no old documents.*

Conscious of time, Michael flung open each drawer of the map cabinet. But inside were just more maps and photos of the night sky.

The first of the two desks that Michael came to was covered in camera equipment. That could be safely ignored, he concluded. However, the second desk was covered in library books, journals and paper. Michael unceremoniously swept the books and paper to the floor with his thick forearm. Underneath the books were a laptop and a small black notebook with well-worn corners and an elastic band around it holding it together. This is more promising, thought Michael. There was a photo stuck to the laptop's lid with sticky tape. The photo was of Doctor Chan standing next to a gray stone statue. According to the plinth at the base of the statue in the photo, the smiling Doctor Chan stood next to a statue of the famous Ming Dynasty ambassador, Admiral Zheng He. Michael stuffed the laptop and the notebook into his duffel bag. *Jerome would understand their significance.*

Michael next pulled out each drawer of Doctor Chan's desk and one by one emptied their contents on the floor. But they contained only stationery. Still nothing old-looking, Michael worried.

But, under the desk, in the corner of the room, Michael found a metal box. He sat down at the chair behind Doctor Chan's desk and ran his fingers over the box. It was a solidly made metal box, with a keypad and an LED display. He had initially thought it was part of the desk, but a closer inspection revealed that it was attached to the wall. This looks important, guessed Michael, it looks like a wall safe. His fingers lingered over the keypad. But he thought better of attempting to guess the password. It might be alarmed. *Better take the whole box.*

Michael looked around the room for something to give him leverage with. The table legs will do, he thought. Michael swung his legs under the desk and pinned the desk leg to the floor with his feet. He then extended his calves slowly and drove his knees into the underside of the desk. The desk was not built to resist force in this direction. Screws popped and the desk top parted company with the legs. Michael caught the metal desk leg before it clattered to the floor.

Michael then cleared what remained of the desk away from around the small wall safe. Setting his muscular legs about shoulder width apart, he hefted the desk leg to measure its weight. *It will have to do.* He then heaved the desk leg over his shoulder and brought it crashing down, as he would a spear, in to the plaster just above the metal box. White chips of plaster and dust flew up from the point of impact. Old buildings look pretty, but they are weak, smiled Michael with a quiet determination. Two more heavy blows and there was a small cavity in the wall behind the metal box. He pushed the table leg into the hole, placed his foot on the wall, leant back and let gravity help. The muscles along his arms rippled as he pulled on the table leg. The table leg acted like a crow bar and struggled with the brick and plaster for its grip on the wall safe. The wall lost. Michael tumbled backwards as the four metal bolts holding the wall safe to the masonry came loose. The safe fell to the floor with a dull thud. Michael grinned. *Jerome will be pleased with Michael.*

CHAPTER 8

Su-Lin grabbed her brown leather satchel before turning off the lights. San offered to carry the flask of hot coffee that Su-Lin had prepared for Doctor Chan, while she locked the research room door.

"You mentioned that you were working toward your doctorate degree. What's your research interest?" asked San, as they walked through the reading room toward the Library of St. Mark's main exit.

"My thesis is on the history of China's maritime trade."

"That sounds quite broad." San held open the door into the tunnel that led from the library lobby to the Piazzetta.

"Well I'm particularly interested in the early Ming period. That's why I transferred to Nanjing University, so that I could work with Doctor Chan," explained Su-Lin. "Maps of China's maritime trade routes start to appear in the Ming period and so my research interests and Doctor Chan's overlap at that point. He's a little eccentric, but he's also one of China's best historical cartographers."

The Doge's Palace, where Doctor Chan had been working overnight, wasn't far. It faced St. Mark's Library across the Piazzetta.

"I think it's his Navy experience," continued Su-Lin, walking out from the arcade and toward the Palace. "Doctor Chan was a submariner you know. He was a navigator in China's People's Liberation Army Navy. I think it gives him an added insight when it comes to analyzing maps."

The Doge's Palace looked awkwardly proportioned, thought San. The top half of the Palace was an almost boringly plain, large, rectangular block. This then clashed with the intricate design of the lower half which was decorated with two layers of finely carved arches. To San it looked unfinished, as though the builders ran out of money.

San followed Su-Lin to the ground floor entrance of the Doge's Palace. A queue of envious tourists looked on as Su-Lin skipped to the head of the queue and presented her staff pass to the guards.

"He's with me," said Su-Lin to the security guard, indicating to San.

"That's fine miss," replied the guard. "But we'll just have to make him with a pass. Can I have your passport sir?"

San handed over his passport and he was issued with a laminated pass that hung from a lanyard around his neck. Once they were through security, Su-Lin and San crossed the Palace's internal courtyard and began climbing the *scala d'oro* to the second floor and to what had been the Doge's personal apartments. The *scala d'oro,* or golden staircase, was designed in the sixteenth century to show off Venice's wealth to visiting dignitaries. The staircase got its name because not only were the walls and ceilings intricately carved and decorated with fine paintings, but the ceiling was trimmed with gold leaf.

"Doctor Chan is taking photographs in the map room," said Su-Lin, as they reached the second floor landing.

The Palace's map room was in the north east corner of the second floor. So turning left from the landing they entered a small antechamber, called the *Sala degli Scudieri,* named after the Doge's personal attendants. The door on the opposite side of the room, and entrance to the map room, had been cordoned off with bollards and rope to prevent tourists from interrupting Doctor Chan's work. Su-Lin moved one of the bollards aside and knocked on the door.

"*Buon giorno!*" Su-Lin called out, in what sounded to San as good Italian as a native would speak. "Doctor Chan?" Su-Lin tried again, this time in English. "I've got coffee!"

But, there was no response.

"He's probably in the middle of taking a photograph," guessed Su-Lin.

Su-Lin pushed open the door and San followed her into a long rectangular room with windows at each of the narrow ends. Immediately in front of the entrance was one of two enormous globes that sat in the middle of the floor. One globe showed a map of the earth and the other showed a map of the stars at night. Between the two globes in the center of the long wall was the *scudo*, or coat-of-arms, of Ludovico Manin, the last Doge of Venice. The Doges of Venice had been the chief administrators of the Venetian republic for over a thousand years. Each Doge was elected to serve for life, and the last - Ludovico Manin, only abdicated when Venice fell to Napoleon's army at the end of the eighteenth century.

San could see that, although the walls were wood panelled for the first six feet or so, above the panelling, the walls were painted with large maps of the world. It was these paintings that gave the map room its name. San noticed that the maps were distorted relative to modern maps. Europe was painted a little bit larger than it should have been and India and China were depicted significantly smaller than they were in reality. Japan, Korea and Taiwan were hard to distinguish at all. The map's distortions were probably caused by European's inability to accurately measure longitude, concluded San. *And a small dose of*

Eurocentricity. But the murals were far more interestingly detailed than modern maps, with pictures of geographical features like mountains and rivers, as well as sailing ships, and the occasional sea monster.

Looking right, San saw that a movable scaffold had been set in front of one of the many maps. There was a camera tripod on the scaffold and white studio lights illuminated a large mural depicting Asia, India, and across the Pacific to North America. The map was odd though, because unlike the two globes or any of the other maps in the room, it showed the southern hemisphere at the top of the map and the northern hemisphere at the bottom. It was like how the Chinese cartographers used to draw their maps, thought San.

Looking left past Su-Lin, San could see a temporary desk had been positioned with its back to windows overlooking the Palace's internal courtyard. Facing the desk was a portable whiteboard to which poster sized photos of maps had been attached.

But there was no sign of Doctor Chan.

"That is odd," Su-Lin remarked. "He's left the lights on." Su-Lin walked over to the scaffold and switched off the studio lights before continuing on toward Doctor Chan's desk.

Approaching the desk they both noticed a dark liquid had been spilled over the desk top, run down its side, and pooled on the floor.

"Looks like he's already had his coffee," smiled Su-Lin.

On the floor, in front of the desk, lay a silver lapel pin. Su-Lin bent down to pick it up, examining it quizzically. The pin was crafted in the shape of a crucifix surrounded by a sword on one side and a branch on the other.

San approached the desk, but then stopped suddenly. There was a sharp metallic smell in the air. "I don't think that's coffee."

On the table, in the dark pool of what was now clearly

blood, lay four severed and disfigured fingers.

Su-Lin dropped the tube of photos that she had been carrying, and screamed.

San ran to the desk and saw Doctor Chan lying face down behind the desk, next to his overturned chair. Kneeling down beside him, San rolled Doctor Chan on to his back.

San recoiled, but the image was seared into his memory whether he looked away or not. Bright white, splintered bone and torn flesh protruded from the blood soaked left sleeve where Doctor Chan's hand should have been. Doctor Chan was quite cold, and long dead.

"Who would do such a thing?" pleaded Su-Lin as she sank to her knees, crying into her quivering fingers.

In the distance, sirens wailed.

CHAPTER 9

Agent Tao Ma looked down the drably decorated corridor in both directions as he slowly approached room four zero seven of the Londra Palace Hotel. Standing to one side of the doorway, he reached out tentatively and rang the doorbell. But there was no response. He couldn't hear any television noise coming from inside the room either. There was no sound at all.

Agent Mei-Li had remained in her position at the other end of the corridor, on the fourth floor landing. She maintained the compact, muscular build of the gymnast she once was. Born in the far west of China, at the age of six, she had been selected for her size and the size of her parents to be sent to a state gymnastics academy in Beijing. Although the slow accumulation of injuries had ended her gymnastic career in her early teens, traveling overseas to compete had helped her language studies, and her service to the gymnastic program earned a scholarship to a university in Beijing. From there she was recruited into the Ministry of State Security.

Mei-Li wore tight, blue jeans and a bomber jacket. Her hair was cut in an aggressively short bob and she wore no makeup or jewelry. There was a small patch of blond in her otherwise black hair, which might have been confused for an affectation, but was actually the result of a training accident in the gym. She had attractively full lips when she smiled, but the width of her jaw combined with her short hair and stature gave a powerful and slightly masculine appearance.

When Tao reached the hotel room door, Mei-Li checked for approaching lifts, and to see if there was anyone on the fire escape. But she found no one to interrupt them. She nodded at Tao, who stood silently, waiting for her signal.

Tao took a deep breath, lifted his leg, and crashed his foot into the lock of the hotel room door. The door frame split around the lock and the door swung open, banging loudly. Tao dropped into a crouch, his left hand held the swinging door open and his right hand was inside his jacket, poised over his firearm. But there was still no sound or movement from inside the room. He gestured to Mei-Li, indicating that she should follow him into San Lee's hotel room.

The room was a modest size, with a queen sized bed facing two large, full length windows. There was a desk in the corner and a small bathroom to the right of the entrance. The windows to a small balcony overlooking Venice's lagoon had been left open, and the sheer, white curtains billowed inwards on the breeze. An empty wine glass sat on top of some Korean *manhwa* on the bedside table.

Satisfied he was alone, Tao began methodically combing through the room. There were still shirts hanging in the closet, toiletries around the sink in the bathroom, and an open suitcase sitting by the bed. Tao was surprised. It seemed as though San had expected to return to his hotel room to collect his belongings. *Or perhaps he still planned to?* And he was definitely here this morning, thought Tao. *That's today's newspaper on the desk.* But there was no sign of

San Lee and no sign of the bronze rat's head sculpture.

"It looks as though San left in a hurry," Tao remarked to Mei-Li as she entered the room. "He's left everything behind."

But she did not respond, because she had a cellphone pinned to her ear with her shoulder as she busily scribbled notes on a pad of paper.

"Sir," reported Mei-Li after she had hung up. "Interpol has reported that the body found inside the Doge's Palace is that of an Asian male, about 165cm in height, medium build, and aged between 50 and 60."

"Have they made an identification?" demanded Tao angrily.

"No, not yet," answered Mei-Li, shaking her head.

"But it's definitely not a tourist?"

"No," confirmed Mei-Li. "They were found in a restricted area, off limits to the visiting public."

There can't be that many Chinese academics working in Venice, thought Tao. *It has to be Doctor Chan.*

"Cause of death?" persisted Tao.

Mei-Li checked her notepad. "At the moment, it's just listed as trauma."

But was San Lee really a murderer? wondered Tao. *You've surprised me San.*

"Any mention of the bronze rat's head sculpture?"

"Negative."

But how on earth does he think he'll be able to sell the bronze rat's head sculpture, now that he's stolen it? thought Tao to himself. *The hardest part of any theft is turning the goods into bankable cash.*

"Let me know when there is a photo of the body available," ordered Tao. "We need to confirm it's Doctor Chan. Until then it seems that we can work on the basis that San Lee is a murderer and his motive for murder was to steal the bronze rat's head sculpture." *Unless he has a deeper political motive?*

"Let's hurry," he urged, pointing Mei-Li in the direction of the desk drawers. "The Doge's Palace was crawling with police when I arrived. It won't take them long to link San Lee to the murder and that will lead them here to his hotel room."

Tao walked around to the far side of the room, picked up San's suitcase, and upended it, emptying its contents on to the bed. Mei-Li began rifling through the desk drawers.

"We're looking for travel documents," Tao continued, sifting through the contents of San's suitcase, "a wallet, or an address book, anything which might tell us where San is heading to next." *Or who he stole the bronze sculpture for?*

CHAPTER 10

Kneeling beside Doctor Chan's ruined body, Su-Lin sobbed quietly. Tears ran down her cheeks, smudging her mascara, and spoiling her otherwise manicured appearance. She tenderly pushed Doctor Chan's unruly, gray hair away from his dull, empty eyes. Gone was the boundless curiosity and ceaseless chatter, she thought, leaving just an empty stare frozen somewhere between terror and surprise.

San didn't know what to say. He put a comforting hand on Su-Lin's shoulder, knowing it was hopelessly inadequate. San had not known Doctor Chan beyond the professional acquaintance he had made the night before. But Su-Lin was clearly distraught. San stared silently at Doctor Chan's injuries and the pool of blood in which he now lay. Bile rose in his throat as he tried to imagine what, or who, had torn the hand from Doctor Chan's arm.

Su-Lin picked up Doctor Chan's remaining right hand, the edges of her eyes red with exhaustion. But as she slowly loosened Doctor Chan's grip, to hold his lifeless hand in her own, a crumpled piece of yellow paper fell from the dead cartographer's grasp.

"What's that?" asked San, pointing at the scrunched up

ball of paper.

Su-Lin picked up the piece of paper and began to unfold it. She sniffed and wiped some of the tears from her face welcoming the distraction from the horror of Doctor Chan's mutilated corpse. She squinted at the piece of paper, trying to make sense of its contents.

The piece of paper was yellow with age and there was a tear down one side, suggesting to Su-Lin that it had been ripped from a book. The old paper was covered with black, but faded Chinese characters arranged in neat columns. San could read a row of numbers at the top of the page, which seemed to function as column headings. But he could make nothing out of the text below. The ancient style of Chinese characters, combined with the faded text, made it difficult for San to decipher.

"Something he was working on?" suggested Su-Lin, holding the paper up to examine it in a better light.

"Anything important?" asked San.

Su-Lin was not sure. She turned the piece of paper over. The other side of the piece of parchment was similarly covered with Chinese characters arranged in neat columns. But unlike the first side, the numbers, "1 5 1 2 5 4," had been daubed in dark, red numerals diagonally across the page. She showed the message to San with a confused frown on her face.

But San could only shrug, not knowing what to make of the message.

Turning back to the paper, Su-Lin touched the dark red numbers and recoiled. It was still sickeningly tacky. She looked to San with wide disbelieving eyes.

San hurriedly picked up Doctor Chan's remaining hand to examine it. The tip of his index finger was the same dark red as the numbers scribbled on the yellow piece of paper. Doctor Chan had written the message in his own blood.

Su-Lin blanched, turned her head and covered her mouth with her hand. She dropped Doctor Chan's piece of paper, doubled over at the waist where she knelt, resting one hand on the ground. For a moment, San thought she was about to be sick.

San knelt quickly beside her, put a steadying hand on her shoulder, and offered her his dark gray handkerchief.

Su-Lin closed her eyes in anticipation. But after a second, she took a deep breath and composed herself. "I'm OK," she whispered, forcing a smile and nodding a thank you.

San took a step backwards and picked up Doctor Chan's piece of paper.

"1 5 1 2 5 4," repeated San, looking at Su-Lin for signs of recognition. "What does it mean?"

"I don't know," answered Su-Lin, equally confused.

"Do you think it's a phone number?"

"It's not long enough," retorted Su-Lin, shaking her head. "Italian phone numbers are seven digits long, not six."

"Map coordinates?" The rising pitch of San's voice betrayed his lack of confidence.

"Possibly," responded Su-Lin, raising an eyebrow. "It could be 15 degrees, 12 minutes, and 54 seconds." But her brow quickly creased again. "But map coordinates usually come in pairs, one for latitude and one for longitude."

"Is it a Biblical reference?" San guessed. "I know that sounds a little bit like pulp fiction."

Su-Lin thought for a moment. "Unfortunately it can't be. The book of Ezra doesn't have twelve chapters. It only goes up to chapter ten."

San gave Su-Lin a curious look.

"One of the side effects of a Catholic schooling," explained Su-Lin, blushing slightly. "I think it looks more like a date."

San nodded in agreement. "But is it January the fifth 1254, or May the fourth 1512?"

"Can you think of anything significant about 1512?"

"Michelangelo finished painting the Vatican's Sistine Chapel?" offered San, digging into his memories of art history classes. "But I've never heard anything as specific as May the fourth."

"Copernicus wrote the *Commentariolus* asserting that the sun is the center of the solar system." Su-Lin looked at San hopelessly.

"It's about astronomy." San wrinkled his nose, trying to see a connection with Doctor Chan. "Astronomy is somewhat nautical?"

But Su-Lin raised both eyebrows and pouted, unconvinced.

"What if it's 1254?" San asked. "All I could think of was that in 1254 the Horses of St. Mark were installed at St. Mark's Basilica in Venice."

"Yes, taken by pilgrims on the fourth crusade who got lost on the way to the Holy Land and sacked Christian Constantinople instead." Su-Lin's voice was tinged with sarcasm.

"Well we are in Venice," suggested San.

Su-Lin and San paused for a moment to mull over the suggestion. But neither of them could see a connection with Doctor Chan.

"It was also the year Marco Polo was born," said Su-Lin more brightly.

"That makes some sense." San was warming to the idea. "Doctor Chan was a cartographer and Marco Polo was one of history's most famous travellers."

"But what about Marco Polo?" asked Su-Lin.

"And why was it the last thing that Doctor Chan ever wrote?" added San.

The wail of the sirens grew louder and louder.

CHAPTER 11

As the plane leveled off after reaching cruising altitude, Inquisitor Jerome opened his eyes. There was something about being on a plane just before take-off that always put him to sleep, he thought. But it might also be the spacious leather seats on the Vatican's private jets. Jerome could not help but grin smugly. The priority that the Prefect had assigned to the search for the *Proditio* meant that Jerome was able to use one of the Vatican's fleet of private jets. *A rare perk of the job.*

Although there were only eight seats on the aircraft, Brother Michael was the only other passenger on the flight. He sat opposite Jerome across a small table. But in a sharp contrast to Jerome, Michael squirmed nervously, clearly uncomfortable with the idea of flying.

"You did well Michael," said Jerome comfortingly.

"Thank you, Your Excellency," bowed Michael awkwardly, since he was still fixed to his chair by a seat belt.

Jerome leant across the plane's center aisle and grabbed Michael's duffel bag from the seat next to him. He opened the duffel bag and placed the items that Michael had collected from Doctor Chan's office, one by one on the table between them. "We have Doctor Chan's laptop and his note book," said Jerome switching on the laptop to ensure that it still worked. "We will learn much from this Michael." Jerome nodded approvingly.

Jerome pulled the rubber band off from around Doctor Chan's small, black notebook and flicked through the pages. The notebook was full of dense Chinese hand writing and geometrical figures. It made little sense to Jerome and he grated his jaw in frustration. His mood deteriorated further after Doctor Chan's laptop powered up, because it was password protected.

"Get the notebook to our translators and the computer to our tech team as soon as we land Michael," ordered Jerome with barely concealed annoyance.

"Yes, Your Excellency." Michael bowed again.

Jerome reached again into the duffel bag. In the privacy of their rooms behind the Basilica di San Giovanni e Paolo, it had been a relatively simple task to open the wall safe that Michael had retrieved from Doctor Chan's office. Especially for a religiously devout locksmith in need of absolution, thought Jerome.

"And last, but not least, we have a bronze sculpture of..." Jerome stared at the sculpture, but was not sure. It was about the size of a rugby ball, but heavier. Jerome turned the bronze sculpture over in his hands, looking for something with which to identify it.

"A mouse?" suggested Michael.

"Or at least its head," agreed Jerome, not sure what to make of the sculpture, nor its significance to Doctor Chan. It's hideous, thought Jerome. *But what was of value to Doctor Chan, may well be of value to us.*

Jerome pulled one of the plane's in-seat handsets out of the armrest. "Now please excuse me Michael. I must report our progress to the Prefect." Jerome waited for Michael to get up from his seat and make his way back to the plane's galley area, before dialing the number. The phone rang once before it was picked up.

"Your Eminence?" asked Jerome.

"Jerome, have you arrived already?" demanded the Prefect impatiently.

"Not yet, Your Eminence, but we should be landing in Rome in less than an hour."

"I have some good news for you Jerome", said the Prefect begrudgingly. "Interpol informs us that one of the suspects they are hunting is a Mr San Lee. He is wanted in connection with art fraud and money laundering. And now he's a suspect in the murder of, God rest his soul, Doctor Chan."

Jerome could almost hear the Prefect smirking.

"So it seems that your carelessness will go unpunished... this time."

"Yes, Your Eminence. That is most fortuitous." Jerome made sure to appear suitably admonished.

"But to more important matters Jerome," snapped the Prefect. "Has there been any sign of the *Jinyi Wei*?"

"No sign, Your Eminence." Jerome spoke as bluntly as he could without appearing disrespectful. But Jerome was dismissive of the idea that this shadowy group of Chinese nationalists would ever pose a significant threat.

"Those enemies of God would like nothing more than to find the *Proditio* before we do," the Prefect warned. "And if they did Jerome, they would embarrass the Church in front of the whole world."

"We remain ever vigilant, Your Eminence."

"With any luck Jerome it will shortly be of little consequence," concluded the Prefect. "Because after searching St. Peter's tomorrow, the *Proditio* should be safety in our keeping."

"But, Your Eminence?" Jerome interjected, hesitant to be as confident as his superior. "What of Doctor Chan's message? 'Toscanelli in St. Peter's' What does it mean? Who is Toscanelli?"

"Ah that, yes!" blurted the Prefect, clearly excited. "It all fits together perfectly Jerome. Paolo Toscanelli was a fifteenth century Florentine astronomer. He was a collaborator with Leone Battista Alberti who was commissioned by Pope Nicholas V to work on the design for the new Basilica of St. Peter's." The Prefect paused, inviting Jerome to share his enthusiasm. "And that's just one of the many potential connections between Toscanelli and St. Peter's."

It was a connection, thought Jerome doubtfully. But what does it have to do with the *Proditio* or its location?

"Even more tellingly Jerome, Toscanelli's letters show that he was in Rome when Pope Eugenesis IV signed the *Proditio.*" The Prefect waited a second for the news to sink in. But his excitement got the better of him. "Don't you see Jerome? It was Toscanelli's astronomical expertise that made him instrumental in disseminating the information that Pope Eugenesis IV earned by signing the *Proditio.*"

Jerome's head swam, as he tried to both absorb the new information, and to remain focused on the task at hand. "But is there anything about Toscanelli's connection with St. Peter's that might reveal the location of the *Proditio* within the Basilica?"

"Of that, we are not yet sure," conceded the Prefect. "We are checking the funeral monuments within the Basilica for any connection to the Toscanelli family. We are examining the records to see whether Toscanelli ever studied at the Vatican archive, whether he was one of the donors, or whether he ever purchased one of the indulgences sold to finance the construction of St. Peter's Basilica."

"Excellent questions, Your Eminence," Jerome muttered with as little sarcasm as he could manage.

"Armed with this information Jerome," said the Prefect firmly, "I have the utmost confidence that tomorrow you will search St. Peter's Basilica and find the *Proditio.*"

"Yes, Your Eminence."

CHAPTER 12

San Lee stared at the cryptic series of numbers that Doctor Chan had written in his own blood, not knowing what to make of them.

"San, did you call the police?" interrupted Su-Lin, as she wiped the last of the tears from her cheeks.

"No." San shook his head, confused by the question. "Why do you ask?"

"Those noises in the distance are Italian Police sirens," explained Su-Lin. "Venetian Police boats most likely."

San had heard the sirens, but it had not occurred to him that they might be heading toward the Doge's Palace.

"Good," declared San. "It's just as well that they are on their way."

"Is it San?" Su-Lin looked out of the window suspiciously. "But why are the Police on their way San?" The pitch of Su-Lin's voice rose as she became increasingly agitated. "Why do they know to come here?"

San felt flustered by the questions and uncomfortable that he did not have a good explanation to give. San and Su-Lin had so far been too distracted by finding Doctor Chan and his message to call for help. So someone else must have called the Police, thought San. "Maybe Doctor Chan called for help before he died?"

"Well quite apart from the fact that there is no phone line in the map room," screeched Su-Lin more aggressively than she had intended. "Doctor Chan has been dead for some time now."

"Maybe the museum staff made the call?"

Su-Lin looked at San sceptically. "And then left Doctor Chan's body here and replaced the bollards when they left?"

San frowned. "I guess that's unlikely."

Su-Lin's expression suddenly changed from incredulous to concern. She stood up abruptly. "We're being set up," concluded Su-Lin.

"That's ridiculous!" retorted San, still kneeling by Doctor Chan's body.

"Is it San?" asked Su-Lin sarcastically. "Why else are Police racing toward the scene of a murder, when the very museum in which the murder has occurred, are unaware of the incident?"

"But why set us up? We haven't done anything!"

"I know that San. You know that. But what do the Police out there think they know?" Su-Lin pointed in the direction of the sirens. "What have they been told San?"

"They might be here for something completely unrelated." San grasped desperately for an alternate explanation. "Maybe some tourist stole something from the gift shop? I don't know." San knew it was unconvincing the moment he opened his mouth.

"I think we should go," said Su-Lin calmly.

"Run?" It was San's turn to raise his voice. "If we run, we'll only confirm whatever suspicions they might have! They'll think we really are guilty."

"Well stay if you like San. But, Doctor Chan is dead!" Tears began pooling in Su-Lin's eyes again. "You wanted his bronze sculpture. That's a motive for murder. We've both got blood on our clothes. That's evidence we murdered him. And we are about to be caught at the scene of the crime."

San did not know how to respond. Everything Su-Lin had said was true, thought San. *But surely they could explain. Surely the Police would understand?*

Su-Lin's face was flushed, frustration mixed with sadness. "Looks to me like a pretty easy day's work for the Venetian Police." She folded her arms and stared at San.

She's right. San gave in. "So what do you suggest we do?"

Su-Lin stared into space for a moment to think. "The exit that's furthest from the canal and the Police boats is the gate over by the Basilica."

San nodded.

"Come on then," said Su-Lin quietly, as she led San back across the map room toward the door through which they had entered. She was going to leave behind the black plastic tube that she had dropped earlier, but she thought better of it, picked it up and hefted it on to her shoulder again. When they got to the map room door, Su-Lin paused listening for any activity in the corridor. But there was nothing unusual. Su-Lin took one last glance in the direction of Doctor Chan and bit her lip before slipping out and into the corridor.

San replaced the bollard and rope barrier after closing the map room door behind them. There was a steady stream of tourists climbing the golden staircase. Periodically they would stop to crane their necks and admire the ceiling. San and Su-Lin headed back the way they had come and toward the Palace's internal courtyard.

But once they got to the first floor landing, Su-Lin did not continue on down the golden staircase, and back the way they had come. Instead, she waved her staff pass at the museum attendant guarding the entrance to the arcaded verandah on the first floor overlooking the courtyard. This part of the Doge's Palace was normally off limits to visitors. But Su-Lin knew that it would allow them to move much faster than through the museum's crowd of tourists.

Just before reaching the end of the veranda, Su-Lin turned sharply left and out from under the first floor arcade and on to the landing at the top of the *Scala dei Giganti* – the Giant's Staircase. It was here that each new Doge of Venice was coronated. Su-Lin passed between the two large statues of Mars and Neptune that had given the staircase its name, before descending the broad marble steps to the Palace's internal courtyard.

At ground level again, Su-Lin headed across to the north west corner of the courtyard, where the Doge's Palace joined St. Mark's Basilica. The Basilica was originally only a temporary chapel within the Doge's Palace. It had first been built almost one thousand, two hundred years ago to house the relics of St. Mark the Evangelist that Venetian merchants had stolen from the city of Alexandria in Egypt. But, when the much larger Basilica was built, it was joined to the Palace, forming a tunnel like exit under the Palace's west wing.

San and Su-Lin hurried toward the exit. But, as they approached, a lone security guard appeared from under the arcade lining the west edge of the courtyard. The guard's eyes scanned the tourists wandering about the Palace's courtyard. Su-Lin slowed herself down to a less conspicuous pace. San tried to relax his thumping heart and avoid any eye contact with the security guard.

"*Mi scusi?*" said the guard stepping out in front of Su-Lin. "Excuse me miss?"

San's eyes widened. His first instinct was to run. But there was no getting past Su-Lin and the guard. And running back the way they had come and toward the Police, was an even less appetizing prospect.

CHAPTER 13

"Still nothing!" fumed Agent Tao Ma, throwing San Lee's empty suitcase against the hotel room wall in frustration. He knew that time was against them. Every minute without a lead meant that San Lee was that much further away from being caught. Furthermore, the longer they risked searching San Lee's hotel room, the greater the risk that they would be discovered by the local Police. Tao moved on to the closet, patting down the hanging shirts and jackets to ensure they hadn't missed anything that San may have left in the pockets.

"Got anything?" demanded Tao.

"Nothing sir," reported Agent Mei-Li glumly, as she went through the small desk in the corner of the room. "Just a map of Venice and a hotel voucher."

"Keep looking." Tao moved on to the bedside table. He picked up the pile of magazines lying on the table. The first couple were Korean *manhwa*. "Childish," he grunted as he flicked through the comics to make sure there was nothing hidden inside them. Tossing them on the bed, Tao next found a brochure for what looked to be gambling machines. Tao couldn't read the Japanese, but the Chinese characters spelling the name of the product were clear enough – Fist of the North Star. More garbage, Tao scoffed. Lastly, he came to a dark gray spiral bound notebook. Opening the notebook, Tao found newspaper articles stuck to the first few pages on top of which San had scribbled notes and highlighted key parts of the text. The newspaper articles all concerned a Taiwanese woman who had died in an accident not so long ago. Tao stared at the photo which accompanied one of the newspaper articles. Where do I recognize that photo from? he wondered.

"Sir!" yelled Mei-Li. "I think I've got something."

Tao snapped out of his thoughts, and looked up from the notebook he was examining.

"Plane tickets," Mei-Li announced loudly, pleased with herself. She opened a small paper folder, took out the ticket and showed it to Tao.

"Where to?" Tao had his hands on his hips, already irritated with Mei-Li's lack of urgency.

Mei-Li studied the green and white card tickets. "San Lee has a reservation on Japan Airlines flight JL400 returning to Osaka via Tokyo tomorrow afternoon."

"Tomorrow?" San scowled, confused. "How can San expect to get the bronze sculpture on to a flight?" *A bronze sculpture that size will set off every metal detector in the airport.*

"It doesn't matter," concluded Mei-Li, "Interpol will pick him up at the airport."

"Focus!" snapped Tao. "We don't want San Lee. He's just a means to an end. And the end is the bronze rat's head sculpture. Although San doesn't know that Interpol are after him yet, he'd probably know how difficult it would be to get the sculpture through security. So he would only plan to go to the airport, if he has already identified a buyer." *And plans to sell the sculpture before he gets on the flight!* "Where's he flying from?"

Mei-Li's eyes flicked to the ticket and back again. "He's departing from Rome's Fiumicino Airport sir."

"And to get from here to Rome," Tao mumbled, thinking aloud. "He could..."

"Drive?" suggested Mei-Li.

"Drive from Venice?" Tao gave agent Mei-Li a withering look. "Have you not noticed we're surrounded by water?"

"I meant..." Mei-Li blushed, berating herself for her imprecision. "I meant after crossing the Ponte della Liberta – the Freedom Bridge, to Port Marghera." Mei-Li grated her teeth, irritated that Tao was always so humorless.

"Of course you did." Tao rolled his eyes sarcastically. "He could also fly from Venice's Marco Polo Airport."

"Or catch a train," Mei-Li added, still smarting from being scolded by Tao.

Tao paced the room for a moment, thinking to himself. "If he checks in to a flight, he'll have to present his passport, and Interpol will pick him up."

But if he travels by train, we might lose him, thought Tao, cursing the liberal rules allowing free movement across borders within Europe.

"Agent Mei-Li," ordered Tao decisively, "We've got to get out of here before the Police arrive. Quickly, grab all the written material and all of San Lee's personal effects that you can carry."

"Yes sir." Mei-Li picked up San's suitcase and began shoveling San's magazines and papers into the bag.

"And monitor the local police radio channels," Tao added. "Contact me immediately if they locate him first."

Mei-Li nodded an acknowledgement. "And what is your plan sir?"

But Tao had already run from the hotel room.

CHAPTER 14

The security guard raised a hand, halting San and Su-Lin in front of the exit at the north west corner of the Doge's Palace. Not only was the guard large, but he had a crew cut and matching scowl. To San he looked permanently angry, unhappy with his lot in life, as though he was frustrated that one too many disciplinary incidents had prevented him from enlisting in the real armed forces. San started to sweat, grasping for things to say, for an explanation, or an excuse.

"Yes?" asked Su-Lin innocently, smiling sweetly.

Flirting? Good idea, thought San, that might work.

"Sorry miss," said the guard more softly than his face appeared capable of. "But I'm afraid your guest here," he continued in a more officious tone, pointing at San. "He will have to return his pass."

"Sorry." San smiled nervously. "I forgot it was only a day pass."

The guard nodded politely at Su-Lin, doing his best impression of a smile. But he eyed San suspiciously. San's hand shook imperceptibly as he handed over his pass.

"Thank you officer," chirped Su-Lin.

"Miss." The guard tipped his hat to Su-Lin, turned on

his heel and headed back to his post. San and Su-Lin exhaled audibly in relief.

After going through the turnstiles, the north west exit from the Doge's Palace led into a short tunnel under the Palace's west wing. Halfway down the tunnel Su-Lin passed the map tube she had been carrying to San. "Could you hold this for a moment?" As they walked, Su-Lin took off her lab coat. "This must look conspicuous," she explained, before scrunching up the lab coat into a ball and throwing it into a garbage bin at the end of the tunnel. "That's better." Su-Lin smiled.

But rather than comfort San, it only served to remind him that they were running away without knowing who they were running from.

The tunnel opened on to St. Mark's Square at the point where the Piazzetta joined the main body of the Square to form an enormous L-shaped public space. Ever since St. Mark's Square was enlarged in the twelfth century for a papal visit, it had been the political, religious, and cultural heart of Venice. San was relieved to find it overflowing with the usual crowd of tourists.

"Where to now?" asked San.

"Somewhere away from here. Somewhere I can think," said Su-Lin. "We need a taxi."

"In Venice?" San gently mocked Su-Lin's suggestion.

"A water taxi San." Su-Lin covered her mouth with her hand trying to conceal a faint, but much needed giggle.

San felt a little foolish.

San and Su-Lin slipped into the camouflage of milling tourists. They weren't quite dressed the part. Neither of them carried an SLR camera, nor was either of them wearing a sun visor. But San suspected Asian tourists probably all looked the same to the local Police. Su-Lin led San out across the heart of St. Mark's Square toward its northern edge, sending pigeons scrambling to get out of their way.

Su-Lin flinched as a flock of pigeons flew uncomfortably close. “Disgusting creatures.”

“Rats of the sky,” agreed San. “I can't say I understand why tourists take photos of themselves feeding pigeons.”

On San's right, they passed a couple of famous pieces of loot captured during the Fourth Crusade. Wedged into the corner of the Basilica nearest to the Palace’s exit they passed the porphyry sculpture of Diocletian’s tetrarchy, while above them, on top of the Basilica's façade were four copper horse statues said to have once adorned Trajan's column in Rome.

On San’s left they passed St. Mark's Campanile - the Basilica's bell tower, which at about four hundred feet in height, was the tallest building in Venice. A particularly unlucky structure, thought San. The bell tower had been struck by lightning, immolated, and finally collapsed before it was completely rebuilt in the early twentieth century.

At the northern edge of St. Mark’s Square, San and Su-Lin entered a narrow tunnel that opened between two cafes and ran under the Procuratie Vecchie. The procuraties were three long, two storey buildings built on the three sides of St. Mark's square facing the Basilica. The Procuratie Vecchie was the oldest of the three and was built in the sixteenth century to house the offices of San Marco’s procurators - the administrators of the Basilica. A far cry from the procuraties’ present use thought San, which now served Europe's most expensive cups of coffee.

The tunnel ended at a tee junction. To the right, the street followed the canal as it passed behind the Procuratie Vecchie. To the left it crossed the canal immediately in front of them and disappeared between a yellow ochre apartment building and one of the *mascherari*'s shops - a mask maker, selling masks for Venice's annual *Carnevale.*

The Venice at the end of the short tunnel was a sharp contrast to the grand, open space of St. Mark's Square. Here, the streets began to twist around tightly packed apartment blocks or leap across the labyrinth of narrow canals. No two walls seemed to be perfectly parallel and everything was coated with in a thin layer of mould and lichen, giving a melancholy impression of decaying grandeur. The streets were narrow, admitting little sunlight to ground level and there were fewer pedestrians away from the popular tourist destinations. It would be very easy to get lost, thought San.

But Su-Lin headed neither left nor right. Instead, she walked to the canal edge and looked up and down its length. A little further down the canal, she saw a small motor boat and its pilot lazily reading the newspaper. Su-Lin leant precariously out from the edge of the canal, whistled and waved.

Eventually the wizened, old boat pilot noticed Su-Lin waving at him. The pilot started up the motor boat's engine, and edged the craft forward until he pulled up alongside Su-Lin. The boat was white with green trim. But the paint was peeling and the trim rusted. Like Venice, the boat had clearly seen better days.

The pilot too was in his seventies at least, and wore a similarly faded naval jacket and shabby white cap atop a well-tanned and deeply lined face. He smiled welcomingly, offering both hands, to help Su-Lin into the boat. But he left San to clamber in after her by himself.

Su-Lin settled into the bench seat just behind the pilot, whereas San was unceremoniously dumped into his seat as the pilot accelerated away from the canal's edge. The pilot looked to Su-Lin for directions.

"Santa Lucia Railway Station please," instructed Su-Lin, before turning to San. "We need to get to Rome."

CHAPTER 15

Agent Tao Ma raced from San Lee's hotel room in the Londra Palace Hotel and along the fourth floor corridor to the lifts. He hammered on the button to call a lift. But both elevators were waiting at the ground floor lobby.

"Damn it!" swore Tao, knowing every precious minute counted. He shoved open the emergency exit door that led to the stairwell. *It will be quicker to use the stairs.*

Less than a minute later, Tao burst out into the street from the hotel lobby before turning right and accelerating along the Riva degli Schiavoni. After arriving from Murano, Tao had left the motor boat outside the Hotel Danieli. But it seemed a mile away to Tao, as he ran along the waterfront to where he had parked the boat. If San tries flying to Rome, Interpol will catch him for us, thought Tao. *But if he escapes Venice by train, we might lose him and the bronze rat's head sculpture forever.*

Opposite the Hotel Danieli, Tao turned left on to a short wooden pier. He unhooked the mooring line from the palina or black and blue striped mooring pole over which he had left it. He pushed hard on the motorboat's bow to start it moving backwards before he jumped into the cockpit. Tao turned the steering wheel hard to the right, so by the time the engine had started, the motorboat had drifted free of the boat parked to its left and Tao could accelerate away from the dock.

Tao ignored the open lagoon to his left, and followed the shoreline to his right, steering the motorboat into the mouth of the Grand Canal. He knew that the Grand Canal snaked toward Venice's main rail terminal – Santa Lucia Station. Tao toyed with the idea of heading up through one of the smaller canals in search of a short cut. But without any experience navigating Venice's canals he knew that he would almost certainly get lost.

The mouth of the Grand Canal was, Tao reckoned, almost a hundred yards wide. There was a line of elegant apartments on the northern side of the canal facing the glistening white domes of the Basilica of St. Mary of Health on the other. The Basilica was a plague church built in the seventeenth century after a third of Venice's population was wiped out by the Black Death. Although whether the Basilica was built to mourn the third of Venice who had died, or for the two thirds who hadn't died to say thanks, Tao was not sure.

Unlike the southern edge of Venice near St. Mark's Square, where it was possible to walk along the edge of the lagoon, the apartments at this end of the Grand Canal were inaccessible on the canal side except by boat. Without access, there were few tourists, giving Tao a rare moment of relative peace and an opportunity to soak in his surroundings.

Some people call the Chinese city of Zhouzhuang, the Venice of the East, thought Tao. But only by those people who have never been to Venice, he sneered. *The old heart of Zhouzhuang is barely the size of a soccer field!* Marco Polo might have written that he admired the thousands of old stone bridges crossing the canals of Suzhou, but precious few of them remained today. They have been slowly consumed by the ever expanding metropolis of Shanghai. But it is progress, thought Tao. *It is good for the state.*

Tao was shaken from his thoughts by an angry gondolier yelling at him. The gondolier was waving aggressively for Tao to slow down because the wash from Tao's motorboat had set the gondola swaying precipitously, scaring two of its passengers. The narrower the Grand Canal became, the greater the density of slow moving gondolas and ferries, and the increasingly frustrated Tao became at the slow pace of progress.

The Grand Canal was at its narrowest at the Rialto Bridge - the geographic center of Venice, where Tao estimated the canal was no more than a hundred feet wide. The high stone arch of the four hundred year old Rialto Bridge was one of only four bridges to span the Grand Canal. It was an unusually broad bridge with two rows of shops along its length, separating three lanes of pedestrian traffic. Despite the season, the bridge was crowded with tourists shopping, or admiring the view down the canal. On both ends of the bridge, restaurants lined the canal, adding to the boat traffic that Tao had to slow down to negotiate.

Beyond the Rialto Bridge the Grand Canal widened again and Tao was relieved to be regaining speed. Tao noticed that the mix of boat traffic began to change too. The further he got from the Rialto Bridge, the number of gondolas diminished, whereas the number of water taxis increased, ferrying passengers between the train station and Venice's better hotels. But even though the Grand Canal was less crowded than before, speed limits were strictly enforced. Tao had to balance his urgency against the interminable delay that being pulled over by a Police boat would incur.

The Grand Canal bent sharply to the left, and from Tao's memory of the maps he had seen, he guessed that he was now well over half way to the train station. A minute later and Tao could see the Church of San Geremia looming up on his right. The Church was a white, stocky building not much taller than the surrounding hotels and apartments. But Tao knew that the same buildings that crowded around San Geremia also blocked his view of the train station, which was now no more than a couple hundred yards in front of him.

Tao slowed the boat as he approached Venice's Santa Lucia Station and steered across to the berths on the right hand side of the canal. The station opened onto a large square whose southernmost edge bordered the Grand Canal. Tourists would typically disembark from their train and catch one of the boat taxis waiting to take them to their hotel. Tao didn't wait for the boat to stop, let alone secure it to a mooring post, before leaping out onto the pier and clambering up the canal wall. Tour boat operators looking to collect tourists arriving by train complained loudly as Tao abandoned his boat in such a busy part of the waterway.

Having reached the top of the canal wall, Tao dashed across the square in front of the station. It was obvious even to the normally disinterested Tao that the Santa Lucia Train Station building was one of the ugliest buildings in Venice, built with a stubborn lack of regard for the surrounding history. He climbed the broad flight of stairs that led up the station building and pushed through one of the many glass doors.

Tao paused for a second to let his eyes adjust to dull interior of the station, and to search out the departure board. The station was hectically busy, a sharp contrast to the leisurely pace of the boat traffic on Venice's canals. There was a constant din of screeching trains, unintelligible platform announcements, and hundreds of people wheeling luggage back and forth.

Tao quickly spotted the departure board, jogged over to it, and waited a few moments for the display to flick from Italian to English. Tao could see that trains were scheduled to leave for Rome every fifteen minutes and the next train to Rome left in two minutes, from platform three.

Tao checked his watch. "Excellent!" he smiled, feeling encouraged by the information on the departure board. He doubted that San could be more than fifteen minutes ahead of him. So while it was only a hunch that San might use a train to get to his flight from Rome, if the hunch was correct, San was in all likelihood in the station, or on his way.

CHAPTER 16

San Lee watched on as Su-Lin paid with cash for two train tickets to Rome at the ticket offices of Venice's Santa Lucia train station.

"We've got to hurry," urged Su-Lin. "The train leaves in a couple of minutes."

San quietly followed her through the crowd of tourists to platform three. He knew that a decision would shortly be made for him, unless he first made one for himself.

They approached the gates separating the platforms from the waiting area. Su-Lin tugged at San's jacket. "That's it." Su-Lin pointed at one of the waiting trains, as she showed their tickets to the ticket inspector. The train was an express, judging by the red, blue and gray striped design and the slightly more aerodynamic shape of the engine car. Hardly a *Shinkansen*, thought San. *But about as fast as one could expect in Italy.*

The train had not yet opened its doors for boarding and so passengers milled about in approximately carriage width intervals along the platform. San smiled to himself. In Japan, the passengers would be far more orderly - standing in neat queues within clearly painted yellow lines on the platform.

Those passengers encumbered with luggage were loath to carry their bags all the way down the platform and so Su-Lin seeing that the nearer end of the platform was more crowded than the other, walked briskly around the waiting passengers and toward the far end of the platform.

Having almost reached the end of the platform, San reached gently for Su-Lin's wrist. It startled Su-Lin, although he had not intended it to, and she abruptly came to a halt.

"Yes, this is far enough." Su-Lin smiled awkwardly, not knowing what to make of San's worried expression.

"Why Rome Su-Lin?" asked San, with a serious look on his face.

"Doctor Chan's date is the only clue we have to go on. If we discover what those numbers mean, if we understand what date he is referring to…"

"If it is a date," interrupted San.

"It might explain why Doctor Chan was killed."

True, thought San, but this is not my problem. He felt guilty, knowing that he was reacting selfishly. Doctor Chan's death was certainly more serious than any of San's problems. *But I have to find the bronze rat's head sculpture.*

Sadness crept back into Su-Lin's face. "And Doctor Chan didn't deserve to die like that San. No one deserves to have died like that. Torn apart like a piece of meat." Tears began to gather in Su-Lin's eyes again. "Who could have done such a thing?"

San patted Su-Lin's arm in sympathy.

"Doctor Chan gave me an opportunity to work with him. He looked after me. He nurtured me," Su-Lin said pleadingly. "I owe it to him to at least try and understand the last thing he ever wrote."

"But why Rome Su-Lin?" San repeated himself, struggling to keep the frustration from his voice. "How is travelling to Rome going to help?"

"The best interpretation of Doctor Chan's numbers that we could come up with was that they referred to the date of Marco Polo's birthday."

San nodded an acknowledgement.

"I know a scholar in Rome - Doctor Stefano Macheda, whose specialty is early Renaissance explorers. If anyone can tell us more about these numbers, it's Doctor Macheda."

She is right, thought San. *She needs to go to Rome.*

Su-Lin was looking straight into San's eyes, and San wondered for a moment whether she could see in his face, the doubt that he felt.

"San, whoever killed Doctor Chan, in all likelihood has also stolen the bronze sculpture," Su-Lin said firmly. "The bronze sculpture that you desperately need to buy."

Desperately indeed, thought San. The commission from a purchase this big was the only conceivable way that San could think of clearing his father's debts. Like most of the Japanese economy, San's father's pachinko arcade business had recently suffered. But whereas larger businesses could borrow from banks when times were tough, smaller businesses could only turn to the extortionate rates offered by consumer finance companies. But since these lenders were being regulated out of existence, it wasn't long before San's father had been borrowing from the four fingered criminal element. And whereas the consumer finance companies would merely suggest you throw yourself from a window to collect on the insurance money, the Yakuza would offer to harvest and sell your kidneys for you. San also knew that his choice of career had always been a disappointment to his mother. A disappointment that had never been put right before her accident, thought San. *I'll be damned if I disappoint my father too.*

"I do need to find that bronze sculpture," San conceded.

"These are the same people that framed us for the murder of Doctor Chan," continued Su-Lin. "If we find out why Doctor Chan was murdered, we also find out who killed him. If we find the killers, we'll also find your bronze sculpture, and clear *our* names."

San fought to suppress a half smile. *She made a good case.*

"And San…" Su-Lin took half a step forward, putting her hand lightly on top of San's forearm. "I could use your help."

There was a sharp whistle of hydraulic pressure as the train doors opened smoothly.

"Let's board the train," said San resolutely.

CHAPTER 17

"Will all remaining passengers bound for Rome on platform three, please board the train now," blared the announcement, first in Italian and then again in English. "This train will be departing shortly."

"Damn it!" swore Agent Tao Ma, checking his watch. *Just my luck to be chasing the only train in Italy that's running on time.*

He turned from the departure board near the ticketing offices and ran toward the platform area of the station, searching for platform three. Santa Lucia station was a large station, because it was the only practical way for all but the very richest visitors, to get to Venice. There were more than a dozen platforms and most of them were busily disgorging tourists. Tao spotted a sign for platform fourteen, and cursed again, realizing he was in the wrong end of the station. Running toward the east end of the station, Tao passed platforms ten and nine, and then seven and eight. *Only a couple more to go.*

Tao slowed as he approached platform three. Ticket barriers at each platform separated the public area of the station from the platforms which were for paying passengers only. On Tao's side of the ticket barriers there was a queue of passengers presenting their tickets to the inspectors. Beyond the ticket barriers, the platform swarmed with passengers struggling to get their luggage up and into the carriages of the train to Rome. Tao stopped to scan the faces of the queued passengers, searching for San Lee. It wasn't as easy as it would be in the rest of Italy, grimaced Tao. Venice's fame and Asia's growing prosperity meant at least a third of the people waiting to pass through the ticket barriers were Asian tourists. And amongst them Tao could see absolutely no sign of San.

Tao approached the barriers to get a better look at those passengers already on the platform. He shaded his eyes from the sun and stood as tall as he could for a better view. About three quarters of the way down the platform, he thought he could see a tall, Asian man dressed in black. Is that San? wondered Tao. He doesn't seem to have any baggage, thought Tao, which would fit with what we found left in his hotel room. But, the crowded platform, the haze of diesel smoke, and the distance meant that Tao could not be sure. He could see that the tall Asian man was standing in a queue waiting to board the train and he was talking to a smartly dressed lady with long black hair. Although only a couple of inches shorter than San, Tao thought she was too slightly built to be Italian. But Tao didn't recognise her either. San may not even have arrived at the Station yet, growled Tao. *He may not even be traveling by train!*

But Tao knew that he wouldn't be happy not knowing for sure and so he joined the queue at the ticket gate that led to platform three. After less than a minute, Tao reflexively checked his watch. The queue didn't feel as though it was moving at all, fumed Tao. He tried pushing, but it drew a strong rebuke from the people standing ahead of him in the queue. He knew what they said must have been rude, because he hardly understood a word of it.

Losing patience with the European respect for queues,

Tao left the line, took a couple of paces to gain momentum, and hurdled the hip-high barrier dividing the waiting area from the platforms and trains. But as soon as he landed, in a well-balanced crouch, two blue uniformed guards stepped away from the queue to intercept him. One guard made an open hand gesture for Tao to stop. The second guard placed his hand on Tao's shoulder and gestured for him to get back in the queue.

In China, this could be resolved easily, thought Tao. For a start, he could have just drawn his firearm and demanded to be allowed through to the platform. *But that would not be viewed as career enhancing, even in China.* Alternatively, in China, Tao could simply contact the stationmaster and have the train stopped and searched. But this was Italy, and Tao was a long way from his jurisdiction. *I shouldn't even be carrying this firearm.*

The guards demanded a ticket. But Tao just shrugged, shaking his head innocently and pretending not to understand. The guards pointed at the ticket office, shepherding Tao back toward the ticket barriers. Then a thought occurred to Tao. He turned to look along platform three, and at the top of his lungs, above the din of the station, Tao shouted, "San!"

The performance further irritated the platform guards who pushed Tao with unreasonable force back toward the gate. But the tall Asian man, now stepping onto the train, turned his head when he heard Tao yell. He was too surprised and too far away to turn exactly in the right direction, but the sign of recognition on his face was unambiguous.

Tao smiled. *I've got you San Lee.*

Tao raised his hands in submission to the guards as the train doors closed behind San and his companion. Innocent men don't run, thought Tao. San Lee's train slowly accelerated from the platform. *And now I know where you're running to.*

Tao pulled out his cellphone. It's at least three hours to Rome by train, thought Tao.

"Mei-Li!" barked Tao, before she had a chance to say anything.

"Yes Sir?"

"Get us on the next available flight to Rome," ordered Tao. *We'll arrive in Rome before San does.*

CHAPTER 18

Su-Lin had been lulled to sleep by the regular sway of the speeding train bound for Rome. San sat opposite Su-Lin, staring out of the window at the remains of a Roman aqueduct whose ruin wound its way across the fields. They sat in one of the older style carriages with separate compartments, and its own door, dividing it from a corridor running the length of the carriage. Because it wasn't too busy, they had an eight seat cabin all to themselves, quaintly decorated with wooden armrests and curtains.

The train rattled its way over a bridge. Su-Lin startled, her eyes opening.

"You're awake," smiled San.

"Sorry." Su-Lin felt a little embarrassed. She rubbed her eyes and stretched her arms like a yawning cat.

"It's alright. You gave me some time to think." San's smile faded. "And you have had a difficult day."

"We both have," agreed Su-Lin.

A couple of seconds later San sought to break the awkward silence. "The page that Doctor Chan's numbers were written on, do you recognize where it was from?"

"Yes, it was an ephemeris table," Su-Lin answered

confidently. "Or more exactly, it was a page from a compendium of ephemeris tables."

"Sorry. Please forgive my ignorance. But it was a what?"

"An ephemeris table." Su-Lin grinned, basking in her area of expertise. "It's like a calendar. But instead of telling you the days of the year, it tells you what the positions of the stars and planets will be on any particular day. But it only tells you the positions of the stars in one particularly place."

"And what are they used for?"

"They are used for navigation. Or at least they were." Su-Lin waited for a moment, not wanting to appear overly condescending. "There are no street signs in the middle of the ocean, and a map would just be a large expanse of blue. So in the days before GPS and laser guidance, you had to navigate by the sun and the stars."

"Sure, but how does an ephemeris table help with navigation?"

"Well if you know where the stars should be on a particular night, in Nanjing for example, you simply measure how far out of position the stars are wherever you do happen to be, to measure exactly how far you are from Nanjing."

San nodded, impressed.

"It was quite an important development, because without being able to use the stars to calculate position, it was extremely dangerous for sailors to cross open oceans. For centuries most boats moved only on rivers or within sight of land. Even if you managed to survive an ocean crossing, without such navigation techniques, there would be no way of getting back, let alone being able to mark it on a map so others could follow your route."

"And I guess any improvement in navigation techniques, not only improved maps, but extended the distance by which traders could travel safely and make money," chimed in San.

"Exactly and that explains why the technology was so valuable. By 1280 the Chinese had observed the position of the stars on every day of a 1,461 day cycle and by 1384 they had produced a calendar for navigators with which they could calculate their position at sea based on the observed position of stars. And it's not just as simple as drawing maps of the stars because to be able to use the technique you needed to understand that the earth not only orbited the Sun, but that it orbited in an irregular ellipse. Europeans wouldn't work out either of these two facts for another couple of centuries."

Su-Lin could sense that while this might be interesting, San didn't quite realize how it related to Doctor Chan's numbers. "This page." Su-Lin held up Doctor Chan's last message. "The page on which Doctor Chan wrote those numbers, was torn from one of those calendars."

San sat there for a moment in thought. "Does that mean," San began, suspecting that he might be about to embarrass himself, "if we have an ephemeris table that shows the positions of the stars, we can work backwards, and figure out the date to which the table refers?"

Now it was Su-Lin's turn to be impressed. "I guess so," she nodded, realizing that San was referring to the piece of paper on which Doctor Chan's message had been written. "Just give me a moment." Su-Lin looked again at the scrap of paper on which Doctor Chan had written his cryptic numbers. A couple of minutes later after deciphering some old Chinese script and making a few calculations, Su-Lin put down her pen. "This page refers to the position of the stars on July the sixth 1439."

"Another date," said San rolling his eyes. "So our best guess for Doctor Chan's numbers was that they should be read as January the fifth 1254, which we suspect might refer to Marco Polo's birthday. And now we have a second date - July the sixth 1439. Does 1439 mean anything to you?"

"It's about the beginning of the Renaissance?"

San frowned. "But the Renaissance is an era, a loose period. It's not something that began on a specific day."

Su-Lin wore a blank expression, not being able to think of an alternative.

"I think it's the year in which Gutenberg invented printing with movable type," suggested San.

"Invented?" sneered Su-Lin, wrinkling her nose. "The Chinese had invented movable type four hundred years earlier. Gutenberg was just the first European to catch up."

"It was just a guess." San pouted, a little surprised by Su-Lin's abrasive reaction. "Although I can't really see a connection between movable type printing and Doctor Chan's research interests anyway."

"Hopefully Stefano will be able to help us figure out this date as well."

"And Doctor Macheda is the historian we're meeting in Rome?"

"Now, he is more of a writer," corrected Su-Lin. "But he used to lecture in history at the British School in Rome. He's one of the foremost authorities on early European exploration," she continued admiringly, "he's written biographies of Marco Polo and other renaissance explorers of the New World."

"And how do you know him?"

Su-Lin blushed. And the more Su-Lin blushed, the more San smiled smugly, knowing he'd stumbled upon an interesting story.

"When I was an undergraduate history student," began Su-Lin, shakily. "I was young and impressionable."

San smiled broadly.

"We were both adults," added Su-Lin defensively.

They both laughed.

"So you grew up in Italy?" asked San.

"Yes and got my undergraduate degree in history here in Rome. But I'm half Chinese, so my Mandarin is fine. In fact, since Doctor Chan has been doing most of his research in Europe, it was actually my language skills that I think persuaded him to take me on as a doctoral student."

"What was Doctor Chan working on anyway?"

"He was taking OCT scans of the maps painted on the walls of the Doge's Palace," explained Su-Lin. "Are you familiar with the technique?"

"Yes, in the study of art providence, optical coherence tomography, and other forms of tomography for that matter, are used to examine a painting's different layers." San felt more confident now the conversation had moved to an area he was familiar with. "We can use tomography to determine whether a masterpiece is authentic or an elaborate fake. Or we can use the technique to determine whether a second artist, an apprentice perhaps, has added to a master's painting at a later date. The technique can also be used to see whether a painting has changed much from the original pencil sketch that lies underneath the paint."

"Precisely," Su-Lin continued. "Doctor Chan wanted to date the separate layers of paint used in the maps of the Doge's Palace."

"But, why? Weren't the maps part of the original building and finished in the early fifteenth century?"

"Yes, you're absolutely right San. The maps were part of the original building. But one of the maps shows the North West coast of Canada and North America."

It took a moment for San to appreciate the significance of what Su-Lin had said. "But Columbus didn't discover America until 1492!" complained San.

"And it would hardly be a discovery if there was already a map of the destination," Su-Lin said sarcastically.

San was shocked. "So is the map a fake?"

"Or was Columbus a fraud?" challenged Su-Lin.

San, like every other high school student, had learnt that Columbus discovered America. "It's such an obvious problem," he mumbled, stunned that he'd never heard any objections raised to it.

"But it's not that simple," qualified Su-Lin. "For a start, the Doge's palace was badly damaged by fire in 1486. And there's always the possibility that the paintings were altered at a later date. So Doctor Chan had hoped to use the OCT scanning technique to examine the different layers of paint and date the order in which the important details were added."

"But if the maps were painted before Columbus returned from the Americas how on earth did they know what to paint?"

But San was interrupted by the ring tone of Su-Lin's cellphone.

"Hello?" Su-Lin covered one ear to block out the noise of the train. "Oh thanks for getting back to me."

"Just a second." Su-Lin scrabbled in her brown leather satchel for a pen. "Lunch at 1:00pm tomorrow, in the courtyard of the Vatican Library. Got it! Thanks again. Bye."

Su-Lin put the phone back into her bag. "We're all set."

"That was Doctor Macheda?" asked San.

"No, his secretary. She's arranged a meeting for us tomorrow at the Vatican Library. If there's anyone who can help us get to the bottom of Doctor Chan's two mysterious dates, it's Stefano."

CHAPTER 19

Inquisitor Jerome knelt in prayer at the foot of the monument to Pope Paul III at the rear of St. Peter's Papal Basilica in Rome. Jerome had abandoned his cane, which now lay before him, and on both knees he closed his eyes and clasped his hands together tightly. Silently, he prayed to St. Dominic, the founder of his order and for the wisdom of those that had gone before him. He prayed to Pope Gregory IX, who had honored the Dominican Order with the task of defending the faith, and to Pope Paul III who had defined their curial jurisdiction and established the Sacred Congregation for the Doctrine of the Faith. With God's blessing we will prevail in this investigation, thought Jerome. *We will find the Proditio… and destroy it.*

But Jerome's silent introspection was interrupted by the hurried clicking of a dozen digital camera shutters from a nearby tour group.

Heathens in the Papal Basilica! "It shouldn't be allowed!" he cursed in disgust.

Jerome opened his eyes and struggled back to his feet. He briefly considered using his cane to teach these disrespectful tourists what the fear of God really meant.

But, he thought better of it. After all, he shrugged, there is work to be done, and instead he turned to walk back down the nave of the Basilica.

St. Peter's Basilica was one of the most holy Catholic sites, because, according to tradition, it was built on the tomb of St. Peter, one of Jesus' apostles. But Jerome did not like St. Peter's Basilica. It's not even four hundred years old, he sneered. The Basilica's construction was finished in 1626 making it less than half the age of the great, Gothic and Norman cathedrals in Paris, Reims, Durham or Salisbury, bemoaned Jerome. *And it has none of their threateningly austere majesty.*

The design was not to Jerome's taste either. The layout of St. Peter's Basilica was heavily influenced by the, *unhealthily secular,* Renaissance interest in perspective. And it was designed largely by Michelangelo. That notorious homosexual shouldn't even have been allowed to receive the sacrament he growled. *Let alone design this house of God.* "That was your fault," muttered Jerome, glancing over his shoulder accusingly at the statue of Pope Paul III.

But what it lacked in age, St. Peter's made up for in size. Jerome looked down the two hundred yard long nave, and up the massive stone columns almost twenty yards in circumference, to a ceiling fifty yards above his head. St. Peter's Basilica was the largest church in Christendom. It covered almost six acres in area, and it was capacious enough to seat sixty thousand worshippers. It contained more than a hundred tombs and thousands of art works. And the *Proditio,* a treaty signed between the Pope Eugenesis IV and the Ming Emperor Xuan De, was hidden somewhere within its walls. Jerome took a deep breath trying not to feel overwhelmed. *And I am tasked with locating it.*

However, despite the Prefect's enthusiasm, Jerome was not entirely convinced by the Prefect's interpretation of Doctor Chan's last words. "Toscanelli in St. Peter's," he repeated. It might mean that the *Proditio* was hidden within St. Peter's Basilica, he thought. But, he had looked over the Prefect's research and had some grave concerns. Toscanelli was not related to any of the Popes either buried or commemorated in St. Peter's. Toscanelli had not worked in Rome and he had certainly not worked on the construction or the design of St. Peter's. Toscanelli had not, nor had any of his family, purchased any of the indulgences sold by the church to finance the construction of the Basilica.

On a more encouraging note, the Prefect's research had revealed that Toscanelli had worked with fellow Florentine Leone Battista Alberti who had been commissioned to work on the design of St. Peter's. But Toscanelli and Alberti's common interest was mathematics and astronomy, not architecture. Ultimately thought Jerome, there was nothing that directly connected Toscanelli with St. Peter's. Despite the Prefect's fervent belief, there was nothing from Toscanelli's history that indicated the *Proditio* was located somewhere within the vast interior of St. Peter's Basilica.

But while Toscanelli's connection with St. Peter's was doubtful, Jerome could not deny Toscanelli's connection with the *Proditio.* Toscanelli's letters to Columbus and the King of Portugal's personal priest - Fernan Matins, showed that Toscanelli had been in Florence and met Pope Eugenesis IV. Furthermore, Toscanelli had also met the Chinese embassy from the Ming Emperor Xuan De with whom Pope Eugenesis IV signed the *Proditio.* Jerome picked out a copy of Toscanelli's letter that the Prefect had sent him and read, "In the days of Pope Eugenesis IV, there came an ambassador to him and I had a long conversation with the ambassador about many things."

Jerome ran his finger down the page to the next line he had highlighted in Toscanelli's letter. Toscanelli wrote that he learned from the Chinese ambassadors that, "a globe could represent the earth," and that, "China can be reached by sailing to the west, even though we usually say to the

East." *Europeans wouldn't learn this for themselves for almost another century after Toscanelli.*

Jerome knew this scientific knowledge and the navigational techniques were of staggering importance and value. It allowed Europe to find, reach and colonize the New World. Whether Eugenesis IV's motive was driven by the prospect of the millions of souls in the New World to whom the Church could deliver salvation, or by the prospect of earning the New World's gold and slaves, was unclear. But either way, the temptation would have been enormous. Moreover, Eugenesis IV would have known that Imperial China did not colonize like the Europeans and there would be little competition for control of the New World's riches.

Instead, Imperial China was an empire of tribute, rued Jerome. Tribute was offered by the vassal states to China, and in turn, China bestowed gifts of wealth and technology to the vassal. So to earn these gifts, Pope Eugenesis IV had only to sign the *Proditio* and concede that the Holy Catholic Church was a vassal - a mere tributary of Imperial China.

"But what a price to pay," sighed Jerome, shaking his head. *It contradicts the apostolic authority of the Church.* The Church was founded by God and the Pope wields supreme power over her. Jerome nodded confidently. It is Di Fide – divine and infallible revelation. *To believe otherwise is heresy.*

There were over ninety popes buried within St. Peter's Basilica. But Pope Eugenesis IV had not been granted that honor. Eugenesis IV had been buried in Constantine's old St. Peter's Basilica. But when the current St. Peter's Basilica was completed in 1626, his body was transferred to San Salvatore in Lauro, until recently a simple parish church on the other side of the river Tiber. "He was lucky to be buried in consecrated ground at all," grimaced Jerome. *For all the trouble he's caused us, for signing the Proditio, for his betrayal.*

CHAPTER 20

San Lee woke up as the mid-morning sun began streaming in through the lounge room windows of Su-Lin's apartment in Rome. The apartment was a small one bedroom loft on the top floor of an old apartment building, just off the Via del Babuino. The building sat about midway between the Spanish steps and the Piazza del Popolo in one of Rome's older residential areas that over the last century had been invaded by small fashion boutiques and al fresco restaurants. There wasn't much of a view, but when San stood on the balcony, and leant dangerously over the railing, you could just about see the dome of St. Peter's Basilica in the distance.

San was a little embarrassed to have fallen asleep on Su-Lin's couch. It reminded him of high school and being relegated to the lounge room when staying at his ex-girlfriend's parent's house. But the alternative of a hotel was impractical. Not because they arrived in Rome particularly late last night after the train trip from Venice, but if he had stayed in a hotel, he would have had to present his passport, advertising his location to the local Police. San thought it was sweet of Su-Lin to have covered him up with a blanket sometime during the night.

San had showered and put the coffee on by the time that Su-Lin emerged. She wore a tight white T-shirt and track suit pants, sheepishly playing with her morning hair as she headed toward the bathroom.

"Good morning," said San, smiling at the contrast to the normally immaculately presented Su-Lin.

"Sorry. I slept in. I'll be ready in ten minutes."

"I hope you don't mind," said San apologetically. "I put the coffee on."

"Help yourself."

"And I couldn't resist the *miyeok guk* in the refrigerator."

"The what?"

"The seaweed soup."

"Oh that?" Su-Lin sounded surprised, having apparently forgotten it was there. "It's not mine."

"Did your Korean boyfriend leave it behind?"

"Ex-boyfriend," she explained. "Where did you think that spare shirt you're wearing came from?"

"Touché," whispered San under his breath. He could hear Su-Lin turning on the water in the shower.

As San finished off the bowl of soup, he wandered around Su-Lin's lounge room, scanning the book shelves. Both ends of Su-Lin's lounge room were lined with bookcases. They were full of histories mainly, betraying her academic background, but also maps and a selection of vampire romance novels. Between the books, were scattered statuettes and antique bric-a-brac.

A pale yellow, oval-shaped stone about the size of a cellphone caught San's eye. It was resting in a purpose-built lacquered wood stand. San picked it up and turned it over. There were three Chinese characters written down its center. But the characters were faded and in an archaic form of script. San could not make them out.

"What have you found there?" Su-Lin walked back into the lounge room rubbing her hair with a towel. She was wearing tight blue jeans, a white long-sleeved T-shirt and a short, but heavily padded, black, leather jacket. "Oh that? It's just a souvenir," she said, taking the stone from San and replacing it hastily on her book shelf. "Are you ready?"

"Yep, let's go."

San put his empty soup bowl in the kitchen sink and joined Su-Lin by the front door. She was slipping on a pair of heavy, knee high boots over her jeans. San grabbed his long leather jacket from the hook on the back of the door. Su-Lin threw back the last of the espresso that San had made for her and collected her keys.

"It's a nice apartment," San commented as Su-Lin locked the door, wondering just how much PhD research assistants were paid these days.

"Thanks. It was a gift from my parents."

"Cool parents," quipped San. "It's a nice part of town."

"They died. It was left to me." Su-Lin spoke in a matter of fact way.

San turned a little red, wanting to bite his own tongue. "I'm sorry. That was insensitive."

"That's OK." Su-Lin shrugged indifferently. "It was a long time ago. I never really knew them. I was very young."

Losing a parent is never easy, thought San to himself. *I don't ever want to learn what losing both of mine might feel like.*

San and Su-Lin made their way to the ground floor in a beautiful old elevator with a sliding cage door.

Su-Lin smiled noticing San admiring the antique lift's polished brass fittings. "It's wonderfully analogue, isn't it?"

When they got to the ground floor San looked to Su-Lin for cues as to which direction they would be taking. "Taxi or walking?"

"Neither." Su-Lin grinned. Instead of heading out on to the street in front of the apartment building, she walked out into the small courtyard at the rear. From the paved courtyard, Su-Lin entered what looked like a large garden shed and emerged a few seconds later. "This is for you," she said, passing San one of two black motor bike helmets. "Try it for size." Su-Lin then ducked back inside the shed and this time returned, pushing a seriously large, red trimmed motorbike - a Ducati Monster.

"I haven't driven a motorbike in ages," reminisced San.

"Don't worry." Su-Lin sniggered. "You won't be driving this one either." Su-Lin straddled the bike and kicked up the stand.

"Funny, I imagined you to be a Vespa kind of girl." San hopped on to the back of the bike gingerly, holding the rear faring as Su-Lin started the engine.

"Don't be shy," Su-Lin teased. "You're just as likely to fall off backwards sitting that upright."

San shifted his weight forward and held Su-Lin's thin waist tentatively.

Su-Lin edged the bike in to the street. "Let's hope Stefano has something to tell us about Doctor Chan's dates," she said, before the acceleration of the bike drowned out any hope of a conversation.

CHAPTER 21

Agent Mei-Li watched over the rear entrance of the apartment block to where she and Agent Tao Ma had followed San Lee and his accomplice the night before. She had been there all night, keeping watch from the driver's seat of her car.

On the previous day, after Tao had confirmed that San was traveling to Rome by train, Mei-Li had arranged a flight from Venice so that they both arrived in Rome before San. It was then a relatively simple task of waiting in Rome's central station for San's train to arrive. From there they followed San and his accomplice to the apartment Mei-Li and Tao were now staking out.

Tao was monitoring the front entrance of the apartment on the Via del Babuino.

"And no doubt enjoying a fresh croissant and a warm cup of coffee at that stand-up cafe he's sitting in," grumbled Mei-Li, yawning.

It had been a long night and there was still no sign of the bronze rat's head sculpture. Mei-Li guessed that her boss wouldn't risk taking San into custody until he already knew where the bronze sculpture was. It would be completely illegal for Tao to make such an arrest. *Although that's hardly likely to stop him.* But there was the small practical issue that if they arrested San Lee, there would be no guarantee that he would have the sculpture in his possession, or that he would reveal the location of the sculpture when questioned. *No matter what Tao did to him.*

Mei-Li stared out of the right hand side of her car toward the fashion boutiques which lined the opposite side of the street. It was still too early for them to be open, but she peered through the shop window covetously. Mei-Li was amazed that while Rome had a full complement of the international brands like Louis Vuitton, Gucci and Chanel, there were also hundreds of local brands that she had never heard of before.

Sadly, Mei-Li also knew that most of these shops sold goods priced far beyond a Ministry of State Security Agent's pay grade. Neither was she the kind of girl who would attract a rich sponsor that could buy them for her as gifts. She wasn't entirely sure whether this fact bothered her or not. It was a lifestyle choice that more than one of her friends back home had made. And while Mei-Li didn't feel particularly judgmental about the issue, she aspired to greater independence.

Mei-Li's headset crackled in her ear.

"Agent Mei-Li?" Tao asked, as he had done regularly since they had taken up their positions the previous evening. "Anything to report?"

"Still nothing Sir," she answered wearily.

The line fell abruptly silent. Tao was never one for civilities. Something to which Mei-Li was now accustomed. He was never bothered whether his subordinates liked him or not. Not that she minded. It was simpler this way. Tao was a hardworking and efficient boss, and while that meant he was correspondingly demanding, he was either uninterested or incapable of playing social or political games.

His behavior on this assignment was no different. Tao had approached the problem methodically. While he could have tipped off the Italian Police or Interpol and have had San Lee arrested immediately, he had not informed them of San's location. It made sense, she conceded, because to retrieve the bronze rat's head sculpture quickly meant preventing the sculpture from ending up in an Italian Police evidence locker. Tao also surmised that San couldn't possibly expect to get the bronze sculpture on to a plane, and therefore San was intending to sell it before he left Rome. *And we just need to be there when he does.*

But Mei-Li found it difficult to sympathize with Tao's determination to find the bronze rat's head sculpture. "What do we want this ugly bronze sculpture for anyway?" she had asked. Sure it was a Chinese sculpture, and sure it had been stolen by foreigners. *But that was hundreds of years ago!* The idea that a notionally Communist Party was idealistically motivated by something stolen from the last emperor was preposterous, grunted Mei-Li. *And I for one can't pretend otherwise.*

Mei-Li was roused from her thoughts, by the gate at the back of the apartment building being pushed open. Once open, she could see two figures in black motorbike helmets. The taller of the two wore a long, black leather jacket much like San Lee had done the night before. The second figure wore blue jeans and a biker's jacket, but was far more slightly built. While Mei-Li couldn't identify her, it could be the woman that they had seen San Lee disembarking the train with last night.

"Sir, there is movement at the rear of the apartment block," whispered Mei-Li into her headset. "Someone has opened the gate at the back of the apartment. It looks as though they are getting ready to leave"

"Is it the target?" asked Tao, excitedly. "Is it San Lee and his accomplice?"

"There are two people. Probably one man and one

woman on a red motorbike."

"Probably?" Tao leapt quickly to anger. "Identify them Agent Mei-Li! Is it San?"

"I can't identify them," she snapped back. "They are both wearing motorbike helmets."

The smaller of the two riders, edged the large red motorbike to the curb, looking left as they prepared to turn right. It looked to Mei-Li as though they were planning on heading in her direction and on toward the Tiber.

"What do you want me to do sir?" asked Mei-Li. "They're leaving, and it looks like they are heading west."

Tao fell silent for a moment, considering the situation.

Mei-Li knew that if it was San on that motorbike and she didn't follow them, they could lose San and the bronze sculpture for good. She started the car in anticipation of Tao's orders.

"Agent Mei-Li," barked Tao, as she revved the car's engine into life. "Follow the motorbike, and contact me as soon as you've got a positive identification."

The red motorbike roared past Mei-Li's car.

"Yes sir!" Mei-Li scrambled to perform a U-turn so as not to lose the motorbike.

"I'll stay here and see if I can find out if San is still in the apartment."

CHAPTER 22

Even on the back of Su-Lin's Ducati Monster, it took San and Su-Lin almost twenty minutes to get through Rome's chaotic traffic to Vatican City. Su-Lin parked the motorbike as close to the Vatican as she could. But the only empty spot that she found was one of the motorbike parking bays on the Via della Conciliazione, Mussolini's contribution to city planning and the major artery joining the Vatican to the heart of Rome. From there, it was a five minute walk to the entrance of the Vatican Museum.

For one of the oldest, largest and certainly among the most famous of all museums, the Vatican museum had a peculiarly modest entrance. A large black wooden door, in an otherwise featureless brick wall surrounding Vatican City was all that indicated the entrance to a five hundred year old museum visited by millions of people each year.

The Vatican Library where Doctor Macheda was working was buried in the middle of the museum. Fortunately, Doctor Macheda had been kind enough to leave two passes at the museum's entrance, and directions for a guide to escort San and Su-Lin to the Vatican Library's courtyard. This let them avoid the infamously long queues which, on a busy day, could stretch for two hours around the stone walls of Vatican City.

"Doctor Macheda's apparently studying a copy of *Marvels of the World*," Su-Lin explained as they followed their guide into the Sistine Hall.

The Sistine Hall, like its namesake the Sistine Chapel, had an elaborately painted ceiling of biblical and ecclesiastical images. Centuries ago, the Sistine Hall had once housed the Vatican Library's collection until more space was required. After the collection was moved to its current location, the hall became one of the museum's many galleries, and the Library's reading rooms were moved to the floor above.

"It's Marco Polo's travelogue from his trip from Italy to China and back in the thirteenth century," she continued.

But San was not listening to Su-Lin. He was thoroughly distracted by the heady density of art and architecture in the museum.

Su-Lin smiled, watching San staring at the ceiling. "Have you not been here before San?"

"I've visited the Vatican Museum a couple of times. Twice while I was at university, and once since, while I was on holiday. For an art history student it's sort of compulsory to go."

"And once an art history student, always an art history student," she joked.

But San's enthusiasm had blunted his humor detectors. "But I've never visited the library."

Their guide led them to the library's reception desk and asked them to sign in. The Vatican Library was not open to the public like a regular library and it was only because Doctor Macheda had arranged their visit that San and Su-Lin were able to enter without the normally lengthy application procedure.

The Vatican Library was one of the oldest libraries in the world, even older than St. Peter's Basilica or the Vatican

Museum in which the library now resided. Pope Nicholas V had established the library in 1475 by bequeathing the books he had inherited from his predecessors. Since then, the library had grown into one of the world's largest collection of medieval manuscripts.

But San and Su-Lin were not here to see the collection. Instead, after they had signed in, their guide led them into a small courtyard, which nestled between the library and the museum's New Wing. The paved courtyard was open to the sky and contained half a dozen small tables around which academics and students read or chatted. It was peaceful, befitting a library thought San, and especially quiet compared to the bustle of tourists percolating through the museum.

San and Su-Lin's guide indicated a table on the other side of the courtyard in front of a row of potted shrubs. At the table sat a balding, contently plump, and well-tanned man whom San guessed was in his early fifties. He wore sunglasses, a brown jacket and while time had eroded the hair on his head, it had done little to diminish the coarse hair on his chest which now clambered over his flamboyantly open necked shirt. He was reading an issue of Classical Quarterly and taking notes in a small purple notebook.

Their guide bid them farewell, leaving San and Su-Lin alone.

"He's a little old," sniggered San, gently nudging Su-Lin with his elbow.

Su-Lin ignored him, but her eyes narrowed.

As they approached it took a moment for Doctor Macheda to notice Su-Lin. But as soon as he did, he hurried to stand up, grinning widely.

"Su-Lin, it's been too long!" welcomed Doctor Macheda merrily in Italian, embracing her warmly and kissing her on both cheeks. "You are as beautiful as ever." Doctor Macheda had a bright smile and a disarmingly open demeanor.

"Stefano, I'd like you to meet a friend of mine," said Su-Lin in English. "San Lee, this is Doctor Stefano Macheda."

"A friend?" Stefano smiled, shaking San's hand firmly while holding San's shoulder in a half embrace. "A special friend I think." Stefano winked at Su-Lin. "No?"

Su-Lin blushed and avoided eye contact with Doctor Macheda.

San smiled, bemused by the exchange.

"You're breaking my heart Su-Lin." Stefano grinned cheekily, gesturing extravagantly at the simple wooden chairs around the table, "Sit. Please sit."

"Stefano thank you very much for seeing us," said Su-Lin in a more serious tone.

"No. I must apologize to you for not being able to meet you in a more comfortable environment. But the library has only recently reopened." Stefano shrugged. "You understand." Doctor Macheda leant forward gently holding Su-Lin's forearm. "And this manuscript... It's beautiful!" Doctor Macheda, oozed enthusiasm. "And not just any copy, this copy of Marco Polo's travelogue has been annotated by the hand of Christopher Columbus himself! There is no doubt in my mind that it was one of the chief inspirations for Columbus' voyages."

"No apologies necessary, please," reassured Su-Lin. "We really appreciate you seeing on us on such short notice."

"Anything for my favorite student. How can I help?"

"Well," Su-Lin began, "you remember Doctor Chan?"

"Yes of course I remember. A great cartographer," agreed Stefano, nodding. "But Doctor Chan is an eccentric historian."

"We have been going through one of his notebooks and we were wondering whether you could help us understand the significance of two of the dates we found?"

"I can try. What are the dates?"

"The first date is January the fifth 1254 and the second

date is July the sixth 1439."

Doctor Macheda leant back in his chair and scratched his chin thoughtfully.

"We made a guess at the meaning of the first date." Su-Lin continued talking while Doctor Macheda concentrated on the two dates. "We guessed it might be the date Marco Polo was born. That's why we thought you might be able to help us."

A puzzled expression suddenly crept across Stefano's face. "But why ask me? What has Doctor Chan said of this matter?"

"I'm afraid..." Su-Lin's expression darkened. "Doctor Chan has passed away."

Dr Macheda's eyes widened and his smile faded. He was clearly surprised. "I am very sorry to hear that Su-Lin. I know..." He searched for the right words in English. "...I know you and he were very close. I know his work meant a lot to you."

"And these dates are the last things he ever wrote." Su-Lin's frown deepened and her voice wavered. "If there is anything that you can tell us, anything at all."

Doctor Macheda wrote the two dates on his notebook in front of him. "Although the year is correct, the evidence for the precise day of Marco Polo's birth is very weak," frowned Doctor Macheda. "I'm not sure there is any compelling evidence to suggest Marco Polo was born on a date as specific as the fifth of January."

Su-Lin bit her lip. She was deeply disappointed.

"But." Doctor Macheda smiled. "The second date, July the sixth, 1439 is an unquestionably famous date."

San and Su-Lin both perked up, relieved that there was something to learn.

"In 1439 Pope Eugenesis IV and the Patriarch Joseph II of Constantinople successfully concluded the Council of Florence and reunited the Latin Catholic and Greek Orthodox churches. After the concluding Papal Bull was composed and signed, it was read aloud at a mass held in the Basilica di Santa Maria del Fiore, more commonly known as Florence Cathedral." Pausing for emphasis, Doctor Macheda leant forward, making eye contact with Su-Lin and San. "That day was the sixth of July, 1439."

CHAPTER 23

Brother Michael approached the prospect of interrupting Inquisitor Jerome nervously, knowing full well that Jerome did not like to be disturbed at prayer. But, Michael had run the short distance to St. Peter's Basilica from the Palace of the Holy Office, because he suspected Jerome would be even angrier with him if he wasn't informed immediately.

Michael leaped up the steps past Charlemagne's sculpture - the first Emperor to be crowned in the Basilica, scattering a gaggle of frightened nuns in his wake. He hurried along the Basilica's portico, only slowing to a more reverential pace before entering the Basilica through one of the five sets of bronze double doors. Once inside, Michael instinctively knelt on one knee, bowed his head and crossed himself.

It wasn't long before Michael found Jerome in the Chapel of The Pieta. The chapel was modestly located in a small alcove at the back of the Basilica in the far right hand corner. The rear of the chapel was covered with an orange marble, detailed in green and red. Against the rear wall was mounted a simple white crucifix above an altar. But behind the chapel's altar, on a red marble plinth, sat The Pieta, possibly the Christian world's most famous religious sculpture. The Pieta was a large, white marble statue of Jesus after the crucifixion, lying in the lap of his mother Mary. It was finished in 1499 by Michelangelo and was the only sculpture that he ever signed.

As Michael approached, Jerome was meticulously studying the inscriptions in the chapel, as he had studied the inscriptions on more than a hundred other tombs and monuments that St. Peter's Basilica contained. Jerome exhaled wearily. Again there was nothing here associated with either Pope Eugenesis IV or Toscanelli, let alone anything that indicated to Jerome the location of the *Proditio.*

"Your Excellency," interrupted Michael tentatively. "We may have a problem."

"Another problem Michael?" Jerome turned toward Michael, scowling and dripping with sarcasm. "But I have not yet dealt with our first problem."

Brother Michael's eyes widened nervously. He knew from past humiliations that Jerome was intimidatingly good with words, and Michael was unsure as to whether Jerome's question was rhetorical. *Or whether it was a question at all.*

"The lady I saw in Doctor Chan's research room…"

"Yes Michael?"

"…In St. Mark's Library in Venice."

"Get to the point Michael."

"She's here!" blurted Michael. "She's here in Vatican City!"

"Are you sure Michael?" Jerome's forehead wrinkled and his eyebrows gathered accusingly.

"I've seen her on the security cameras." Michael began to sweat nervously. "I'm certain that it's her."

Jerome considered this for a moment. She can't have followed us to Rome, he thought. She must have been scheduled to be in Rome anyway. *But it would be a strange coincidence indeed.* "What is she doing?"

"She's in the Vatican Library, Your Excellency."

But Jerome spoke before Michael could form the next sentence. "Have you gone back through the security recordings? Where has she been?"

"She went directly to the library," stuttered Michael, feeling rushed.

She may be an academic herself, thought Jerome. She may have simply been sharing St. Mark's Library's resources with Doctor Chan. She may not even know of Doctor Chan's fate. *She may not even care?*

But Jerome knew it was unwise to rely on such wishful thinking. It was just as likely that she was a colleague of Doctor Chan and intimately familiar with work. *And if that proves to be the case, we may have need to talk to her later.*

"What should we do Your Excellency?"

"Just watch her Michael," ordered Jerome. "For now, we need to focus on finding the *Proditio.*" Jerome turned back to finish studying Michelangelo's La Pieta.

"Yes Your Excellency." Michael bowed and turned to go back to the Palace of the Holy Office.

"But Michael."

Michael halted at the sound of Jerome's voice.

"Speak to our allies in the Vatican Library. See if they can help us find out who she is exactly, and why she is here." Jerome paused before another thought occurred to him. "Oh and find out what manuscripts she was examining or which books she was trying to borrow."

"Yes, Your Excellency." Michael bowed again. "Immediately."

Jerome stared at Michelangelo's La Pieta. This sculpture is horribly out of proportion, he sneered. *Our Blessed Virgin Mary would have to be nine feet tall for these proportions to make sense. Or our savior a child!*

Jerome stalked away from the chapel, his metal cane echoing down the nave of the Basilica. As enormous as St.

Peter's Basilica was, it wasn't obvious where anyone would hide a document like the *Proditio.* He had searched the sacristy, the Basilica, and the catacombs. He had paid strict attention to anything written or inscribed on its interior. But so far, he had found nothing. Jerome was beginning to suspect that Doctor Chan's last words were a code of some sort. *If they mean anything at all.*

CHAPTER 24

San Lee leaned back in his chair in the courtyard of the Vatican Library, trying to absorb what Doctor Macheda had just told them. San knew as little about Pope Eugenesis IV as he did about the sixth of July, 1439, let alone any attempt the Pope may have made to reunify the church. But Su-Lin fidgeted excitedly, invigorated by Stefano's explanation of the second of Doctor Chan's two mysterious dates.

"That's the connection!" exclaimed Su-Lin. "Pope Eugenesis IV received an embassy, in Florence, from the Ming Emperor Xuan De in 1434." Su-Lin's eyes flicked from San to Doctor Macheda.

While Stefano smiled warily, San's expression was blank.

Su-Lin pressed on. "You remember that Doctor Chan was working on pre-Columbian maps of the Americas, and in particular, the possibility that the map of the Americas in the Doge's Palace had been based on one?"

San nodded dumbly.

"His hypothesis was that Europeans, and ultimately Christopher Columbus, had a map of the Americas long before any European had rounded Africa and sailed into the Pacific, let alone crossed the Atlantic Ocean to discover

America." Su-Lin gave San and Doctor Macheda a piercing look. "But the obvious question remained, where did they get such a map?"

But despite her enthusiasm, Su-Lin was met with blank expressions.

Su-Lin became frustrated that she alone understood the implications of Doctor Chan's last message. "Doctor Chan is telling us how it happened!"

"OK," nodded San, keen to show he was listening, if not completely comprehending.

"In the fourteenth century before the European Renaissance, China was by far the largest, richest and most technologically advanced country in the world. They had the astronomical knowledge to navigate the oceans, and Doctor Chan is telling us that the Chinese embassy gave that information to Pope Eugenesis IV!"

"But Su-Lin," interjected Doctor Macheda. "There is no evidence that an embassy from the Ming Emperor ever visited Rome or Pope Eugenesis IV."

"Not true!" Su-Lin snapped. "The Florentine astronomer Paolo Toscanelli wrote in two separate letters that he had met a Chinese embassy to Pope Eugenesis IV in Florence. He specifically stated," Su-Lin tapped on the table aggressively, "the Chinese had explained to him that it was possible to sail west from Europe to China. He also said that he had copied a Chinese map showing the route to the Americas and included it with the letter that he sent to Columbus."

"You overstate your case." Doctor Macheda folded his arms. "The providence of these letters, supposedly written by Toscanelli, is unclear. There is no evidence from Columbus to suggest that he ever received such a map, or any other kind of help from Toscanelli."

"But what would be the point of Toscanelli sending such a letter to Columbus after he returned?" she asked critically.

San felt as though he was watching a tennis match.

"Even if there was a Chinese embassy and even if Toscanelli had met them," continued Doctor Macheda calmly, "there is no evidence for a pre-Columbian map of the Americas."

"No evidence?" Su-Lin screeched, exasperated. "What about the map of the Americas painted on the wall of the Doge Palace's map room?"

"It was painted later. The original was destroyed by fire."

"What about Pope Innocent VIII's tomb claiming that the New World was discovered during his life despite the fact that he died before Columbus ever got to America?"

"A small error of tense by the sculptor."

"What about Marco Polo's map from 1297 that shows Alaska?"

"A forgery."

"What about the Pizzagaro chart drawn in 1424 which shows Guadeloupe, an island in the Caribbean, long before the Americas were ever *discovered* by Europeans?"

"Another forgery."

"Why did the Portuguese Prince, Henry the Navigator, issue an order to find Guadeloupe in 1431, sixty two years before the island was discovered by Europeans?"

Doctor Macheda looked weary.

But Su-Lin bristled with energy, as though she was only just getting started. "What about Schoner's globe that shows the straits of Magellan in 1515, five years before the straits were found by Ferdinand Magellan - the first European to sail through the straits and into the Pacific. Or explain to me why Waldesmuller's green globe showed the South American Andes mountains in 1506 before any European had ever seen the South American mountain ranges."

While San was no expert, he was surprised by the weight of evidence.

"Magellan and Antonio Galvao both clearly write that they had seen a map of the Straits of Magellan in the library of the King of Portugal, long before Magellan ever discovered them. In fact, Magellan was sent specifically to find the Straits of Magellan shown on the King's map!" Su-Lin raised her hands palms up as though asking a question. "Where did these pre-Columbian maps of the Americas come from?"

"All right, all right." Doctor Macheda smiled, raising his hands in mock surrender. "Enough of this irresolvable speculation."

"Speculation?" Su-Lin reacted as though she had been insulted. "That's a lot of maps which all have to be forgeries for you to be right."

"You're being stubborn Su-Lin." Doctor Macheda waved his finger at Su-Lin, accusingly.

"You're ignoring the evidence because it doesn't fit with your prejudices," she riposted.

"So the provenance of some maps is not fully understood," admitted Doctor Macheda. "It could be new maps drawn on old paper. Who knows? The facts are that historians for five hundred years have understood that Columbus discovered America and that Magellan was the first to circumnavigate the globe."

"European history, written by Europeans," sulked Su-Lin.

CHAPTER 25

Agent Tao Ma crossed the street wondering if it was San that Agent Mei-Li had seen leaving the apartment building on the back of a motorbike. If it was San Lee, with any luck he hoped, they may have left the bronze rat's head sculpture behind. Conversely, if it wasn't San on the back of that motorbike and if he is still in the apartment, thought Tao, *this could be an ugly altercation.*

To Tao, the exterior of the apartment block looked every one of its three hundred or so years of age. But the lobby interior was very modern, with plain white walls, polished concrete floors and brushed aluminium details. Tao surveyed the letter boxes in the ground floor lobby. None of the letter boxes were marked. But, there was only one apartment per floor on the first three floors. These apartments must be huge he thought. *Three thousand square feet at least!* However, on the top floor, there were two apartments. Since San Lee is single, and so too presumably was his girlfriend, reasoned Tao, she would most likely be living in one of the two smaller lofts. *I'll start there.*

Tao climbed the stairs toward the fourth and highest floor, not trusting the antique elevator around which the stairs wound. When he reached the fourth floor landing, he stopped to listen. It was very quiet. Tao drew his firearm, but it was little comfort. He hardly feared a physical confrontation with San. He's a harmless art buyer, he laughed. But because Tao was only a consular attache assigned to the Chinese Embassy, it wasn't within his jurisdiction to arrest San. So if San was still in his apartment he would have to rely on intimidation. *Or something even less savory.*

Tao's headpiece crackled into life.

"We have a positive identification Sir!" yelled agent Mei-Li excitedly. "It was San Lee on the back of the motorbike. San is with the female companion we saw him get off the train with last night."

"Where are they?"

"They just entered the Vatican Museum."

Tao relaxed and holstered his weapon. That's a stroke of luck he thought, they're at least 20 minutes away. *And it should mean that their apartment is empty.* "Any sign of the bronze rat's head sculpture?"

"No sir. Not yet."

Even better, he smiled, if I can find their apartment and break-in, we will have recovered the bronze sculpture without confrontation. *And without having to pay an agent.*

"Stay on them Mei-Li," ordered Tao. "Contact me immediately if they leave the Vatican Museum. I'm going to have a look at their apartment."

Tao then hung up on Mei-Li. He approached the first of the two apartment entrances in the short corridor on the top floor. Tao bent toward the keyhole and listened. He could hear the faint babble of an Italian drama on TV. Somebody's home here, he concluded. *So it's more likely to be the other apartment.*

Tao repeated the procedure at the second door. He listened. But this time heard nothing. Tao knocked twice. But there was still no response. He peered over his shoulder to check the corridor was clear before pulling two small metal tools from his pocket. The tools looked like large pins or unusually small screwdrivers. Tao inserted both tools into the lock, and began feeling for the lock's pins. A couple of seconds later, the door clicked opened. Tao stepped into the apartment and closed the door behind him.

The door opened on to a long lounge room with book shelves at both ends spanning the width of the room. A large, low leather couch and a Le Corbusier recliner sat perpendicular to the bookshelves and facing the floor to ceiling windows opposite the door. Next to the entrance was a crowded shoe rack. An Asian house, surmised Tao. *I'm in the right place.*

Tao walked across the polished timber floor to survey the book shelves. The shelves were crowded with histories, atlases and rolled up maps. They were written in English, Italian and Mandarin Chinese. Definitely the right place, he nodded. *But still no sign of the bronze rat's head sculpture.*

Tao flicked through some of the books and maps on the shelves and examined the couch. But he found nothing. The room was very open. There were no cabinets, boxes, or drawers, no place in which the bronze rat's head sculpture might have been hidden.

Feeling increasingly frustrated, Tao moved on to the kitchenette and bathroom. But they were both tiny, designed for a single person who spent most of their time eating out. Tao banged about among the pots and pans, searching the kitchen. But again he found nothing, leaving only the bedroom.

Like the rest of the apartment, the bedroom was simple and modern. A king sized bed dominated the room, covered in dark purple and red sheets. An empty bottle of wine and a single, lipstick stained glass rested on the floor by the bed. On either side of the bed were wardrobes. On one side there was a narrow wardrobe between the two windows overlooking the street. On the side closest to the door the wardrobe stretched the width of the room.

Tao slid open the doors of the larger wardrobe. Inside, he found designer jeans, fur coats and leather jackets, some cocktail dresses still in their dry cleaning bags, a couple of yukata and an extensive collection of shoes. No surprises here, he thought, remembering San's companion to be expensively well dressed. Although it's not exactly consistent with an academic's salary, Tao wondered. *But maybe an art thief's?*

Tao crossed the room to the other wardrobe. On closer inspection Tao could see that the narrower wardrobe was an antique, black lacquered cabinet with two doors opening from the center. Tao ran his fingers over the surface of the cabinet admiring the faded red Chinese characters carved into the lacquer surface. Tao removed the iron pin from the rusted latch and opened both doors.

"What's this?" Tao did not know what to make of what he saw.

Resting on a mannequin's torso in the center of the cabinet was a suit of armor. Tao couldn't help but reach out and touch the hundreds of metal plates meticulously sewn into a padded leather jacket. When worn, the heavy suit of armor would have protected the wearer from the chin to below the elbows and knees. On the mannequin's head perched a metal helmet, with a cheek guard and a faded red chin strap. Tao tested the weight of the material. "It's real," he gasped. And judging by the cracked and faded leather and the dull oxidized metal, it was an original Ming Dynasty suit of armor.

Below the mannequin sat a separate wooden stand holding a thick bladed sword, a little less than three feet in length. The leather grip had long since decayed and the metal pommel was also dull with age. *But the edge…* Tao knelt to run his finger along the blade. *Someone had been keeping this sharp.* Along the fuller of the blade Tao noticed some writing. But he couldn't read the writing in the darkness of the cabinet. So Tao lifted the blade out carefully and took it to the window to examine it more closely.

In the better light, Tao saw three unmistakable Chinese characters 錦衣衛 - *Jinyi Wei*. Founded in 1368, by the first Ming Emperor Hongwu, the *Jinyi Wei* were the secret police of China's Ming Dynasty emperors. But the *Jinyi Wei* were disbanded three hundred years later when the Qing Dynasty succeeded the Ming, Tao thought. *So what on earth are they doing in twenty first century Italy?*

CHAPTER 26

Su-Lin and Doctor Macheda sat silently in the courtyard of the Vatican Library. Both nursed their wounds from the earlier verbal sparring. Doctor Macheda folded his hands, and stared at his feet, regretting having repeated an old argument. Su-Lin had a sullen, school girl look on her face as though she resented being ignored or condescended to.

San sought to break the awkward silence. "Doctor Macheda, it seems you've figured out that Doctor Chan's second date was a reference to Pope Eugenesis IV's Council of Florence. But can you shed any light on the meaning of the first date?"

Doctor Macheda returned to the dates he had transcribed to his pad of paper. "As I mentioned earlier, you were correct to identify this as the year of Marco Polo's birth. Furthermore, as Su-Lin knows well, Marco Polo fits with Doctor Chan's research interests." Doctor Macheda shrugged. "But it's overly precise. We just don't know exactly on which say Marco Polo was born. That long ago, it was very rare for anyone outside of a royal family to have had their birth date recorded. Even as recently as a hundred years ago, the best records we have for many people are christening dates and not specific dates of birth."

"So we should consider other possibilities?" concluded San.

"Yes." Doctor Macheda nodded. "I would suggest so."

"Well 1254 is also the year in which the Mongols invaded the Korean kingdom of Goryeo," San suggested. "General Jalairtai Qorchi is meant to have taken hundreds of thousands of prisoners. But I am not sure whether this would have been of any interest to Doctor Chan."

"And while we are on the topic of Mongols," added Doctor Macheda. "1254 is also the year that Pope Innocent IV died. Earlier in his papacy he had sent an embassy to Guyuk, Khan of the Mongols." Doctor Macheda suddenly looked tired. "We could go on. But it would be highly speculative as to whether Doctor Chan was referring to any of these alternatives."

"The reply from the Great Khan Guyuk to Pope Innocent IV still survives," Su-Lin said absently, re-joining the conversation. "He wrote a letter back to Pope Innocent IV. But the letter is hidden away in the Vatican Secret Archives."

San knew that the Vatican Secret Archives was a separate repository within the Vatican Library that contained the Catholic Church's most sensitive materials. Access to the Secret Archives - the Vatican's diplomatic records, Papal correspondence, and accounts was even more strictly limited than access to the Vatican Library. It was nearly impossible for all but a handful of sufficiently Catholic scholars to gain access. Copying materials from the Vatican Secret Archives was absolutely forbidden.

"If the Chinese embassy gave anything to Pope Eugenesis IV," continued Su-Lin, "a map of the Americas for example, like the one Toscanelli sent to Columbus, it might still be locked away in the Vatican Secret Archives."

Doctor Macheda rolled his eyes, but said nothing.

On this point, San sympathized with Doctor Macheda.

While such a suggestion was plausible, it was also hopelessly impossible to verify.

"But why conceal it?" asked Doctor Macheda. "Why go to all the trouble of hiding the origin of this supposed pre-Columbian map of the Americas?"

"Perhaps the church was embarrassed by how they obtained the information?" Su-Lin suggested. "Or perhaps, more simply, they knew exactly how valuable colonizing the New World would be, and sought to conceal the prize from others."

Doctor Macheda sighed, giving up.

"Why else later that same year, after receiving news of the New World from the Chinese embassy, and on the eve of the European voyages of discovery, did Pope Eugenesis IV issue a series of Papal Bulls that made it clear that while Christians should not be enslaved, the pagans of the Americas were enemies of God, and fair game?"

"Perhaps he was trying to defend the recently baptized pagans in Africa from being enslaved," protested Doctor Macheda.

"Or perhaps he was preparing the legal groundwork for the conquest of the Americas," retorted Su-Lin. "A conquest made possible by the Chinese maps of the Americas."

"I think again." Doctor Macheda stood up slowly. "We may have to agree to disagree."

Su-Lin pouted, both irritated with Doctor Macheda and embarrassed that she may have been overzealous.

"Su-Lin, it's always a pleasure." Doctor Macheda bent low to kiss Su-Lin goodbye. "But the Vatican Library's manuscripts demand my attention."

San stood up to shake Doctor Macheda's hand. "It was a pleasure to meet you too. We appreciate all your help with the dates."

"I am sorry I couldn't be of more help San." Doctor Macheda picked up his jacket from the back of the chair and pushed his chair under the table. "Please enjoy your time in Rome." Doctor Macheda collected his journal and pad of paper. But before he left he turned back to San as though he had remembered something important. "If you haven't had the chance before San, I suggest you go and enjoy the museum. Every one of the Vatican Museum's fifty four *sala* are magnificent!"

"I will." San shook Doctor Macheda's hand again.

"And I wish you luck San." Doctor Macheda chuckled, leaning close to San and whispering. "She is a feisty one."

After Doctor Macheda left, San sat back down and looked at Su-Lin.

"Doctor Chan had always believed that Europeans had obtained pre-Columbian maps of the Americas," stated Su-Lin firmly. "Doctor Chan's date is telling us that he found proof that those maps were brought to Europe by the Chinese embassy to Pope Eugenesis IV. From there, Toscanelli passed the maps, and the Chinese technology to use them, to Christopher Columbus enabling him to be the first European to discover America." Su-Lin looked at San resolutely. "All we have to do, is find Doctor Chan's proof."

CHAPTER 27

Inquisitor Jerome had abandoned his search of St. Peter's Basilica and retreated to his study in the Palace of the Holy Office. The Palace was a five storey building to the left of the Basilica as one faced it from the square, just past the Petriano entrance to Vatican City. This innocuous sandstone building housed the Congregation for the Doctrine of Faith. It was here that Pope Benedict XVI, then Cardinal Joseph Ratzinger, worked as Prefect of the Congregation for the Doctrine of Faith for twenty four years.

The Congregation of the Doctrine of Faith was formed in 1542 making it the oldest of the nine congregations of the Roman Curia – the administrative apparatus of the Holy See and government of the Catholic Church. The role of the Congregation for the Doctrine of Faith was defined most recently by Pope John Paul II as one of safeguarding the doctrine of faith and morals throughout the Catholic world.

Jerome's office was on the top floor of the Palace. He headed a department specializing in the investigation of *delicta graviora*, the most serious crimes of all - crimes against the Eucharist, crimes against the sacrament of Penance and crimes against faith itself. He reported directly to the Congregation's leader, the Prefect.

Having searched the Basilica but finding nothing, Jerome was now convinced that Doctor Chan's message was not to be taken literally. After reaching this conclusion he had been angry at first. He was annoyed with himself for having been seduced by the Prefect's overconfidence. But most of all, he was embarrassed to have been duped by the last words of a dying man. *His last intelligible words anyway.*

But Jerome's experience suggested that there was still something of value to learn from Doctor Chan's last words. The art of this craft, thought Jerome, was separating the begrudgingly conceded facts from the desperate misinformation and lies. *Perhaps Doctor Chan has given us a code?*

"Toscanelli in St. Peter's," said Jerome quietly to himself. It was the last thing that Doctor Chan had ever said. For good measure, he wrote out the message on a fresh sheet of paper. He stared at the letters. One sentence of three words, thought Jerome. *Three words or twenty letters.*

But a knock at the door broke Jerome's concentration. He looked up. "Yes Brother Michael?"

"Your Excellency." Brother Michael bowed his head to apologize, conscious of disturbing Jerome for the second time today.

"Yes Michael?"

"I have spoken to our friends in the Vatican Library." Michael hesitated trying to remember what he had planned to say. "As you instructed."

"And what did they say Michael?"

"The lady I saw earlier on the security cameras," mumbled Michael, staring at his shoes. "The same lady I saw in Venice."

"You have identified her?" Jerome struggled to remain patient.

"She signed into the library as a Miss Su-Lin Wong."

"Good work Michael. What were you able to find out about Miss Wong?"

Brother Michael was pleased with his work, but he thought it best to avoid appearing smug. "She's twenty six years old. She carries a European passport." Michael recited steadily and flatly as though he was reading from a shopping list. "She speaks Chinese, Italian and English. And her photo looks like she's a half breed."

"Interesting," thought Jerome aloud. But it was not yet enough to establish how familiar she was with Doctor Chan's research. "And her work?"

"We have her resume from the University of Nanjing website." Michael offered a piece of paper to Jerome.

But Jerome waved it away. "What does it say Michael?"

"She is a PhD student." Michael consulted his notes again. "She has had a couple of articles about Chinese cartography published in obscure academic journals."

Jerome nodded. He had guessed earlier that she might have been another academic and was pleased that this intuition had been confirmed.

"What's her relationship with Doctor Chan?"

"She transferred to Nanjing University's PhD program two years ago, to study under Doctor Chan."

Jerome would have scolded Michael for not getting to the point faster, if he wasn't already digesting the implications. So she may be familiar with Doctor Chan's work, thought Jerome. *But how familiar?*

"Where did she transfer from?"

Michael suddenly looked worried. "We don't know," he conceded.

"Nothing?" Jerome rubbed his chin, not sure how concerned he should be.

"Before two years ago, we found no academic history, no residential address and no record of any bank accounts, either in China or here in Europe."

"Am I to believe she was conjured out of thin air?"

Michael was fairly confident that Jerome's question was rhetorical.

"Anything else?"

"Apparently she was not here to examine the Vatican Library's manuscripts."

Jerome sat up straighter, confused by Michael's comment.

"Our allies in the Vatican Library said she was there to meet someone," Michael continued. "A professor." Michael checked again the notes he had been given. "Doctor Stefano Macheda."

Jerome thought for a moment. But he did not recognize the name. "And who is he Michael?"

"Our contacts in the library tell us that he was a professor of history. And he is now a well-known author and biographer."

"A biographer of whom Michael?"

"Explorers like Marco Polo and..." Michael blushed. He had earlier memorized a fuller list. "Christopher Columbus."

Jerome froze. *What does she want to learn from Christopher Columbus' biographer?* This was too much of a coincidence, thought Jerome. *Does she too know of the Proditio - the document that sent Christopher Columbus to the New World?*

Michael could sense Jerome's unease.

"Michael, watch her. Watch her closely," urged Jerome, a hint of concern entering his voice. "Let me know if she tries leaving Vatican City."

"Yes Your Excellency." Michael waited by the door. But after a few seconds of silence, Michael knew that he was dismissed. He bowed and left Jerome to his thoughts.

Jerome felt uncomfortable. He put his elbows on the desk, folded his hands and leant them against his lips. Was this Su-Lin Wong, like Doctor Chan before her, searching for the Proditio?

He stared at Doctor Chan's message with even deeper concern than before. "Toscanelli in St. Peter's." On the face of it, the sentence meant nothing. Not in this order anyway, thought Jerome. *But what about in another? An anagram perhaps?* Jerome was no mathematician, but even he knew that there were thousands of possibilities. *But it's still worth a try.*

Jerome took out his pen and began writing a new sentence with the letters contained within Doctor Chan's original message. "Peter is Toscanelli," wrote Jerome before putting his pen down and studying the new sentence. It may be grammatically correct, thought Jerome, but it has no meaning. *And there is a T, N and an S left unused.*

Once again, Jerome considered Doctor Chan's message as a collection of letters. He formed the word, "Persistent," from the letters in front of him, and wrote it down. A good start, he thought.

"Latin so persistent," wrote Jerome and then paused. *Again it's meaningless, and there's an E, and a C left over.*

"Persistence not a slit." *Still meaningless.*

"Praise intellect snot." *Meaningless and childish!*

Jerome knew that his frustration and desire to act, was interfering with his ability to focus. So for a moment, Jerome stopped what he was doing, breathed slowly, close his eyes and prayed. A couple of minutes later a far calmer Jerome reopened his eyes and began rearranging the letters of Doctor Chan's message once again.

Four words slowly took shape on his pad of paper. When Jerome was finished, he stared at the finished sentence. Jerome began grating his teeth. His face reddened and the veins in his neck began to bulge. Anger boiled over into rage.

"Get in here now!" screamed a red-faced Jerome. He stood up, quivering with fury. "Now! Brother Michael, now!"

"Toscanelli in St. Peter's," was indeed an anagram. And

with it, Doctor Chan had taken one last swipe at his torturers, determined even in death to uncover the truth of the *Proditio.* Rearranging the letters of Doctor Chan's message, Jerome now read its hidden meaning. "Cannot let lies persist." *Doctor Chan had been playing with us.*

CHAPTER 28

San and Su-Lin approached the Vatican Library's reception desk to sign themselves out.

"I'm sorry San. I hadn't intended to put you through that." Su-Lin looked at San guiltily. "The conversation with Doctor Macheda didn't go quite as smoothly as I had hoped."

"There did seem to be some history between you two on that subject." San had felt more than a little uncomfortable while Su-Lin and Doctor Macheda were arguing. "But at least we now understand the meaning of Doctor Chan's second date."

"Although nothing about the first date," noted Su-Lin glumly.

San sensed that Su-Lin was still a little embarrassed by her behavior in front of Doctor Macheda because she continued in an apologetic tone. "It's an important topic for me San, and Stefano knows exactly how to rub me the wrong way about it."

After leaving the Vatican Library, San and Su-Lin turned right toward the museum's entrance. The next room they entered was called the Gallery of Tapestries. It was a long corridor in which both long walls were covered by sixteenth century Flemish tapestries. Originally decorating the Sistine chapel, the tapestries depicted biblical scenes drawn by the pupils of Raphael. The tapestries had an interesting history, thought San, some had been stolen, some melted down for their gold thread, and one depicted a face whose eyes seemed to follow you around the gallery.

"History is Eurocentric at the best of times," complained Su-Lin.

San had thought that Su-Lin might have given up, but she seemed determined to try and draw him into an argument.

"But to stubbornly stick to one's prejudices in the face of new evidence." Su-Lin shook her head. "It's not scholarly." Su-Lin was working herself up toward anger. "It smacks of chauvinism at best, and racism at worst."

From the Gallery of Tapestries they passed into the Gallery of the Candelabra. From the crowd milling about the corridor it looked to San to be one of the busier sections of the museum. The hall was littered with Roman sculptures, but San could not see any candelabra that might have given the hall its name. It wasn't until San consulted a plaque on the wall that he learnt the corridor got its name from two massive, white, marble candlesticks, built into niches, and facing each other on opposite sides of the hall. They were ridiculously large, thought San. *You could be forgiven for thinking the candlesticks were columns holding up the ceiling.*

"It was exactly the same treatment that Doctor Chan received at the hands of European academic journals when he tried to publish his work."

San nodded a polite acknowledgement.

But Su-Lin was determined to corner San into offering an opinion. "San, what did you think of the evidence for pre-Columbian maps of the Americas?"

San's forehead wrinkled. At first he was irritated by Su-

Lin's insistence that he take a side in an argument he was ill prepared to make. But it took San back to the conversation with Doctor Macheda. San began sifting through his memories.

"San? I said..."

But San interrupted Su-Lin. "What did Doctor Macheda say to us before he left?"

"Goodbye," guessed Su-Lin unhelpfully. She scowled, feeling as though she was being ignored.

"No." San gave Su-Lin a withering look. "What did he say before that?"

"Something about the Vatican Museum."

San stopped. "Do you have a map of the museum?"

"Yes, I picked one up at the entrance." Su-Lin started digging around in her jacket pockets for the map. "But we didn't need one because Stefano had kindly provided us with a guide." Su-Lin pulled out a small brochure. "Why?"

"It's something Doctor Macheda said." San hesitated for a moment before committing to the thought that had occurred to him. "He said there were fifty four *sala* in the Vatican Museum."

Su-Lin unfolded the map and examined its legend. "Well *sala*, or salon in English, simply means room. And yes, there are fifty four galleries in the museum. But so what?"

"We figured out the significance of Doctor Chan's second date, but not the first. What if the first of Doctor Chan's two mysterious dates isn't a date at all?"

Su-Lin was intrigued, but didn't follow San's logic.

"What if it's a location?"

"You mean the first date? The fifth of January 1254?" Su-Lin frowned, still unsure as to what San was suggesting. "How could that be a location?"

"Doctor Macheda didn't see any significance in the fifth of January 1254 as a date."

"Right."

The pitch of San's voice grew as did his enthusiasm. "So

perhaps the numbers aren't meant to indicate a month, a day and a year. Perhaps it's a code. Perhaps Doctor Chan's numbers are meant to be read as 15 of 12 of 54."

Su-Lin suddenly understood what San was suggesting. "You mean Doctor Chan is leading us to the twelfth gallery of the fifty four galleries in the Vatican Museum?"

"It seems possible." San shrugged. "Although I have no idea what the fifteen might indicate in the context of the Vatican Museum's twelfth gallery."

"Nor can I imagine what could Doctor Chan might have actually discovered in a gallery of the Vatican Museum?" added Su-Lin.

"Particularly since the museum is visited by millions of people every year."

"So where's the twelfth gallery?" asked Su-Lin eagerly.

San smiled. "You tell me. You've got the map."

CHAPTER 29

Sitting in the Palace of the Holy Office's security room, Brother Michael watched Doctor Chan's associate - Su-Lin, on the security feed from the Vatican Library. He could see Su-Lin at the reception desk signing a document. He wondered if she was about to leave. Jerome will need to be informed, thought Michael.

It wasn't yet that late, but Michael was already alone in the security office. He didn't mind though. He was used to his colleagues avoiding him. Even as a youngster at a Catholic boarding school his classmates had kept their distance. Threatened by his physique, and impatient with his inability to put a coherent sentence together, he had not been easy for other boys to befriend. It was only his sporting endeavors which were celebrated by his peers, although indiscipline on and off the field sharply curtailed his participation. After a particularly ugly and physical altercation with his own coach, it was politely suggested to his guardians that further schooling would do little to improve Michael's employment prospects. Not knowing exactly what to do with Michael, the state encouraged him to exercise his physical talents in the military. Michael permitted himself a satisfied grin. *And there I excelled.*

Michael's thoughts were interrupted by a loud scream. At first Michael was surprised; it seemed so out of place, in the normal peace and tranquility of Vatican City. It didn't sound to Michael like a desperate, tortured scream. He was very familiar with what that kind of screaming sounded like. This was more a scream of venomous anger, he thought. It was another moment before Michael even considered that the scream may have come from inside, rather than outside the Palace.

"My God!" Michael recognized the voice. *It was Jerome.*

Michael leapt from his chair and ran from the security room. As Michael turned out of the security room, he heard Jerome scream his name and he accelerated toward Jerome's office. *Jerome hasn't been this angry in a very long time.*

As Brother Michael ran, he heard the sharp, tinkling of breaking glass from Jerome's office. The noise was attracting the puzzled expressions of other agents of the Holy Office who poked their heads out of their own cubicles to nose around in the corridor, only to pull them hurriedly back in as Michael charged past.

Michael skidded to a halt outside Jerome's corner office, breaking his momentum by leaning heavily on the door frame. Jerome's office looked out toward St. Peter's Basilica and the large square beyond it bearing the same name. The office was austerely decorated with dark, wood paneling and a large oak desk in front of bookcases at the end of the room opposite the door. The dull, yellow lamp on the desk and the dark, red carpet gave the room a threateningly warm glow.

Although Brother Michael would not enter uninvited, he could see Jerome standing with his back to the door. Jerome was looking out the window toward the setting sun. His hands were folded loosely behind his back, suggesting a calmness that Michael had not expected given the sound of his voice. Shattered glass covered the carpet, apparently from the large, jagged hole recently smashed through one of the windows. One of Jerome's desk lamps was missing from an otherwise painfully well-ordered desk. A car alarm droned from somewhere in the street below.

"Your Excellency?" Michael swallowed anxiously, trying to maintain composure despite panting heavily.

Jerome did not turn around. "Doctor Chan lied to us Michael." Jerome's voice betrayed only the slightest residual anger. "He took us for fools and he laughed at us."

Michael knew that Doctor Chan was dead. But he could not remember him having laughed. Jerome is very good with words, he thought. *I should probably remain silent.*

"Michael, bring me Doctor Chan's whore." Although Jerome spoke calmly, there was an edge to his voice, thought Michael, as though Jerome was struggling with something. "Bring her to me now."

"Yes Your Excellency." Michael bowed.

"No need to worry about her condition Michael." Jerome was nodding slowly, thinking to himself. "We won't be needing her for very long."

"Yes Your Excellency," reiterated Michael. "Should I bring her to the Palace?"

"No, of course not," snapped Jerome, his fury emerging at the slightest provocation. "We will be conducting this investigation offsite." Jerome glanced at Michael to ensure that he understood the instruction. "I will meet you there."

"Of course, Your Excellency." Brother Michael turned to leave.

But Jerome raised his hand as though to bring Brother Michael to a halt. "And Michael?" His voice had returned to a more even temperament. "Bring me my tools."

CHAPTER 30

"Which way is it to the twelfth gallery?" asked San.

Su-Lin searched her copy of the Vatican Museum tourist map. San couldn't help but smile, as Su-Lin rotated the map ninety degrees to orientate herself with her surroundings.

"Back the way we came," Su-Lin concluded. "If we go back to the Vatican Library's entrance and turn left toward the Sistine chapel, instead of right toward the entrance, gallery twelve should be the first room we come to." Su-Lin set off at a faster pace than before, excited by the possibility that they may be on the verge of understanding the other date that Doctor Chan had left behind.

"There's the reception." San pointed ahead after they had retraced their steps through the Gallery of Tapestries.

But this time they passed the library's reception on their left and carried straight on into the Gallery of Maps. At almost a hundred yards long, the Gallery of Maps was the Vatican Museum's longest if not largest single room. The gallery was given its name from the walls being covered with murals of maps and cityscapes. Painted by the Dominican priest and mathematician Ignazio Danti, it took over three years to complete all of the paintings.

"It's just like the map room of the Doge's Palace in Venice." San was in awe of the quantity of painting that had gone into the decoration of the gallery. "I can imagine that, as a cartographer, Doctor Chan would have loved this place."

Su-Lin nodded in agreement. While they stood at the entrance to the gallery, Su-Lin read the brief description that was included within her tourist map. "It says here that the gallery contains forty murals representing different Italian regions and the dominant city of each region."

"Forty murals?" murmured San. "That explains the rest of Doctor Chan's first date." San turned to Su-Lin. "It wasn't a date. It was a location. Doctor Chan was referring to the fifteenth mural in this gallery."

"Doctor Chan's message was 15 12 54," repeated Su-Lin. "The fifteenth map, in the twelfth gallery of the fifty four galleries of the Vatican Museum." Su-Lin beamed, happy that they had finally made sense of Doctor Chan's date.

"So which map is number fifteen?" wondered San. "I can't see any numbers on them."

Su-Lin shrugged. "Let's just count them."

San and Su-Lin walked slowly down the Gallery of Maps, counting the maps as they passed. Each map was a couple of yards wide showing the geography, major cities and roads of a particular region of Italy.

"This is it," announced San, after walking more than halfway down the gallery. The fifteenth map was a large, predominantly green and brown mural of the Italian region of Tuscany, North West of Rome. To one side of the map was inserted a smaller painting of Tuscany's largest city - Florence.

"Doctor Chan has led us to a map of Tuscany and in particular the city of Florence." But San did not sound confident, because while he was now sure of the meaning of Doctor Chan's date, he wasn't sure of the implications of a map of Tuscany.

Su-Lin could sense San's questioning tone. "Doctor Chan's second date – the sixth of July 1439 was telling us how pre-Columbian maps first came to Europe."

"When the embassy from the Ming Emperor Xuan De met Pope Eugenesis IV and maps of the Americas and the technology to use them were given to Toscanelli who then passed them on to Columbus," repeated San. "An elegant solution to the problem of pre-Columbian maps of the Americas for sure. We just need to find some proof."

"Exactly," agreed Su-Lin. "And Doctor Chan's first date, or more precisely, this series of numbers, is telling us where we can find the proof." Su-Lin turned excitedly toward San. "Doctor Chan's proof is located in Florence."

"Miss Su-Lin Wong?" interrupted a gruff voice from behind San.

"Yes?" responded Su-Lin instinctively.

San and Su-Lin span around to see two men, in bright blue, red and orange striped uniforms. One of the two men wore a metal helmet with a red feathered plume running down its center. He also carried an intimidatingly long, wood-handled halberd. The other man wore a similar uniform except for a black beret and a sword in a leather scabbard at his waist. They were members of the Swiss Guard, the mercenary regiment responsible for security at the Apostolic Palace and the personal safety of the Pope.

The older of the two, wearing the black beret, stepped forward. "Miss Su-Lin Wong, come with us."

CHAPTER 31

Agent Mei-Li had followed San Lee and his female companion from their apartment near the Via del Babuino to Vatican City. It had not been difficult. They had not seemed to be in any particularly hurry and they had parked out in the open, close to St. Peter's Square. Keeping an inconspicuous distance, Mei-Li had pulled her car into a parking space about twenty yards from where San and his companion had left their motorbike. From where she had parked, Mei-Li could look up toward St. Peter's Basilica and monitor their motorbike. But once San's companion had locked up the motorbike, they had both headed toward the Vatican Museum, leaving Mei-Li with a dilemma.

Mei-Li could have followed San and his companion into the museum and perhaps have learnt a little bit more about what they were doing. I may even have discovered where San was hiding the bronze rat's head sculpture, she thought. But she knew that the Vatican Museum was enormous and she also had to consider, that if she followed them in, she might lose San and his companion among the tens of thousands of visitors, hundreds of rooms, and multiple exits.

It had been obvious to Agent Mei-Li that on the back of the motorbike neither San Lee nor his companion had brought the bronze sculpture with them. So Mei-Li had reasoned that there was no increased danger of losing the bronze sculpture if she waited for them to return to the motorbike. Furthermore, if she followed them into the museum and lost them completely, she would risk serious damage to her career. This risk, relative to only a small chance of learning something about the bronze sculpture's location, was not a risk that Mei-Li had been prepared to take.

So instead, the day had passed slowly for Mei-Li. She sat in the car and waited for San and his companion to return to the motorbike. "Almost twenty four hours sitting in this car," she cursed, rubbing her sore back.

Eventually in the orange glow of the late afternoon light, Mei-Li caught herself nodding off to sleep. To remedy the situation and to stretch her tired legs, she decided to buy a coffee from the café on the other side of the road. Tao would probably be very angry if he knew that she had left her post. But it was only a short walk, she reasoned, and she would have line of sight to San Lee's motorbike all the way from her car to the café.

Having bought her coffee, Mei-Li returned to the car. She put the cup of coffee on the roof, while fishing in her brown bomber jacket's pockets for her keys. Habitually Mei-Li's eyes flicked from her car keys to the motorbike. But the motorbike was still there, and there was no sign of either San or his companion.

However, as Mei-Li opened the driver's side door, she noticed a man running diagonally across the street from St. Peter's Square. She lifted her sunglasses and squinted at the man. He was still some distance away and the setting sun made it difficult to see any details. But he ran quickly, as though panicking, or at least completely oblivious to the heavy traffic around him. *Why is this guy in such a hurry?*

For a moment, Mei-Li couldn't pull her eyes away. She was sure that, at any moment, the man would be mown down by the busy traffic. A small, white sedan locked up its brakes as the man stepped out in front of the car. Mei-Li winced. *That was close.* The white sedan skidded, the driver beeped the horn angrily, barely missing the man as he sprinted across to Mei-Li's side of the road. The man was tall, wearing black pants and a long, black, leather jacket. She watched him for a few moments before realizing that she may have seem this man before. *Not in the flesh though.* But Mei-Li suddenly recalled the ministry's copy of his passport photo. "That's San Lee!" Where's he going? she wondered. *And why is he in such a hurry?*

Mei-Li abandoned the coffee and jumped into the driver's seat, scrabbling to get the car started. She didn't think San had seen her. He looked way too preoccupied. San leapt on to the back of the motorbike and donned his helmet. What's he doing? thought Mei-Li. *And where's his companion?*

As soon as San had the motorbike started, he revved the engine impatiently, and pulled out at a ninety degree angle to the traffic, preparing to make a U-turn. Mei-Li threw her car into reverse, cursing at the European habit of parking so dangerously close. She didn't have time to be gentle. She reversed firmly into the car behind her and shattered its headlights. But it bumped the car far enough backwards, to make room for her to pull out from the curb.

San shot across the road, merged with the traffic flowing back toward Mei-Li, and passed her heading east on the Via della Colizione, toward the Tiber. Mei-Li span the wheels of her car performing an inelegant U-turn. It was hardly fair, she thought, to be chasing a motorbike in her pokey European hatchback. But there was no choice but to follow, and Mei-Li ignored the blaring complaints of car horns as she forced her way across the road and into the traffic behind San. The Via della Colizione was relatively wide for a street in central Rome, and one of the few streets that wasn't permanently jammed with traffic. Mei-Li tortured the wailing Fiat's motor, in a desperate struggle to keep up with San. *That motorbike's engine is probably bigger than the one in this car!*

San's motorbike turned sharply left toward the Castel San Angelo and Mei-Li scrambled to follow. Diving into the corner, the front wheels of her car chirped loudly as they lost traction for a second. The rear end of the car slid dangerously wide, scaring the pedestrians crossing the road. But through the turn and having wrestled to straighten the car, Mei-Li could breathe a sigh of relief. The traffic nearing the river was its normally agonizingly slow self, and she could see San caught behind a large black minivan trying to enter the roundabout surrounding the Castel San Angelo.

The Castel San Angelo was a large, circular fort built on one of the sharp bends in the Tiber River. Originally built as a mausoleum for the Roman Emperor Hadrian, after the Castel San Angelo was sacked by Goths, it was converted into a castle and then into a prison. Little of its original shape remained.

Mei-Li sat impatiently waiting for the traffic to inch its way over one of the many bridges crossing the Tiber and into the older parts of the city of Rome. Street lights were slowly filling the grayness left by the setting sun. She stuck her head out of the car window and craned her neck to try and keep San in view. But he was similarly trapped just a few car lengths ahead. Mei-Li wondered why San wasn't using the motorbike to zip along the road in between the lines of traffic. He had been in a hurry to get to the bike she thought. *Why isn't he in a hurry now?*

The question continued to gnaw at Mei-Li as she followed San through the narrow streets of Rome. Like tailing anything, she was constantly balancing the chance of losing San against the risk that San might realize he was being followed when determining just how far behind him she should drive. She was pretty confident that San didn't know he was being followed because he continued to drive at a normal speed. But it bothered her that he seemed so much calmer than he had been before he got on the motorbike. *What's changed San Lee?*

Mei-Li began to panic as she waited at an intersection to pass in front of "the type-writer" - the Altare della Patrie, an ugly and unnecessarily large monument to the first King of a unified Italy – Victor Emmanuel II. The lights had changed before she could follow San through the intersection and for a moment she couldn't see San at all. But at the second exit, she was relieved to find San's path blocked by a black minivan.

"A black minivan." Mei-Li squinted and looking closer. "Is that the same black minivan I saw outside the Castel San Angelo?" she wondered. *Is San following that minivan?*

When the lights changed, and the minivan accelerated, Mei-Li noticed that San did as well. When the minivan signaled right, moments later Mei-Li noticed that so would San. It took Mei-Li another three minutes before she was convinced that San Lee was following the well-kept, black minivan. But why? She wondered. *Who's driving the minivan?* While Mei-Li's questions were unanswerable for the moment, once the pattern had been established, she allowed herself to relax and hang back because the minivan was a far less nimble target than San's motorbike.

Another ten minutes winding through the streets of Rome and the black minivan slowed again approaching the large piazza in front of the Papal Basilica Santa Maria Maggiore. At first Mei-Li thought it was simply slowing because of the red light up ahead. But it was soon obvious that the minivan was slowing too quickly and it pulled up short of the lights. The minivan turned into a parking space adjacent to the piazza. From San's hesitation on the back of his motorbike, he seemed as confused as Mei-Li. For a moment San slowed conspicuously, following the minivan.

But he seemed to change his mind thought Mei-Li, because he suddenly surprised her by accelerating around the minivan and toward the other side of the piazza.

Another decision to make, thought Mei-Li. *Follow San or stay here with the minivan?* San obviously didn't have the bronze rat's head sculpture with him on the back of the motorbike, she reasoned. *But that minivan might have the bronze sculpture inside.* So Mei-Li decided to compromise. She parked on the opposite side of the road to the minivan where she could watch both the minivan and where San Lee might be heading. *If San was in such a hurry to follow the minivan all the way from the Vatican Museum, he's not likely to leave now.*

Mei-Li switched off her head lights and waited.

It wasn't long before a large, white suited man got out of the driver's side of the minivan and walked around to the rear of the vehicle. After the white suited man opened the back door, two, no three, more men stumbled out of the back of the minivan and moved toward the Basilica's entrance. Two of the men were dressed in a blue, red and orange striped uniform. It seemed to Mei-Li that they were assisting a third person. But it was dark, and she couldn't make anything out about their faces, let alone identifying who they were. The white suited man grabbed a large brown leather case from the van before shutting the door and following the other men into the Basilica. That bag would be just about the right size for the bronze rat's head sculpture, thought Mei-Li. *Tao will be pleased.*

Mei-Li pulled out her cellphone and punched the number for her boss - Agent Tao Ma.

"Yes?" demanded Tao abruptly.

"Sir!" Mei-Li ignored his tone. "I'm at the piazza in front of the Papal Basilica Santa Maria Magiorre."

"What are you doing there?" snapped Tao. "I told you to watch San…"

"I followed San here!" she blurted out indignantly.

"Does he have the bronze sculpture?"

"I can't be sure, but they may have it with them."

"They?" Tao was confused.

"Yes, he's here with four other men who have entered the Basilica."

"I'll be there in ten minutes," ordered Tao with renewed energy. "Don't do anything until I get there."

CHAPTER 32

Su-Lin slowly came to her senses, her consciousness gradually pushing through the disorientating dizziness of a splitting headache. The first thing she noticed was the darkness. She couldn't see a thing. So instead, she kept her eyes closed and listened. But she couldn't hear anything either, except for the slow beat of a single pair of footsteps on a stone floor. The footsteps echoed deeply as though she was in a vast but enclosed space.

As Su-Lin's head slowly cleared, she tried again to open her eyes. But it was still very dark. No! she thought. She could feel a cloth on her face. *There's a bag over my head!* Su-Lin leapt up and tried to rip the bag away from her eyes. But all she did was twist wildly because her hands were bound with a tightly wound rope, to the arms of a wooden chair. *What the hell?*

The footsteps grew steadily louder. Su-Lin began to panic. *Why am I bound?* "Who's that?" she yelled. "Where am I?" Her voice echoed like the footsteps. *It's like being inside a cave.*

The footsteps stopped not far from Su-Lin.

"Help me!" Su-Lin pleaded. She then saw bright

blinding light, as the black felt bag covering her head was ripped away. Su-Lin squinted and turned her head away from the light. As her eyes slowly adjusted, she opened them just a little. Su-Lin could see that she was tied to a small wooden arm chair, in the middle of a ring of four tall candles. Looking beyond the small circle of light, she could see a square patterned ceiling above her head, and two lines of tall marble columns disappearing into the darkness. Inside the two lines of columns were two lines of pews separated by a central aisle. I'm inside a very large cathedral, thought Su-Lin. *But why am I here?*

Su-Lin tried to remember what had happened. She could remember the Vatican Museum, and being in the Gallery of Maps. She could remember being with San. She could remember being happy. *Florence!* That's it, she thought. *We had just deciphered the meaning of Doctor Chan's first date.* But after meeting the Swiss Guard, she couldn't remember anything, let alone how she got here. *Wherever that is?*

Su-Lin had almost forgotten the approaching footsteps, when a slightly built man, with a bearded, angular face, walked into her field of view. He walked slowly, with the aid of a brushed aluminium cane, but any limp he might have suffered was imperceptible to Su-Lin. The man circled deliberately, but at a distance, studying Su-Lin with cold eyes. He wore a smart white suit, a black shirt and on his lapel was pinned a small silver crucifix bordered by a branch and a sword. *Like the one we found next to Doctor Chan's body!*

"Who are you?" blurted Su-Lin.

"I am Jerome," the man said calmly. "And this is my colleague, Brother Michael." He gestured to his right.

An identically dressed but younger and far larger man stepped from the shadow cast by one of the large marble pillars and into the light of the circle of candles. The younger man looked like a solid mass of muscle and he carried a large, dull metal rod in one hand. If Jerome's eyes looked cold and calculating, Brother Michael's looked empty to Su-Lin. *What do they want with me?*

Jerome resumed circling, speaking in a slow measured voice. "And you Miss Su-Lin Wong, are a student of Doctor Chan's, a historian, a Chinese..."

How do they know who I am?

Jerome stopped circling and stared impassively at Su-Lin, "...and an enemy of God." Jerome pursed his lips and nodded imperceptibly. "This we know," he declared confidently. "But what we do not know." Jerome halted, raising his finger. "What we do not know, yet. Is…" He paused for emphasis. "Are you, or are you not, a member of the *Jinyi Wei*?"

"What?" Su-Lin recoiled in shock.

Jerome's nostrils flared. His lower lip quivered with displeasure. Jerome turned to the larger man ushering him forward. "Brother Michael." Jerome pointed at Su-Lin. "The hand."

A broad, hungry grin spread across Michael's face. He strode forward purposefully. A couple of feet in front of Su-Lin, Michael drew back the metal rod to shoulder height, and swung it down into the back of Su-Lin's hand. Skin tore and Su-Lin screamed. Sweat broke out on her forehead and the colour drained from her cheeks.

"Help me!" screamed Su-Lin at the top of her lungs. Blood trickled between her fingers. "Someone please help me!" She struggled again with her bonds. But she could not break the rope.

Jerome gestured around the interior of the Basilica smiling. "Your friends may well know that you're missing Miss Wong. They may even be looking for you." He leant closer, smiling evilly. "They may even know where you are."

Su-Lin could only watch Jerome as she fought to bring her breathing back under control and push the pain of her injury from her mind.

"But they won't come here." Jerome shook his head. "No. They're not allowed to come here. Not even the

Police can come here."

Su-Lin mouth sagged open in disbelief.

"You're not in Italy now," said Jerome shaking his head. "You are in the Papal Basilica di Santa Maria Magiorre, an extraterritorial property of the Holy See. And the Holy See does not maintain any diplomatic relations with you Chinese... you deniers of Christ."

"This is..." Jerome thought for a moment. "What do the Americans call it?" He searched his English vocabulary. "This is extraordinary rendition."

"And whereas America might not approve of torture." Jerome licked his lips. "The Congregation for the Doctrine of Faith has been doing God's work for over a thousand years." Jerome watched Su-Lin, waiting for the inevitable fear to set in. "So perhaps we can try that again," he proposed. "Are you Miss Wong, a member of the *Jinyi Wei?*"

Su-Lin stared defiantly, and bit her tongue.

Jerome stared right back at Su-Lin. "Brother Michael… the arm."

Again the hulking Michael stepped forward.

Su-Lin desperately leant away. But she was helpless, unable to escape from the chair. This time, Brother Michael swung his club with considerably more force. With practised precision, Brother Michael brought the club down midway between Su-Lin's wrist and her elbow. The bones in Su-Lin's left forearm snapped with a sickeningly audible crack. Su-Lin screamed again, significantly louder than before. Her cries slowly trailed off and her head dropped limp. Su-Lin's hair fell over her face. A bruise began to form where the splintered ulna had torn the surrounding muscle.

Jerome smiled. He stepped forward, as blood ran from Su-Lin's arm and down the front left leg of the chair. Jerome lifted Su-Lin's chin sympathetically. "Oh come now Miss Wong, you're stronger than that," he chided. "I don't believe you would have passed out that easily."

Su-Lin's eyes flashed open and she spat, screaming, "What do you want from me?"

But Jerome did not recoil, he screamed right back into her face. "I want you to know, that we will find out what we want, when we want, and whether you want us to or not." He stepped quickly away from Su-Lin, gesturing again at his colleague. "Brother Michael, her shirt!"

Michael leered at Su-Lin as he approached. His eyes lingered over her body until her skin crawled. But Michael did not hit her again as he had previously. Instead, he stepped past Su-Lin and behind her.

Su-Lin grunted in panic, struggling to keep him within her field of vision. But it was impossible for her to move in the chair.

Michael's calloused fingers caressed Su-Lin's delicate neck.

Disgusted, Su-Lin flinched involuntarily.

Angered, Michael grabbed Su-Lin by the neck with his meaty fingers. The muscles across her shoulders bulged and squirmed in resistance. But Michael relentlessly tightened his grip, squeezing the breath from her. She began to gasp, fighting for breath. Tears welled up in her eyes. Su-Lin feared the worst.

But instead, Michael, with his free hand, grabbed the collar of Su-Lin's white T-shirt and violently tore his hand away. Her T-shirt ripped from the collar, all the way down her back to her waist, falling open like a split pear.

Michael looked up to Jerome and smiled. He threw Su-Lin to the ground. The force of the impact shattered the wooden chair to which she was tied. Su-Lin fell face down, gasping for air in the dust, her arms still bound to the broken remains of the chair. With her T-shirt torn, Su-Lin's back was left naked for Jerome to see, that the delicate white skin of Su-Lin's shoulders was decorated with a striking tattoo of nine five clawed dragons surrounding three large Chinese characters. The Chinese text read "錦衣衛." Su-Lin was a member of the *Jinyi Wei.*

CHAPTER 33

Agent Tao Ma slammed on the brakes and screeched to an abrupt halt behind Agent Mei-Li's parked car. He leapt out of the car, shut the door, and ran across the piazza in front of the Papal Basilica di Santa Maria Maggiore. Tao's eyes searched for Mei-Li. She had called him ten minutes ago with the news that, after leaving the Vatican Museum, San Lee and four others, had driven to the Basilica. This could be how San plans to sell the bronze rat's head sculpture, he thought. *This could be our chance to take it back.*

One of only four Papal Basilicas, Santa Maria Maggiore was built in the fifth century, following the council of Ephesus, to celebrate the council's proclamation that the Virgin Mary was in fact the Mother of God. An odd thing to have to determine in hindsight, thought Tao. The Basilica had closed several hours ago, leaving the piazza now empty of the normally ubiquitous tourists and souvenir stands. Abandoned soft drink containers and yesterday's newspaper blew lazily across the square.

"Agent Mei-Li?" whispered Tao into his mouth piece. "Where are you?"

From the shadows around the base of the Marian

column in the center of the piazza stepped the muscular silhouette of Mei-Li. Tao ran over to meet her.

"Where are they?" he demanded.

"In the Basilica sir." Mei-Li pointed toward the entrance.

"And how many are there?"

"About ten minutes ago, four men entered the church. The one in a white suit carried a leather bag, about the size of a gym bag."

"That's probably the bronze rat's head sculpture." Tao smiled in anticipation of recovering the sculpture. "This could be San Lee's meeting with the buyer or at least a fence who could sell it for him."

"The two in uniform," she continued, "carried a third person into the Basilica."

"Carried?" Tao wrinkled his brow, not knowing what to make of that.

"It was dark Sir, so it was difficult to be sure." Mei-Li hesitated. "The third person was not resisting. But it didn't look like they were moving voluntarily either."

"So four of them?"

"No. Two minutes after I called you, the two men in uniform left again in the minivan."

"That could have been the sale of the sculpture Mei-Li!" Tao's anger flared. "Did they take the sculpture with them?"

"No, not that I could see. They weren't carrying anything with them when they left. I would have followed them if they had." There was a hint of resentment in her voice.

"Did you see San Lee or his companion?" asked Tao.

"I think he was…" she paused, having lost track of her original quarry. "I followed San Lee here from Vatican City. But no, I cannot be sure that he entered the Basilica."

"You can't be sure?" complained Tao, sarcastically. "So we have two or three people in the Basilica, none of whom you've identified?"

"It was dark." Mei-Li pursed her lips.

"We'll talk about this later," he muttered, indicating toward the Basilica. "Lead the way."

Mei-Li led Tao up the Basilica's steps to the five large iron gates that protected the Basilica's arched entrance. In the faint light, Mei-Li could see that the gate's heavy padlock had been left unlocked. Slipping past the gate Mei-Li waited for Tao by the vestibule door. Tao took one last look around the piazza to see whether they were being followed, before joining Mei-Li in the shadows cast by the Basilica's imposing facade. At the vestibule door, they could both hear muffled voices coming from inside.

Slowly pushing open the door, Tao stepped into the nave of the Basilica. It was very dark, except for a small pool of light half way down the center aisle. Tao turned to Mei-Li, placed a finger on his lips, and gestured for her to move slowly. Once both inside, Tao and Mei-Li took a couple of tentative steps forward and knelt down, out of sight, behind the last pew in the Basilica. From there they surveyed the interior.

The nave was lined by two rows of large marble columns that seemed to run the length of the Basilica. On the outside of the two rows of columns ran a narrow aisle around the perimeter of the church. On the inside of the two rows of columns were rows of pews separated by a wide center aisle. About half way down the center aisle, the pews were divided again by an aisle running across the Basilica, perpendicular to the center aisle – the transept. Where the two aisles intersected, in the center of the church, Tao could see a dim circle of candle light. Inside the circle of light, two white suited figures were remonstrating loudly with a third person kneeling on the ground. But it was too dark and we are still too far away to identify anyone, thought Tao. *We need to get close enough to hear what's going on.*

The darkness of the Basilica's interior, the large columns

and the rows of pews would provide ample cover from which to approach, thought Tao. But any misstep on the cold stone floor would echo, giving them away. Tao indicated to Mei-Li that they should circle to the right, past the baptistery, and down the right hand perimeter aisle. This would keep the right hand row of marble columns and a row of wooden pews between them and the people gathered in the circle of light.

The back rests of the wooden pews were almost three foot high. So crouching down, Tao and Mei-Li could move behind them without being seen by either of the two white suited men. Progress was awkward and slow since both Tao and Mei-Li were careful to ensure that their footsteps could not be heard. Five or six pews down from the dim circle of light, the voices of the two white-suited men became loud enough to hear. Tao stopped to listen to what was being said.

"*Quoniam punitio non refertur primo et per se in correctionem et bonum eius qui punitur, sed in bonum publicum ut alii terreantur, et a malis committendis avocentur,*" a deep voice intoned in Latin.

"Very good Michael," crooned a second and older voice, approvingly.

"Shall I translate?" asked the older voice, smugly and rhetorically.

Tao guessed that he was addressing the third person who he had seen kneeling on the floor.

The voice paused, but there was no response. "Your punishment is not for your correction, but so that others will be terrified of the evil that they might otherwise commit."

What the hell is going on here? Tao looked at Mei-Li, with a questioning glance. But she shrugged, just as confused as he was. With his back to one of the columns, Tao edged upwards, and risked a peek over the top of the pews.

Two men in white suits stood over a young lady kneeling on the floor. Tao immediately recognized the lady from the train station in Venice and again in Rome last night. It was San Lee's companion. The older and shorter of the two men paced within a circle of four tall altar candles. The younger and far larger man stood outside the circle, his neck and shoulders tensed as though primed for action. Although half in shadow, Tao could see that the younger man held a metallic cudgel in one hand, flexing his arm impatiently. Both men wore white suits, and black shirts, which combined with the silver crucifix on their lapels, gave them the appearance of being priests.

San Lee's companion, bound hand and foot, knelt on the ground, surrounded by wooden debris. Her head was bowed, and her sweat soaked, white T-shirt hung from one shoulder. Blood seeped from an ugly wound on her arm and pooled on the floor. But there was no sign of San Lee, thought Tao. *And no sign of the bronze rat's head sculpture.*

"Our Holy Father Eugenesis IV struck a most unholy bargain," barked the older priest. "Faced with the opportunity to bring God to the heathens of the Americas, he offered tribute to China's Ming Emperor Xuan De and signed the *Proditio.*"

"Faced with the opportunity of gold and slaves more like," screamed the young lady kneeling on the floor, sobbing.

The older priest sneered and struck the young lady viciously across the face with the back of his fist. She fell limply to one side, blood and spittle spraying from her lips. Her head dashed against the granite floor.

The priest grimaced, seemingly annoyed with himself for the momentary loss of control.

"By signing the *Proditio*, Pope Eugenesis IV subverted the authority that God invested in the Holy Catholic and Apostolic Church to… to heathen savages…" The priest stuttered his face reddening. "It was an outrage against all natural order… a betrayal of the most heinous kind." The priest picked up a handful of the girl's hair and lifted her head off the ground at a most awkward angle. The girl sobbed, scrabbling with her uninjured hand to both relieve the pressure on her hair and pin what remained of her shirt to her chest.

"So Miss Su-Lin Wong," continued the priest, holding her hair in one hand, and gesturing to his companion for the metal club, "you must help us find the *Proditio...*" The priest took the heavy metallic club from his companion. He leaned in, his nose inches from the young woman's face. "You will help us find the *Proditio…*" He traced an imaginary line down her forehead, across her cheek, and across her lips with the club. "...so that we can destroy it." The priest drew the club back threateningly.

The young lady's eyes were wide open, her face flinching in fear from the touch of the priest's club. Her head swam with pain and confusion. She just wanted it to stop. Blood oozed between her teeth and spilled over her bottom lip as she mumbled, "Florence."

The priest let go of Su-Lin's hair, and her head thudded wetly against the floor. "There Michael," announced the older priest, pleased with himself. "I told you she could be reasonable."

The elder of the two priests walked out of the circle of candles and retrieved a gray cloth bag from the nearest pew. He returned to the circle of candles and opened the drawstring bag while staring intently at Su-Lin.

"There is one last thing that you can help us with." The priest pulled a shiny bronze colored rat's head sculpture from the bag. "What is this? And why was Doctor Chan concealing it?"

They have the bronze rat's head sculpture! Tao reacted instinctively. He drew his pistol and took a steadying breath. Tao stood up from behind the pews and stepped away from behind the column, screaming, "Don't move!"

But the larger and younger of the two priests reacted with unnatural speed. In one fluid motion, the younger priest dropped to one knee, concealing himself behind a pew, span around, and drew a machine pistol from his jacket, spraying bullets wildly toward Tao and Mei-Li.

Tao's jaw dropped and his eyes widened as the Basilica filled with the explosive cracking of gun fire.

It was impossible for Brother Michael to have moved so quickly and taken care aiming. But it had the desired effect. Tao threw himself back behind the pillar, as bullets ricocheted off stonework and lodged in wooden pews.

CHAPTER 34

San Lee watched over the piazza in front of the Papal Basilica di Santa Maria Maggiore from the shadows of the lane in which he had left Su-Lin's Ducati Monster. San's heart raced. It was partly because he hadn't ridden a bike in years and he had managed to scare himself on more than one occasion following the black minivan from Vatican City. But San was also scared for Su-Lin. He had seen her abruptly snatched away by the Swiss Guard and bundled into the back of a minivan. But for what reason? wondered San. He had no idea.

San watched the short haired Asian woman malingering suspiciously by the Marian column in the center of the piazza. She had arrived shortly after Su-Lin and her captors, he estimated. *But what is she doing?* San desperately wanted to get inside the Basilica and find out what had happened to Su-Lin. But he knew that if he tried to enter the Basilica, he'd be spotted by the curious Asian woman. He checked his watch again. It had only been ten minutes, but he was frustrated by not knowing what was going on inside the Basilica. *Su-Lin could be in trouble.*

San was thinking about whether he could sneak past the

Asian lady, when an Asian man ran across the road on the opposite side of the piazza to join the lady who San had been watching. Damn it! cursed San, knowing that this doubled the chance of him being seen if he tried sneaking across the piazza. Who are they? The two seemed to speak briefly before crossing the piazza and entering the Basilica through the high metal gates, just as Su-Lin's captors had done earlier. *And why are they also following Su-Lin?*

San left the safety of the shadowy lane, and nervously crossed the piazza to approach the Basilica's front gate. He was familiar with the Basilica from his study of art history. The Basilica's mosaics were famous not just because they were over sixteen hundred years old, but because they included one of the first representations of the Virgin Mary. The gate had been left open, and he hurried up to the vestibule door, wondering what the penalty for breaking into a Papal Basilica might be.

San leant on the door handle gently, slowly testing to see whether the door could be opened silently. But suddenly, he heard shouting, followed by the sharp hammering of machine gun fire.

"Oh my God!" he gasped. *Please not Su-Lin!*

San tumbled through the Basilica door, into the dark interior of the Basilica. Gathering himself on the other side, he could see two white suited men in the center aisle of the Basilica, hiding behind a line of pews and illuminated by a dim pool of candlelight. The larger of the two men looked to be armed with a small machinegun. Angry muzzle flashes lashed out from behind the row of columns on the right hand side of the church. Although San could not see them, he guessed that the two Asians that he had followed into the Basilica were hidden in the shadows behind the columns and exchanging gun fire with the two white suited men. *But where is Su-Lin?*

The rapid cracking of machine pistols was periodically followed by the louder but slower pulse of pistols in response. The sound echoed hauntingly throughout the Basilica. Splintered wood and chips of candle wax flew through the air. One of the candles lighting the center of the Basilica shattered as it was hit in the crossfire and went out.

San edged along behind the last pew of the Basilica toward the relative safety of the left hand row of marble columns. He paused before crossing the center aisle, knowing that while it was dark at his end of the Basilica, he might be spotted when he dashed across the aisle. But thankfully, as he prepared to run, San saw the white suited men backing their way gradually down toward the far end of the Basilica. *And further away from me.*

San waited for a blaze of gunfire before diving across the central aisle. But he stumbled when he landed, disturbed by what he had seen. In the center of the Basilica, illuminated by two tall candles, San saw the silent, bleeding body of Su-Lin. *She's been shot!*

Panic flashed through San's mind at the thought of how badly Su-Lin might be hurt. But he took two deep breaths and tried to focus on the task of getting to her first. Having crossed the center aisle, he could now move behind the line of pews on the left hand side of the Basilica. He ran along the outside of the left line of marble columns, or at least as fast as he could bent down low below the level of the pews. San halted just before he got to the transept and considered his next move.

As far as San remembered, not daring to take a look, Su-Lin lay at the other end of the pew behind which he now crouched. But there was a big problem he thought, as gunfire erupted again. Su-Lin was lying in the center of the Basilica where the center aisle and transept crossed. Reaching her would involve wandering out into the middle of a pool of light, where four apparently angry people with guns would see him.

San crawled along on his hands and knees, in the small

space between the first and second pew facing the transept. When he reached the end of the pew that emptied into the center aisle, he peeked out. Just as he had recalled, Su-Lin lay not far from where he knelt. She lay curled up, quite still, her arms limp by her side. Her blood and sweat stained T-shirt was torn and San could see bruising on her arms and neck. But, San could also see the slow, gentle rhythm of her chest rising and falling. *She's still alive!*

San's eyes flicked about looking for a way to cross the dangerously exposed pool of light cast by the two remaining upright candlesticks. The two Asians continued to fire on the two white suited men who had now retreated to the main altar at the far end of the Basilica.

San picked himself up into a crouch, still concealed below the top edge of the pew. He reached his arm out toward one of the candlesticks. He grunted as he stretched his fingers as far as he could, just far enough to grasp the base of the first candlestick. Slowly and quietly, he secured his grip on the candlestick as another chorus of angry gunfire exploded around the Basilica. San took a deep breath to steady himself and tensed his muscles in readiness. *This will have to be done quickly.*

CHAPTER 35

Brother Michael continued to fire, even though the two intruders had retreated back behind the marble pillar from which they had suddenly appeared. He only ceased firing after Jerome had managed to run across the transept and take cover behind the pews on the right hand side of the Basilica, nearer to the altar. Once satisfied that Jerome was safe, Michael calmly ducked down below the height of the pews, ejected the machine pistol's empty clip and inserted another. He strained to hear any sign of movement from the two intruders. Michael was quietly pleased with his muscle memory. It has been a while, he thought. *But no signs of rust.*

With his back against the end of the pew closest to the center aisle, Michael was not perturbed by the inevitable response. The deep thud of pistol fire shouted out from where the intruders hid. Wood splintered from the pews around Michael. Wax flew from shattered candles as bullets flew over his head. The racket is helpful, he thought, smiling peacefully. "Now I know exactly where you are." Waiting for the return of fire to exhaust itself, he slowly began to unsheathe his hunting knife from inside his jacket.

He focused on any footsteps that might indicate the enemy was moving under cover of gunfire.

But Michael's concentration was broken by Jerome screaming at him in Latin. "*Regredere in altari!*"

Michael grimaced with disappointment. "This will have to wait." He replaced his knife in its sheath and moved to obey Jerome.

From behind the pew, and with no pretense of carefully taking aim, Brother Michael again sprayed bullets toward the two intruders. This sent them scurrying back behind the marble columns. But two thirds of the way through emptying his clip, he stood up and began to run. Firing behind himself as he ran, he passed through the circle of candles, across the transept, to where Jerome was crouching further up the center aisle. He knelt down behind the pews for cover, just as Jerome had done moments earlier.

"Did you see them Michael?" Jerome was breathing heavily. "Did you get a look at them?"

"Two shooters." Michael struggled to concentrate with the adrenalin coursing through his veins. "One Asian male." He thought for a bit. "I did not see the other one." But he had misunderstood Jerome's interest in the question.

"It's the *Jinyi Wei!*" Jerome's eyes lit up, partly due to the excitement of being shot at, but partly in surprise that the Prefect's fears had been realized. "They've come to rescue one of their own."

Fire again erupted from behind the marble column. Michael made sure he positioned himself between Jerome and the intruders.

"We'll take cover in the crypt," said Jerome crouching in preparation to run again. He knew it would be risky, because the entrance to the crypt was in the middle, and therefore the most exposed part of, the center aisle. While the wooden pews offered some degree of protection, they would be hopelessly exposed if the intruders crossed to the center aisle. "On my mark Michael."

Michael nodded, preparing to fire again. He waited until Jerome tapped him on the back, before leaping to his feet and firing again on the two intruders. Under the cover of Michael's suppressing fire, Jerome ran down the center aisle toward the crypt.

Dug into the ground, in the center of the aisle, at the foot of the high altar, lay the Crypt of the Nativity. The crypt was so called because it contained one of the Catholic Churches most precious relics – a few pieces of wood, kept in a beautiful silver reliquary, believed to be from the crib in which Jesus lay during his nativity. The crypt was elaborately decorated in marble and dominated by a large sculpture of Pope Sixtus V facing the reliquary. It was also where the remains of St. Jerome were said to have been buried after being transferred to Rome from Bethlehem.

Stepping away from the cover of the pews, Jerome threw himself toward the stairway that led down and into the crypt. He landed heavily and slid on the smooth granite floor. He came to rest against the stone bannister that ran along the side of the stairs that led down into the crypt. Jerome dragged himself down a couple of steps before feeling comfortable that he was fully protected by the bannister. He said a short prayer in thanks to St. Jerome, the church father buried just a few feet, after whom he was named, A great man, thought Jerome proudly, as he searched his memory for his favorite quotation. "Permit not a woman to teach, nor to have dominion over a man, but to be in quietness," he remembered. *A man who knew the place of women in the church.*

While holding off the two intruders, Michael glanced at Jerome to confirm that he had made it safely to the crypt. It was now Michael's turn to run. Without waiting to empty his clip, Michael took off up the aisle. A couple of yards from the crypt, he dropped to his hip, and skidded to the stone bannister behind which Jerome was hiding. With the firing having stopped, the intruders tentatively emerged again from behind the column. They began shooting at the crypt, but the bullets bounced harmlessly off the stonework.

Jerome crept up a couple of steps to join Michael who had assumed a defensive position at the top of the steps. Jerome looked back down the center aisle toward the circle of candlelight at the intersection between the center aisle and the transept.

"You have done well Michael," said Jerome approvingly, patting Michael on the back. "We got the information that we came here to learn."

"Thank you, Your Excellency."

"But there is one more task for you before we make good our escape." Jerome pointed over Michael's shoulder and back down the central aisle toward the bloody figure of Su-Lin. She lay still, between the last two remaining candles. "Kill Doctor Chan's bitch."

Michael smiled, fishing inside his jacket for another magazine. "Yes, Your Excellency." He punched the clip into his weapon and prepared to take aim.

But then the Basilica went completely dark.

CHAPTER 36

San Lee leapt from the pew behind which he had been hiding and into the center aisle of the Basilica di Santa Maria Maggiore. He brandished one of the two remaining candlesticks in his hand. He knew that he was painfully exposed in the dim pool of light in the center of the Basilica. I must move quickly. San swung the candlestick he was carrying at the last candlestick still standing. The two candles shattered on impact. Molten wax arced through the air. The candle wicks sparked as they hit the ground, smoked briefly, and went out.

The gunfire ceased as the Basilica was engulfed in darkness. San's heart was pounding. He fell to his hands and knees, surprised to be still alive. He could hear muffled shouting in Chinese.

"Su-Lin," San whispered, groping blindly on the floor in the direction of where he remembered Su-Lin's body to be. He scrambled desperately because although it was impenetrably dark, San knew the darkness wouldn't be enough to stop a bullet. Shuffling forward San felt Su-Lin's sweat covered arm. She was cold and shivering. Is that shock? he wondered. *But at least she's alive.*

San wanted to wrap Su-Lin's fragile body in his warm leather coat. But he was in a hurry. "Come on Su-Lin, I could do with some help," he begged, rolling Su-Lin on to her back. But she was unconscious. Taking hold of both her arms, he stood behind her and unceremoniously dragged Su-Lin away from the center of the Basilica and into the left transept.

Having reached the end of the transept, San was a little more confident that it would be difficult for anyone to find them without light. Furthermore, now away from the center of the Basilica, the pews and the left hand row of columns offered some protection should the shooting start again. San used the cover to pause and catch his breath. Not wanting to linger long enough for someone to find a torch, he heaved Su-Lin up and into his arms. San guessed that Su-Lin couldn't be much more than half his body weight. But her unconscious body was completely limp and he knew that she would still slow him down considerably. *Especially relative to the unencumbered men with guns.*

San could remember that the Papal Basilica di Santa Maria Maggiore had an unusual feature. Below the famous mosaics of the apse's triumphal arch, were two doors, one on either side of the altar. These doors led out into the street behind the Basilica. It would be heading toward the two white suited men with guns, he worried, weighing the danger. *But they're as blind as I am now.*

Su-Lin mumbled faintly as San stood up again.

"Shhh," whispered San. He could feel Su-Lin's sticky, warm blood soaking into his shirt. "Just stay with me Su-Lin," he pleaded.

But there was no response.

San headed down the left hand perimeter aisle of the Basilica, toward the apse. He moved as fast as he could without making any noise. But it felt to San as though the darkness made his hearing more acute and the slightest shuffle made an unnervingly loud noise. He could only accelerate when the sporadic gun fire drowned out the sound of his footsteps.

Hurrying through the opaque darkness San almost ran straight into the rear wall of the Basilica. He shook his head and cursed his foolishness, hoping he hadn't alerted anyone to his location. In the darkness, he wasn't sure whether the door was to his left or right. But in order to search for the door he would need to free one of his hands. So from cradling Su-Lin in his arms, he threw Su-lin's arms over his shoulders and rested her head on his left shoulder freeing up his left arm to search for the door. It was a slow process of patting down the cold stone wall until he found the wooden door at the rear of the church.

San fumbled with the door handle, but it wouldn't budge. It was locked. His adrenalin spiked again. It didn't make it any better that he had expected that the door would be locked, but now that he had found the door, he had to worry about getting through it.

San took three steps back and a second to collect himself. He knew that the first attempt on the door would be loud enough to signal his location to everyone else in the Basilica. So he knew that he had to commit. *I'll only get one chance at this.*

San charged. Protecting Su-Lin as best he could, he barreled into the door with all of his and Su-Lin's weight behind his right shoulder. The noise of splintering wood and the loud bang of what was left of the door hitting the wall behind it, echoed throughout the Basilica. Street light spilled in through the doorway. San staggered, his bruised shoulder screaming with pain. He lost balance and tumbled down the steps at the rear of the Basilica, spilling Su-Lin to the ground.

Back to his feet again, San pushed himself for one last effort. He didn't look back, certain that those inside the Basilica would come running into the street at any moment. San pulled Su-Lin back off the ground and into his arms.

Roma Termini - Rome's main intercity train station was only four blocks away. *I've got to run!*

CHAPTER 37

San Lee sat on the edge of the bed, where Su-Lin lay sleeping. It looked to him as though some color had returned to her skin, and her breathing was definitely deeper and more regular. But the bruise high on Su-Lin's cheek was still an angry purple and blood was still seeping into the tape covering the split in her lower lip. Su-Lin turned quietly in the clean white linen. But she did not wake up.

Of most concern to San was Su-Lin's arm. It had been clearly fractured, and San's knowledge of first aid was, by his own admission, limited. But at least the bones had not broken through the skin he thought, and they seemed to be fractured only in a single place. After pulling her forearm along its length to a more normal position, San had made a makeshift splint. He had folded a thick cardboard sheet into a U-shaped pipe the length of Su-Lin's forearm, lined it with a towel, and then bandaged it around her arm. He had then slung the splint to Su-Lin's shoulder to stop it moving about too much. It will do, he hoped. *At least until we get to a hospital.*

San yawned, rubbing his bleary eyes and stretching his

bruised shoulder. He felt exhausted. He hadn't properly rested since charging through the rear door of the Basilica di Santa Maria Maggiore last night and sprinting to Rome's intercity train station. It had only been a couple of blocks, and Su-Lin was not that heavy. But with a sore shoulder and only so much adrenaline, he had been relieved to flop down into a train seat for a couple of hours. He could have fallen asleep right there on the train. But he had been too anxious about Su-Lin's injuries. Even wrapped in San's jacket she had been shivering uncontrollably in a semiconscious daze. San had guessed it was only shock. *I hoped it was only shock.* For a while he had felt guilty dragging her on to the train without first seeking medical attention. But San's first priority had been her physical safety and that meant getting her as far away from the white suited men as possible. All he could do was try to keep her warm and watch over her until they reached their destination.

Only after San had checked them into a hotel and washed and dressed Su-Lin's wounds had he a chance to relax. He had slumped down in the arm chair at the end of Su-Lin's bed. The chair had been comfortable enough, and he had fallen asleep almost immediately. But he had not slept deeply. There had been too much to worry about. Who were the white suited men who had abducted Su-Lin? *And why had they hurt her so badly?*

"I feel awful," moaned Su-Lin, stirring weakly.

"You're back." San sighed in relief.

Su-Lin squinted at the morning light streaming through the bedroom window. She seemed a little disorientated. "Where am I?"

"You're in a hotel in Florence. We spent the night in a pension, just north of the Piazza della Signoria." San pushed the hair out of Su-Lin's eyes. "Well it's not really a hotel. It's not even a pension. It's more like a retired couple's spare bedroom."

"Florence?" Su-Lin was startled, her brow furrowing.

"How did we get here?"

"Last night, we travelled up by train. You were barely conscious for most of the journey." San paused, not wanting to burden Su-Lin with the detail, or his questions, just yet.

"I don't remember much." Su-Lin continued to look puzzled.

"I carried you to the station in Rome." San wore a mournful expression. "I didn't know where else to go," he explained. "My top priority was to get you as far away from the Basilica di Santa Maria Maggiore as possible. But they knew your name, so going back to your apartment wasn't an option. Without a better alternative, I headed in the direction that Doctor Chan's date had pointed us in. So after our discovery in the Vatican Museum I got us on a train to Florence." San searched Su-Lin's face for any possible sign of disapproval. He was not sure whether he had taken liberties by bringing her to Florence.

But Su-Lin's expression was pained, and all she did was nod dumbly. Arguing with San looked to be the furthest thing from her mind.

"Once in Florence, I just asked a taxi driver to take us to the smallest place we could stay in the center of the old town. Somewhere that wouldn't be too fussy about identification. This pension is probably run by the taxi driver's parents."

"You carried me?" asked Su-Lin meekly.

"Heh! Don't sound too surprised."

"No." Su-Lin couldn't help but smile. "I just can't remember anything much after…" Images of the Basilica, and of questions - *painful questions* - flashed through Su-Lin's mind. "...after being in the Basilica."

San could see her flinch. "Just relax Su-Lin, you're safe now."

"I must look awful." Su-Lin gently dabbed the tender side of her mouth.

San smiled kindly. "I've patched you up as best I could. The split lip and bruising on your cheek bone will fade in time. But I am a bit worried about your left arm."

Su-Lin used her right arm to gingerly push herself into a sitting position. She pulled her broken arm out from under the bed sheets, surprised by its weight. Seeing the splint, Su-Lin gritted her teeth at the memory of just how it was broken.

"I'm afraid the splint isn't very professional," apologized San. "But it should do the job until we get you to a real doctor."

Su-Lin examined San's makeshift splint. "It will do." She flexed her fingers tentatively. "But it hurts like hell." Su-Lin closed her eyes and leant back into the pillows again.

San gave her a moment, happy to see her healthier and awake again. He walked over to his jacket hanging on the back of the door. Last night, he had gone to a pharmacy and bought some painkillers along with the disinfectant, bandages and tape. He retrieved two tablets from his jacket pocket and returned to the bed, unscrewing a bottle of mineral water. "Here." San offered her the tablets. "Take this."

But as he watched Su-Lin take the painkiller with some water, the questions that had been nagging at him since he carried Su-Lin from the Basilica in Rome, intruded on his thoughts again. "Su-Lin, who did this to you?"

What was left of Su-Lin's half smile faded and her eyes reddened. "Two priests called Jerome and Brother Michael. The same people who killed Doctor Chan." Her eyes moistened as dark memories of Doctor Chan's ruined body flooded back. The memories mixed uncomfortably with the guilty relief that she had avoided a similar fate.

"How do you know?"

"Remember the lapel pin we found near Doctor Chan?"

"Yes. It was on the floor. A crucifix surrounded by a branch and a sword if I remember correctly?"

Su-Lin nodded. "The two priests last night were wearing exactly the same pin." Su-Lin winced, staring at San regretfully. "I should have recognized the design when we found the pin in Venice. The crucifix surrounded by a branch and sword was a symbol of the Inquisition - an organization which is better known today as the Congregation for the Doctrine of Faith. They killed Doctor Chan."

"But who are the Congregation for the Doctrine of Faith?" He thought he had heard the name before, but he had no idea what interest they'd have in beating Su-Lin half to death.

"They're old fashioned, witch-burning inquisitors San."

"The Inquisition? In this day and age? Isn't burning heretics a little medieval?"

"The Catholic Church has never taken very well to modernity," scoffed Su-Lin. "The Congregation was established in the sixteenth century to defend the church from heretics and false doctrines. But the Congregation for the Doctrine of Faith didn't drop the term Inquisition from its name until the twentieth century."

"The change of name doesn't seem to have tempered their methods."

"The Congregation has descended from a long tradition of religiously inspired violence – the Roman Inquisition, the Spanish Inquisition, the suppression of the Albigensian Heresy. They were often little more than thinly veiled pogroms against Jews, Muslims or any other minority the church took a dislike to."

"But what did they want with you?"

"They're searching for a document."

"A what?"

"They're searching for Doctor Chan's proof."

Su-Lin could see the confusion in San's face. "Doctor Chan's proof was a document signed by Pope Eugenesis IV. In return for the Chinese embassy's gifts of maps and the technology to reach the New World, Pope Eugenesis conceded the tributary status of the Catholic Church to the Chinese Emperor.” Su-Lin looked down and her shoulders shook as she sobbed. “They must have killed Doctor Chan when he refused to tell them where the document could be found.”

San put his arm around her shoulders. “So somehow they must have figured out that you worked with Doctor Chan.”

Su-Lin looked downcast. “And now they will be looking for me.”

“But you don't know where Doctor Chan's proof is.”

“They don't know that!”

“Heh, don't worry.” San squeezed Su-Lin's shoulders reassuringly. “You're safe now, and they have no idea where we are.”

But Su-Lin only burst into renewed tears. “I’m so sorry San. I’ve put you in terrible danger.” She leant into San, afraid of what might happen. “I couldn’t help it San. I told them what little we know about the location of Doctor Chan's proof.” Su-Lin looked up at San guiltily. “I told them that the document could be found in Florence.”

CHAPTER 38

Inquisitor Jerome sat down in the refectory of the Basilica Santa Maria Novella. He was served a rich breakfast prepared by some of the most junior novices. But he did not feel like eating. He was too busy wondering where in Florence he should begin searching for the *Proditio*, especially now that he knew that the *Jinyi Wei* were searching for it too.

Jerome and Brother Michael had driven up from Rome to Florence the night before, based on the information they had collected from the previous evening's investigation. It had only taken them a couple of hours, and when they arrived, they had taken rooms for the night in the monastery attached to the Basilica di Santa Maria Novella, the principal Dominican church in Florence.

Jerome wore a grim expression. Previously he had always considered the *Jinyi Wei* to be more myth than real. The *Jinyi Wei* had been an unhealthy preoccupation of the Prefect, he thought. But now, the situation had changed. *Now they were a much more significant threat.*

It wasn't simply that the *Jinyi Wei* had emerged so soon after rumors of the *Proditio* had returned to haunt the church. Although the speed with which the Jinyi Wei had appeared was in itself a cause for concern, because it suggested to Jerome, that they were surprisingly well informed. But most worrying was the fact that two of the Jinyi Wei had interrupted an interrogation and freed one of their own, from the grounds of the Holy See. It was deeply humiliating for the Congregation, and personally embarrassing for Jerome. I have been too patient, he thought, too ill disciplined. *I will not be making that mistake again.*

After brooding over his tea and barely touching his breakfast, Jerome left the refectory in search of some fresh morning air. The Green Cloister linked the refectory, the convent and the Basilica. It was one of four arcaded squares that made up the complex surrounding the Basilica. The Green Cloister surrounded a pleasant garden with a fountain in its center. He began pacing its perimeter. At least we were able to recover the name of the town in which the Proditio is located, he thought. *But now that we have narrowed the location down to Florence, where should we begin our search?*

Jerome bowed his head, knelt as low as his cane would permit, and crossed himself as he passed from the cloister into the Basilica. Although the facade of the Basilica di Santa Maria Novella was decorated in a similarly green, white and pink marble, to Florence's other larger and more famous Cathedral - the Duomo, the Basilica di Santa Maria Novella was even older. And far more religiously significant, he thought.

Jerome walked across the front of the Basilica's altar to the Rucellai Chapel in the far end of the right transept. It was the Basilica's quietest chapel and his favorite place for prayer and introspection. The chapel was reached by one of two small stone staircases that rose up and over the Rucellai family tombs. The Rucellai family had been wool merchants and bankers. One of the leading families in Renaissance

Florence, they had intermarried with the Medici's, could count at least one Pope within their family, and like the Medici's were prolific patrons of the arts.

Jerome knelt at one of the short pews in front of a narrow gray stone altar in an otherwise empty chapel. But what the chapel lacked in furnishings, it made up for in color. Light flooded through two tall windows behind the altar, illuminating brightly colored frescoes covering the walls and ceiling. Jerome clasped his hands together and closed his eyes. He prayed to Leonardo Dati, who six hundred years ago was the Master General of Jerome's Dominican Order and now buried in Rucellai Chapel. He prayed for the strength to find the *Proditio* and to end the torment it had caused the Church.

But Jerome's mind wandered to more immediate, practical matters. His anxiety regarding the location of the *Proditio* and the emerging *Jinyi Wei* threat made it difficult for him to clear his mind for prayer. After several minutes of trying to concentrate, he opened his eyes, irritated with his own ill-discipline. He vented his frustration by sneering at a painting of the martyrdom of St. Catherine that hung to the left of the altar. It was by Michelangelo, Jerome recalled, disgusted by his least favorite painter. He then looked right, toward the tomb of Patriarch Joseph II of Constantinople. The Patriarch had, with Pope Eugenesis IV, united the Catholic and Orthodox Churches at the Council of Florence in 1439. It was about that time that Pope Eugenesis IV had met the embassy from the Chinese Ming Emperor Xuan De. "Did you too know of the *Proditio* too?" asked Jerome, of the long dead Patriarch. *If so, where the hell did you put it?*

Jerome's phone began to vibrate, snatching from him what little chance remained of concentrating on prayer. He pulled the phone out of his pocket irritably. But when he looked at the number, the irritation in his face faded into apprehension. He lifted himself up and off his knees and sat upright on the pew, before answering the phone.

"Your Eminence?" asked Jerome humbly.

"A fire fight Jerome?" the Prefect shouted, ignoring any pleasantries. "In a Papal Basilica! Are you completely mad?"

But Jerome knew better than to respond. He closed his eyes and waited.

"It may well be the sovereign territory of the Holy See, but it is extremely embarrassing for our Holy Father to have to explain away the sound of machine gun fire to the Italian Police."

"Yes, Your Eminence."

"The Basilica had to be closed this morning, until the debris could be cleared." The Prefect paused. "Do you have anything to say for yourself Jerome?"

"We were questioning Doctor Chan's colleague," he explained. "We did not know that she was one of the *Jinyi Wei*. Not until we were ambushed by another two of her kind."

The Prefect had no immediate response.

Jerome guessed that the Prefect too was ruffled by the *Jinyi Wei*'s sudden appearance. "It was uncharacteristically brazen of them," added Jerome.

"It was uncharacteristically careless of you to allow yourself to be ambushed in a House of God Jerome!"

"Yes, Your Eminence. We would have taken extra precautions if we had known, Your Eminence."

"I did warn you Jerome," continued the Prefect shrilly.

Jerome was forced to concede that this was embarrassingly true. "You did Your Eminence."

"And what of the *Proditio*? It can scarcely be more urgent now that we know that the *Jinyi Wei* are searching for it too."

"The *Jinyi Wei* whore was less resilient than Doctor Chan." Jerome smiled to himself, flexing his knuckles and enjoying his recollection of his conversation with Su-Lin. "Our inquiries revealed the city in which the *Proditio* is hidden."

The Prefect remained silent. He was pleased with the news, but irritated that Jerome had been holding back this important piece of information.

"Florence, Your Eminence. The *Jinyi Wei* witch said that the *Proditio* was hidden in Florence."

It was a second or two before the Prefect responded. "It fits, I suppose. Pope Eugenesis IV was in Florence, when he met the Chinese embassy in 1434 and signed the *Proditio*." The Prefect warmed to the idea. "And Toscanelli was a Florentine who likewise probably met the Chinese embassy in Florence too."

"But Your Eminence, Doctor Chan's comment regarding Toscanelli has been shown to be..." Jerome paused, trying to be diplomatic. "...Unhelpful at best."

But the Prefect was no longer listening to Jerome. "Florence. Yes, I will divert the plane."

"What?" Jerome was surprised and unsettled by the looming proximity of the Prefect. "You're coming here?"

"Yes, and I expect some progress from you by the time I arrive." The Prefect enjoyed the fear in Jerome's voice. "I am no more than two hours away."

CHAPTER 39

Su-Lin wiped the tears from her eyes as her sobbing slowly subsided.

"I'm so sorry San. I had no right to put you in such danger."

San put a hand on Su-Lin's shoulder. "You have nothing to be sorry for. It wasn't you who chose to bring me to Florence."

Su-Lin felt comforted by San.

"And as you suggested before," San continued. "The people who killed Doctor Chan, the priests who are coming after you, are the people most likely to have the bronze rat's head sculpture that I need."

"They do," Su-Lin said enthusiastically, grasping at the silver lining. "I saw it with them."

San was surprised. "Where did you see it?"

"They brought it to the Basilica with them. They didn't seem to know what it was."

"See. I'm where I need to be." San gave Su-Lin a confident smile. "You concentrate on getting better."

The pain in her forearm did feel a little better. Su-Lin guessed that the painkillers were doing their work and driving the pain into the background. Anxious to be a little more active again, she sat up and tried stretching her injured arm to see whether it was the sling or the pain which would inhibit her movement the most. She was pleasantly surprised. "You've done well San." She knew that her injury meant she couldn't do anything energetic like swimming, but it was only clenching her fist or rotating her wrist which was unbearably painful. "You're not just a pretty face then."

Encouraged by her new found strength and mobility she tentatively performed a few stretches of her shoulders and back. But in doing so, the bed sheets fell from around her shoulders. Su-Lin's eyes widened as she realized her shoulders were bare. Her eyes darted about the small hotel room until she saw her torn white T-shirt hanging at the end of the bed. Su-Lin scrabbled with her uninjured right hand to see whether her back was covered. But except for the straps of her bra, her back was almost entirely naked. Su-Lin looked nervously at San.

"I'm sorry Su-Lin," San fretted. He assumed that Su-Lin was embarrassed that he had washed and dressed her injuries while she was unconscious the previous evening. "I meant no disrespect. But you were bleeding. I had to clean and dress your wounds."

"No San, it's not that." Su-Lin pulled the sheet back up under her chin, wrapping her arms across her chest and covering her shoulders with her hands. "Did you see it?"

"Did I see what?" San was confused. "The tattoo?" He was not sure why a tattoo might be something that needed to be concealed. "Yes, I saw it. Three Chinese characters surrounded by nine, five clawed dragons. I think the Chinese characters were the same as those on the stone sitting on the shelf in your living room."

There was an awkward silence. San wasn't sure whether Su-Lin looked ashamed because she had a tattoo, or because San had discovered it.

"But I don't know what it means," San admitted.

Su-Lin looked toward the window wistfully. “In English the three characters would translate directly as *brocade clad guard.* In Chinese they are pronounced *Jinyi Wei.*” She then turned to look at San. “My family has worn its mark for over six hundred years.”

San sat quietly, trying to understand what he was being told.

“The dragon was the symbol of the Ming Emperor. The number of dragons one wore was a symbol of someone’s status. Only the Emperor and those closest to him could wear the nine dragons. The *Jinyi Wei* were elite soldiers and the Ming Dynasty Emperors' personal body guards. They were sworn to protect the Emperors, with their lives if need be, earning them the right to wear his mark.” Su-Lin watched San closely. “You remember that I told you I was Chinese, but that I was raised in Italy?”

San nodded.

“My ancestors were sent to Italy by the Ming Emperor Xuan De,” Su-Lin explained with a mix of pride and weariness. “When the Ming Emperor Xuan De sent an embassy to Pope Eugenesis IV, the *Jinyi Wei* were naturally sent with the embassy to protect the interests of the Ming Emperor and enforce compliance with his will.”

“But that was hundreds of years ago?”

Su-Lin nodded slowly, her face determined. “The embassy was sent to announce the Emperor Xuan De’s succession to the throne after the death of his father, and establish the tributary status of the Catholic Church. Gifts were presented to Pope Eugenesis IV - rare silks and ceramics. But most importantly the embassy brought maps and books describing the technology needed to use them. The map of the Americas and the technology were far beyond anything Europeans had yet discovered. It would be this knowledge that led Christopher Columbus to the New World, enriching the Catholic Church, and spreading its influence for centuries to come.”

"Why? What did the Emperor get in return?"

"What China has always wanted," stated Su-Lin flatly. "Respect. Respect commensurate with China's achievements."

"But what did that mean in practical terms?"

"The Chinese Empire had never been one of conquest and colony. The Chinese empire was one of vassal and liege, tribute and protection. In return for these gifts, Pope Eugenesis IV was asked only to pay tribute to the Ming Emperor by conceding the vassal status of the Catholic Church. He was asked to make this commitment in writing, by signing a treaty."

"And did he?"

"For the wealth of the New World? For all of its slaves and its gold?" Su-Lin asked sarcastically. "Of course he did." Su-Lin folded her arms testily. "But Pope Eugenesis IV never honored the treaty, despite the protestations of the *Jinyi Wei*. He never intended to. He probably thought that China was too far away for there to be any serious repercussions."

"And he was right."

Su-Lin flashed San a dirty look. "Eugenesis' successors were embarrassed that he had subverted the authority of the Church to a heathen Empire. They branded the treaty the '*Proditio*.' which is Latin for..."

"Betrayal." San finished the sentence for her.

"Since then, the Vatican has officially denied that the treaty ever existed." Su-Lin's voice hardened, feeding on a festering anger. "But in the meantime, the Inquisition hunted down the *Jinyi Wei* and killed all those that they found."

"So what happened to the *Jinyi Wei* who were left in Italy to enforce the treaty?"

"China was by far the largest, richest, and most technologically advanced nation in the world during the fourteenth century. The early Ming Emperor's built

Beijing's Forbidden City, used woodblock printing to spread Chinese technology and culture, and sent the treasure fleets out to map the world and expand the tributary system. But, just a few generations later, even before the Emperor Xuan De's succession, China had begun distancing itself from the world. Wars broke out in the east, the Chinese fleets were dismantled, and interactions with foreigners were strictly limited." Su-Lin saddened. "The *Jinyi Wei* in Italy were cut off. They were abandoned."

"And your family were among them?"

"The few of my ancestors that survived the wrath of the Inquisition went in to hiding. The *Proditio* was lost, and all memory of it suppressed by the Church."

"And since then?" asked San, astonished.

Su-Lin was humbled by the determination of those who had gone before her. "We have tried to protect the history and dignity of the Chinese people and the memory of their achievements." Su-Lin clenched her fist. "And to that end, we will finish what Doctor Chan has started, and find the *Proditio*."

CHAPTER 40

Agent Mei-Li stared at Agent Tao Ma across the conference room table as he hung up the phone. But, she kept quiet, not wanting to antagonize Tao after such a difficult call. Their superiors had made it painfully clear that it was a fireable offense to be carrying a firearm without authorization on a foreign posting. *Let alone discharging those firearms in a public place.*

As they both had hastened to point out to their superiors, it was the two catholic priests who had opened fire on them first. Not the other way round. But it seemed to matter little to their superiors, convinced as they were that Tao had done something to provoke them.

Mei-Li was thankful that they still had some hope of recovering the bronze rat's head sculpture. Otherwise they would have been sent back to Beijing on the first available plane, she thought. *To face severe disciplinary action.*

"If we recover the statue, we'll be all right." Mei-Li looked at Tao expectantly. "Won't we sir?"

But Tao did not answer. He stood up and stared out of the third floor consulate window. He took one last drag from his cigarette before tossing the butt out of the window. The Chinese Consulate in Florence had made office space available to them, after they had driven up from Rome during the night. Tao crossed his arms and studied the slowly waking street below. The neighborhood was a little distant from the center of Florence, but it too was lined with seventeenth century apartments. In contrast, the Chinese consulate was a modern, concrete monstrosity that clashed with the otherwise pleasant surroundings.

Neither of them understood why the two priests that they had met in the Basilica di Santa Maria Maggiore in Rome, had wanted to be in Florence. But the ferocity with which they had beaten the information out of that poor girl last night, suggested that they would be heading to Florence as soon as they could. And what choice did we have, thought Mei-Li, the priests had the bronze rat's head sculpture. *And that meant we had to follow them wherever they went.*

"Politics!" snarled Tao, smacking the glass of the window with the palm of his hand.

While Tao had focused his efforts and those of the team entirely on securing the bronze rat's head sculpture, it was the larger political ramifications of the confrontation in the Basilica last night that bothered his superiors the most. Political ramifications that Tao was not well equipped to grasp, Mei-Li thought. It had not occurred to him, as his superior's carefully pointed out, that the Catholic Church may have stolen the bronze rat's head sculpture precisely for the purpose of embarrassing the Chinese leadership. *Or at least improving their negotiating position.*

The Catholic Church had never had much success in China. And probably never would, doubted Mei-Li, not seeing the appeal of this particular apocalyptic cult of human sacrifice. Strategically, the church had largely refused to accommodate the Chinese Confucian custom of honoring deceased ancestors. And so ever since the Ming Emperor Hongxi, father of Emperor Xuan De, began the process of closing China to the world, foreign missionaries were for many centuries, barred from entering China or martyred if they did.

For the last sixty years or so, since the establishment of the People's Republic of China, the Catholic Church had fared even worse. Since the Catholic Church refused to operate under the supervision of the state, the Church had been condemned as illegal by the Chinese Communist Party and its priests imprisoned or tortured. China could not accept that the Pope - the head of a foreign state, was the only one with the power to appoint bishops in China. And why should China accept it? thought Mei-Li. *It's just another form of western cultural imperialism.* So instead, China promoted its own, state sanctioned alternative to the Catholic Church, much to the chagrin of the Vatican.

But could the Church really believe that the bronze rat's head sculpture could be used as a bargaining tool? wondered Mei-Li. There was no chance of formal diplomatic relations with China while the Holy See maintained an embassy in Taiwan. Not only was this an affront to the Chinese people, but it should be an embarrassment for the United Nations that the Catholic Church was allowed to masquerade as a nation. *If Utah put a large wall up around its largest Mormon church, would we have to call that a country too?*

"If this is all about the politics of the bronze rat's head sculpture, why were those priests torturing San Lee's companion?" interrupted Mei-Li. "They already had the sculpture. What else did they want?"

But again Tao did not have an answer.

It did not surprise Mei-Li that her superiors ignored the Catholic Church's torture of a Chinese citizen. If they were alarmed every time someone was tortured, thought Mei-Li, we'd never get any work done. But she did not know what to make of how little surprise her superiors exhibited when they were told the news. *It was as though this had happened before.*

"Maybe they're not after the sculpture," suggested Mei-Li. "Maybe that explains Beijing's seeming lack of surprise." *Maybe these abductions have occurred before.*

Tao threw her a dirty look, but said nothing.

Mei-Li knew it was unbecoming to express such doubts in the chain of command. But since Tao did not respond that angrily, she guessed he shared some of her suspicions.

Tao lit another cigarette. "Maybe. But so what?" Tao snarled. "We are only after the sculpture." Tao spoke firmly, as though he expected it sufficient to end the conversation. "The priests' motives are academic. The facts are that these priests have the bronze rat's head sculpture and that they are now most likely to be found in Florence. We must therefore pick up their trail to have any hope of recovering the sculpture."

CHAPTER 41

San and Su-Lin walked out from their accommodation and into Florence's narrow cobbled streets. Although the morning sun shone brightly, the air was brisk, and they both exhaled plumes of steam.

"Hungry?" asked San.

Su-Lin rubbed her left arm. It had not been easy getting Su-Lin into a leather jacket without hurting her or disturbing the splint. But, despite San's objections, she had insisted on discarding the sling. "We'll get something to eat on the way." Su-Lin turned north without hesitation.

San was pleased that Su-Lin's confidence was returning. "Your home town?"

"Yes. I grew up here." Su-Lin smiled, pleased to be in familiar territory. "I was born here."

Although it was mid-morning the streets were far quieter than they had been in Rome. The cobbled streets in the center of old Florence were far too narrow for cars, and because it was still quite early, the tourists were not yet out in force either.

"Wouldn't it have been difficult for the *Jinyi Wei* to have hidden themselves in Florence?" San knew there was no politically correct way of asking his question. "Particularly with such a strikingly different physical appearance?"

"Not really. Fourteenth century Florence was an even more metropolitan than it is today."

"Why was that? I don't imagine there were any tourists or international art history students in those days."

"Slavery mainly."

"Huh?" San hadn't expected that would be the explanation that Su-Lin gave. He had never heard much about slavery in Europe.

Su-Lin noticed his quizzical expression. "They started bringing slaves to Florence after the decree of 1363. The people of Florence had been weakened by severe famine and then decimated by plague. Laborers were desperately needed and so the Priors of Florence permitted slaves to be imported from the East."

"Where did the slaves come from?"

"Mainly from Tana and Caffa, two slave markets on the edge of the Black Sea. Tana was on the European end of the Silk Road that led all the way to China. From here Chinese goods made their way into Europe long before any European knew how to sail to China by ship. From Tana, Genoese and Venetian merchants brought spices, porcelain, silk, and slaves into Europe."

"And isn't Caffa now called Feodosiya, the Ukranian city close to Sevastopol?"

"Yes. Caffa was similar to Tana, except that Caffa was actually ruled by Europeans. It was first ruled by the Venetian Republic and then later by the Genoese, who bought it from the leaders of the Mongol Golden Horde. In Caffa, Europeans bought Russian, Bulgarian, Alan, Zik, and Chinese slaves. Most of them had been enslaved by the Mongol Golden Horde as they ravaged their way across the Russian steppes."

"That is ironic," grunted San. "Importing slaves to solve a labor shortage from the same cities from which Europe imported the plague that caused the labor shortage in the first place."

"Yes I suppose so," agreed Su-Lin. "But with such a plethora of races serving as slaves, when the Chinese embassy from Emperor Xuan De left Florence, it was easy for the remaining *Jinyi Wei* to blend in with the local population. They initially hid as either slaves or slave traders."

"And while they might start as slaves," San added. "Slaves could become freedmen."

Su-Lin indicated to a small cafe further up on the left. Outside, four simple chairs had been set up around two small tables. But, it was cold, so San guided Su-Lin gently inside, preferring to keep her warm. Inside there was a short stand-up bar and a couple of stools overlooking the street. Su-Lin found a space in the corner while San ordered two cappuccinos and a couple of sweet pastries.

"Thanks." Su-Lin gripped the coffee cup tightly in both hands, enjoying the warmth. "But I'm not hungry."

"You have to eat Su-Lin," said San in a serious tone. "You lost a fair amount of blood last night."

Su-Lin considered this for a moment, with an increasingly broad smile. "OK, it's a good excuse. Just one then." Su-Lin grinned at San appreciatively.

"Sorry I must sound like my mother. She was a typical Asian mother. Always eat, eat, eat."

"No." Su-Lin patted San's arm. "It's sweet of you."

San felt slightly awkward, and it was moment before he managed to fill the silence. "You don't hear much about slavery in European history. How much of it went on?"

"Tax records suggest that at least two thousand slaves were being brought into Venice every year," Su-Lin explained. "And given that Venetian merchants were just as unenthusiastic about paying taxes as we are today, that's probably a low estimate."

"That's probably enough people to show up in the

genetic record?"

"It certainly would be. Records from the foundling hospital in Florence show a huge upsurge in illegitimate children born to Asian slaves at about this time."

"Prostitutes?" wondered San.

"Or maybe just prettier," joked Su-Lin.

San drained the last of his cappuccino. "Shall we get going?"

But Su-Lin seemed distant, as though she was staring in to the past. "I shouldn't make light of it. Some of the slaves were men, but they were mostly women. Some of the women were adults, but they were mostly children." Su-Lin looked aggrieved.

"If not taken by force, the children were often sold by their own parents," she continued. "They were sold to be housekeepers, kept pregnant for wet nursing, or rented out as prostitutes. But they were rarely Christians. The church only allowed Europeans to enslave us heathens."

San left some money in the saucer to pay for the coffees. The cafe's doorbell tinkled again as they pushed back out and into the cold.

Su Lin barely had to look up to get her bearings, before heading north again. The narrow street twisted slowly to the left, turned back once to the right, before opening into a large open square. Dominating the square and towering over the surrounding buildings was an enormous Cathedral. San was amazed that they could have approached so closely to such a large building without catching a glimpse of it earlier.

"The first date that Doctor Chan left us with has led us to Florence," said Su-Lin confidently. "Doctor Macheda suggested that Doctor Chan's second date was the date on which Pope Eugenesis IV held a mass to celebrate the reunification of the church."

San shielded his eyes from the sun as he looked up at the Basilica's impressively large dome.

"I can't think of a better place to start searching for Doctor Chan's proof, than the church in which that mass was celebrated - The Basilica di Santa Maria del Fiore. In English, it's more commonly known as Florence Cathedral, or most simply, the *Duomo.*"

CHAPTER 42

Inquisitor Jerome sat at the rear of the Basilica of Santa Maria Novella waiting for Brother Michael to return. He stared at the delicately thin columns that lined the Basilica, and the black and white stone arches that merged the columns with the high ceiling. He wondered what it was exactly that made the nave look longer than it actually was. Is it something about the spacing between the columns, pondered Jerome. He glanced at his watch. *Where is Brother Michael?*

Jerome especially admired the Basilica's pulpit. To the left of the central aisle, a delicate stone, spiral staircase had been carved onto one of the Basilica's columns. It was designed by Filippo Brunelleschi, the same artist who eventually managed to complete Florence Cathedral's impossibly large dome. The balustrade wound around the column, terminating in a circular platform decorated by four bass reliefs of Biblical scenes. It would have given the priest a commanding view over his flock, he thought. But as attractive as the stone work was, it was its historical importance that resonated with Jerome.

It was from here that the Dominican friar Tommaso

Caccini in late 1614 launched the first attack on Galileo. "Caccini was a hero of our order," thought Jerome admiringly. He denounced Galileo's support for the Copernican theory that the earth revolves around the sun, as contrary to scripture and therefore heretical. He inspired the Catholic Church to try Galileo on the charge of heresy. And we, Jerome remembered proudly, the Congregation of the Doctrine of Faith, confirmed his guilt - vehemently suspect of heresy.

Galileo was sentenced to imprisonment and his works were banned. But imprisonment was eventually commuted to house arrest for the rest of his life. Such a lenient punishment should not have been countenanced by the Church, Jerome grumbled. *He was damn lucky not to be burnt at the stake for questioning the authority of the Church like that.*

Jerome heard a slow and unusually heavy plod of footsteps and knew that Michael was approaching. Jerome did not stand, but with both hands resting on his cane, he turned to look at Michael impassively.

"Your Excellency." Michael bowed. But the gesture was somewhat futile, because even after bowing deeply he still towered over the seated Jerome.

"Brother Michael, have our allies among the Florentine priesthood been informed?"

"Yes, Your Excellency." Michael thought this response would be sufficient. But when he looked up, Jerome was staring at him expectantly. "Photos of Doctor Chan's whore have been circulated…"

"Language Michael."

Michael blushed, having forgotten where he was. "Apologies, Your Excellency." Now flustered, Michael lost his train of thought for a moment. "And descriptions of the other *Jinyi Wei*, the ones who attacked us in Rome, have also been distributed."

"Good work Michael." Jerome nodded. "And they will contact us immediately if any of them are seen?"

"Yes. Orders have been given to that effect."

"Any word as yet?"

"No. Not yet."

Jerome was confident, that if the *Jinyi Wei* were to enter a church in Florence, they would hear of it. "Thank you Michael. That will be all." Jerome turned back toward the pulpit. "Oh and Michael, could you have the car brought round to the front of the Basilica? We will have to leave for the airport soon."

Michael bowed again and was gone.

Jerome imagined Tommaso Caccini in his pulpit railing against the heresy of Galileo and the need to maintain the authority of the church in all spiritual matters. Ever since the Renaissance, the Church has been making a mistake by trying to accommodate these unhealthily secular temptations, he thought bitterly. *Culminating in the abject humiliation of the second Vatican Council.*

"But not today," muttered Jerome. "Not on my watch." *It is with vigilance and discipline that the Church will prevail.*

CHAPTER 43

San gazed admiringly up at Florence Cathedral. It was hard not to be impressed, he thought. It was one of the largest Renaissance cathedrals in the world, and it towered above the three or four story apartment buildings which surrounded the Piazza del Duomo in which the Cathedral was situated. Unlike the gray, weathered stone walls of the countless gothic cathedrals that San had seen throughout Europe, the exterior walls of Florence Cathedral were decorated in a bright, white, pink, and green marble that caught the morning sun. Furthermore, whereas the great gothic cathedrals were usually held up by an external skeleton of flying buttresses, the exterior of Florence Cathedral was a sheer vertical surface, giving it an impressive visual weight.

"They started building it in the thirteenth century." Su-Lin was pleased with San's interest in her hometown's most famous monument. "But it took almost two hundred years to complete, and another four hundred years for the marble exterior. They were still finishing the roof when the *Jinyi Wei* arrived with the Chinese embassy from Emperor Xuan De to Pope Eugenesis IV."

San walked the short distance across the narrow piazza between the lane from which they had emerged and the Cathedral's outer wall. He reached out and felt its cool marble exterior.

"We're going this way." Su-Lin set off, walking clockwise around the Cathedral.

To get to the entrance of the Cathedral, San and Su-Lin had to pass through a narrow gap between the Cathedral and Giotto's Campanile - the bell tower. San stood at the narrow base of the bell tower and looked up. The bell tower rose well above the height of the Cathedral's nave, to about a three hundred feet San guessed. It was so tall, relative to its width, that looking up felt dizzying to San because the structure seemed so precariously thin. "It has stayed up for over five hundred years," he mumbled to himself. "There's no reason to think it would choose today to fall over."

"See the hexagonal sculptures." Su-Lin pointed at a ring of sculptures decorating the ground floor level of the tower. "They celebrate the birth of the sciences, but in a Biblical context."

"An early attempt to resolve the emerging conflict between science and religion?" San, picked out one panel in particular, a sculpture of Noah the first farmer and Tubalcain the first blacksmith.

"Isn't it odd that they built the bell tower so close to the Cathedral?" Su-Lin gestured at the few feet separating the two buildings through which they now passed. "But without actually connecting it to the Cathedral."

"It's unusual, but not unheard of," answered San. "The most interesting example I've seen of a separate bell tower is a church in Berkeley."

"Where?"

"It's a small town in Gloucestershire, rural England."

"Nothing to do with California?"

San winced, but pressed on. "The town has a wonderful local legend to explain why the bell tower was separated from the church."

Su-Lin turned back to San, inviting him to share the story.

"In Berkeley, the small parish church, St. Mary's I think it was called, has a bell tower about fifty yards from the church. The local legend says that when the church was being built in the early thirteenth century, they tried building the bell tower adjacent to the church as you would expect. But every night, a witch would appear and move the church's foundation stones fifty yards away to another location. This process continued for a number of weeks. Eventually the townsfolk gave up and built the tower where the witch had put the stones each night."

"A true story?" Su-Lin raised a sceptical eyebrow.

"Sadly not," admitted San. "If the tower had been built next to the church, it would have overlooked the walls of Berkeley Castle."

"I see. So if anyone had besieged the castle, the church bell tower could have been used as a platform from with which to fire missiles over the castle walls."

"So unless the witch was a local's metaphor for Lord Berkeley who lived in the castle..."

"It was just a simple matter of siege engineering," interrupted Su-Lin.

"And just as well, because three hundred years later, during the English Civil War, the Parliamentarians did besiege Berkeley Castle."

"But at least they couldn't use the bell tower as a firing platform."

"No." San smiled. "They just used the roof of the church instead."

Turning right after passing the bell tower, Su-Lin was happy to see that the winter weather was suppressing the number of tourists, and there was no queue waiting to enter the Cathedral. The Cathedral's elaborate facade was pierced by three large portals. The left most set of bronze doors had been set open. San and Su Lin stepped through them and into the nave of the Cathedral.

Like most old churches, the interior was quite dark and it took a second for San and Su-Lin's eyes to fully adjust. Two lines of stone pillars stretched away down the hundred and fifty yard long nave of Florence Cathedral. Although there were not as many pillars as in the older Cathedrals of Europe, they were far larger, and the distances between them greater, increasing the sense of scale. Between the top of the enormous pillars and the ceiling, although still some hundred feet above San's head, the interior of the cathedral became much lighter than it would have been in a similarly sized gothic cathedral. Sunlight streamed through odd, nautically-shaped round windows high in the external walls. The visual effect was to make the ceiling seem even more distant, as though it was somehow floating above the walls.

"I don't know where to start," confessed Su-Lin anxiously. "Where could Doctor Chan's proof be hidden?"

San squeezed Su-Lin's hand for a moment in reassuring encouragement. But it was as much for his benefit as it was for hers. "This Cathedral is enormous."

CHAPTER 44

Inquisitor Jerome and Brother Michael waited patiently at the rear of one of the private hangars at Florence's Amerigo Vespucci Airport. The twin engine Learjet, for which they had been waiting, turned sharply in past the hangar bay doors and rolled to a stop. As the pitch of the whining from the aircraft engines slowly subsided to a more bearable level, Jerome adjusted his suit nervously, and approached the plane. The plane carried no markings except for the sign of the Roman Curia on the fuselage door - the Papal seal of a gold crown over two crossed keys on a red shield.

Jerome could see movement in the cockpit. After a moment, the door of the plane folded gently outwards and down to form a flight of steps. First to emerge from the plane was one of the Prefect's bodyguards. The bodyguard wore a black suit, black shirt and tie, sunglasses and the same silver pin on his lapel that Jerome and Michael wore – a crucifix surrounded by a sword and a branch. He was tall, athletically built and inappropriately youthful, thought Jerome. *Too perfectly presented to be someone hardened by experience.* He stared malevolently at the bodyguard. Jerome did not approve of lay people, without the convictions of his order, having such significant responsibilities for the Prefect.

The bodyguard waited at the bottom of the aircraft steps and looked back toward the door. There, from the shadowy interior of the plane, emerged the Prefect. The Prefect wore the blood red robes and cap of a Cardinal. Over his robes he wore a black velvet, hooded cloak. His back was slightly bent over and the skin around his eyes and throat was loose and sun spotted with age. The Prefect descended from the plane slowly, one step at a time, gripping the aluminum bannister tightly. He bore a scowl, as though he was frustrated by his own immobility. But the Prefect's deeply set eyes jumped around the hangar sharply, betraying a mind far more capable than his body.

When the Prefect reached the last step, Jerome fell to his left knee and bowed his head low. Michael followed Jerome's example, a respectful distance behind him. The Prefect slowly shuffled toward Jerome and offered his right hand, his palm facing the ground. While kneeling, Jerome quickly took the Prefect's hand in both of his own, closed his eyes, and reverently kissed the Prefect's large gold ring. On the Prefect's bulky gold ring was carved a crucifix, surrounded by a sword and a branch.

"Jerome my son," said the Prefect fondly. "Come and walk with me."

Jerome stood, leaning heavily on his cane, and followed the Prefect toward the waiting car. "Your Eminence, you must be tired after such a long flight."

"There is no salvation without suffering Jerome," said the Prefect dismissively. "Do not concern yourself. Tell me, what progress has been made with your inquiries?"

"We have distributed photos of Doctor Chan's colleague – the woman we interviewed in Rome, to all of our allies in Florence. We have also distributed descriptions of her co-conspirators from the *Jinyi Wei* who attacked us in Rome."

The Prefect nodded silently and without expression.

"We should pick up their trail again, as soon as they renew their search for the *Proditio*."

"Are you sure that they will come to Florence?"

"Very sure, Your Eminence." Jerome tried to project even more confidence than he felt. "Doctor Chan's whore was most reluctant to divulge the location of the *Proditio*."

The Prefect stopped for a moment, his eyes narrowed, as he studied Jerome's face. "I hope you are right."

Jerome couldn't help but feel he was being threatened.

"But it sounds awfully passive Jerome." The Prefect shot Jerome an accusing glance. "Can't we do anything ourselves to find the *Proditio*?"

"We would if we could, Your Eminence. But we got nothing more from our investigation than the name of the city in which the *Proditio* is hidden." Jerome didn't want to sound overly defensive. "That is, we got nothing more before we were interrupted by the *Jinyi Wei*." Jerome shrugged. "We have nothing more to go on."

"What about Doctor Chan's message?"

"It meant nothing." Jerome spoke more bluntly than he had intended, and was suddenly concerned that he may have insulted the Prefect.

"Don't be so hasty Jerome." The Prefect overlooked Jerome's transgression. "Toscanelli was from Florence, and there may be a connection there worth exploring. Maybe, his home, his place of work, or one of the projects he worked on?"

"We will look into it, Your Eminence."

A large, black sedan waited at the hangar exit. A similarly well groomed bodyguard held the rear door open for the Prefect. Jerome tried to help the Prefect, who was struggling to get into the car gracefully. But the Prefect shooed him away. Once seated the Prefect leant back, tired from the short walk from the plane to the car. The Prefect's bodyguard went to close the door behind him, but the Prefect held up his hand, signaling for him to wait.

"Jerome? There is one more thing that I would like you to do."

"Yes? Your Eminence."

"Bring one of the *Jinyi Wei* to me." The Prefect licked his lips. "I would like to question them personally."

"Are you sure, Your Eminence?" Jerome gasped, surprised by the request. "It would be most irregular." For a moment, he was lost for words. "And it would entail some unnecessary risks."

The Prefect's face hardened, staring at Jerome. "That was not a request Inquisitor. Don't doubt that there is life enough left in these hands to do God's work."

"Yes, Your Eminence." Jerome swallowed hard. "No doubt Your Eminence," he added, without the slightest trace of sarcasm.

CHAPTER 45

San Lee stared up and into the inside of Florence Cathedral's enormous dome. San and Su-Lin had split the task of searching the Cathedral. San had taken the right-hand side of the church and Su-Lin had taken the left. San worked his way down the Cathedral, reading the dedications, examining the funeral monuments and all of the artwork. He felt as though he was in an art gallery. There were sculptures by Donatello, paintings by Uccello, and busts of the builders Giotto who built the Campanile and Brunelleschi who finished the Cathedral's dome. But nothing seemed obviously related to Pope Eugenesis IV and the Chinese embassy, he thought, let alone the location of the *Proditio*.

Su-Lin approached San, from the opposite side of the Cathedral. She wore a disappointed frown on her face. "Nothing," she said in an ambiguous tone, halfway between a statement and a question. She looked to San for confirmation.

But San wasn't paying her much attention. "It's amazing. It's even larger than I had imagined."

Su-Lin looked up in the same direction, slightly irritated

at being ignored. "Yes, it's about fifty yards across, the largest masonry dome ever constructed."

"That would make it larger than the Pantheon in Rome. Although to be fair to the builders, the Pantheon was built more than a thousand years earlier."

"And larger than the Hagia Sophia in Istanbul," added Su-Lin. "It wasn't for more than a hundred years after the Cathedral was started that Filippo Brunelleschi managed to figure out how to build the dome without scaffolding."

San thought about this for a moment. "There wouldn't have been enough timber in Italy to build it with scaffolding from beneath."

"The trick to the design was ringing the dome with three stone chains, to prevent the force of gravity on the dome, causing the walls to collapse outwards. Like metal hoops on a very large wine barrel."

"Stone rings or not, there must be hundreds of tons of stone in the dome, held up there without support."

"Thirty five thousand tons, apparently." Su-Lin glanced into the dome, but she did not share San's intense interest. "Brunelleschi had to invent an ox-powered hoist especially for the purpose of raising the stone up and into the dome. It was later sketched by a young draftsman, Leonardo da Vinci, and ever since it's been commonly misattributed as an invention of Leonardo's."

San's interest was piqued as Su-Lin wandered into his field of art history.

Su-Lin continued. "Leonardo da Vinci has been credited with all manner of inventions – helicopters, parachutes, and the tank. But they were all copies from earlier artists. Even his most famous image – the Vitruvian Man, was a copy of an earlier work by Taccola. Leonardo was a good draftsman, but there's not much evidence he invented anything very much."

"That might be a little harsh. He was a pretty decent painter."

"OK, maybe I am being a little unfair," conceded Su-Lin. "But have you ever compared the drawings of the so-called Renaissance inventors, like Francesco di Georgio and Leonardo, with Wang Chen's *Nung Shu*? Some of the drawings are identical!"

"So what are you saying? Are you suggesting that Leonardo copied from the *Nung Shu*?"

"Well the *Nung Shu*, or Writings in Agriculture in English, was written in 1313. That's more than a century before Europeans started making suspiciously similar drawings. It was also one of the first books printed with movable type. Again long before European's would discover the technology of printing."

"It sounds interesting, I should take a look." San was genuinely interested. "My art history covered drawings by great artists, but we didn't cover the technical drawings of Asia's great inventors."

"Now I'm not sure if Leonardo copied from the *Nung Shu*, or whether Leonardo copied from Francesco who copied from the *Nung Shu*. But I am sure that the similarities between the European drawings and the *Nung Shu* are compelling evidence of imitation. I'm also sure that the Chinese embassy from the Emperor Xuan De would have brought a copy of such a condensed compilation of Chinese technology as a gift for Pope Eugenesis IV."

"And from there it would have percolated into the hands of the artists of Tuscany," suggested San.

"Just as the Chinese maps found their way from Pope Eugenesis IV to Christopher Columbus via Toscanelli."

San squinted at the ceiling over three hundred feet above him and wondered at the futility of Vasari's painting on the inside of the dome. Vasari had been commissioned by Cosimo de Medici to paint a depiction of the last judgment on the interior of the dome of Florence Cathedral. But it was an image that no one could ever get close enough to actually see, he thought.

"Where do you think we should look next?" asked Su-Lin impatiently.

But San the art historian was thoroughly distracted. "What's that up there?" he asked, pointing at a small aperture in the center of the dome, through which sunlight lit the dome's interior.

"It's the lantern." Su-Lin folded her arms. The words came out sounding a little more impatient than Su-Lin had intended, and so she added, "It lets in light and supports the bronze sphere and cross you can see from the outside."

"I've read something about that I think. Wasn't it used for an experiment?"

"Yes, Paolo Toscanelli," mumbled Su-Lin, thinking instead that they should be searching for the *Proditio*. "In 1475, he used the Cathedral's dome as a giant *camera obscura*, by covering the lantern with a bronze plate. This allowed only a thin beam of light to enter the Cathedral through the lantern. Toscanelli could then measure the movement of the sun by the path that the beam of light traced on the floor."

But San wrinkled his nose, struggling to see the significance.

"You have to remember that in the fifteenth century Europeans hadn't yet managed to standardize their calendar. Nor had Europeans figured out that the Earth rotated around the sun, let alone with an elliptical orbit."

"True," conceded San. "The Inquisition would be torturing scientists for at least another two hundred years for going anywhere near that topic. But, I can't see any connection between this Cathedral's dome and the Chinese embassy to Eugenesis IV, let alone the *Proditio*."

But it was Su-Lin's turn to have her interest piqued. "Navigation perhaps," she suggested. "The Chinese astronomer Guo Shoujing had understood as early as about 1280 that since the earth rotates about the sun in an ellipse the position of the sun relative to the earth at any given time of the day changes. The effect is the same at night and the position of the stars relative to the pole star and earth also changes. Guo Shoujing produced star maps for each day of the 1461 day cycle enabling navigators a far more accurate way to estimate their position. In effect, until the Chinese arrived in Florence, the Chinese could navigate to Europe, but the Europeans couldn't have navigated back."

"So you're suggesting that Toscanelli's experiment in the Cathedral was to test the science that produced the star maps he had recently received from the Chinese?" San considered the idea.

"It's possible. Perhaps even advisable," added Su-Lin. "Especially if you were planning to sail into an open ocean based on the star map's advice."

"What was the date that Doctor Chan gave us?" asked San, toying with an idea inspired by Su-Lin's discussion of star maps.

"January the fifth, 1254."

"No, that was Doctor Chan's date that led us to Florence. I meant the second date, the date from the ephemeris table. The date we don't yet understand."

"The other date Doctor Chan left us with was the sixth of July, 1439. The day that Doctor Macheda identified as the day a mass was conducted here in Florence Cathedral by Eugenesis IV to celebrate the reunification of the western and eastern churches."

"Again, it might not be a date." San squinted, weighing the idea. Su-Lin could almost hear the cogs in his brain rotating. "It also looks like a date. But again, I think Doctor Chan is trying to tell us where his proof is hidden."

"I don't understand?" complained Su-Lin.

"You remember that we thought the first date referred to the date of Marco Polo's birth when in fact it turned out to indicate that Doctor Chan's proof - the *Proditio* - was hidden in Florence?"

"Yes." said Su-Lin excitedly.

"I think the second date is similar!" San was now convinced of his conclusion. "It doesn't indicate when the mass to reunify the church was celebrated by Pope Eugenesis IV. Doctor Chan's second date indicates a place here in Florence."

"Where San?" Su-Lin bubbled with enthusiasm. "Where?"

"While the reunification of the church was celebrated with a mass on this famous date in Florence Cathedral, it was also celebrated in a different way in another church in Florence." Su-Lin's eyes widened eagerly as she waited for San to explain. "Leon Battista Alberti painted a picture of the night sky in Florence exactly as it was on the night of the sixth of July, 1439." San paused for a second, knowing that the wait was unbearable for Su-Lin. "Alberti painted this picture on the ceiling of the old sacristy in the Basilica of San Lorenzo and Doctor Chan is pointing us in its direction."

CHAPTER 46

Agent Mei-Li continued to circle the piazza in front of Florence Cathedral. She searched for the two priests who they had seen with the bronze rat's head sculpture in Rome the night before. The Chinese consulate in Florence was mainly organized for visa work and to help Chinese tourists in trouble. Unfortunately, that meant they had only limited equipment and no trained personnel to help with surveillance work. So Tao and Mei-Li had little option but to monitor the churches in Florence themselves, and hope to pick up the trail of at least one of the two priests. But there are perhaps a hundred churches in Florence, she thought. *All we can do is monitor a couple of them.*

In the center of the piazza in front of Florence Cathedral sat the Cathedral's Baptistery. Mei-Li circled the Baptistery for the second time that morning. The strange octagonal building had three enormous sets of bronze doors covered with castings depicting Biblical scenes and the Fathers of the Church. The doors on the north side of the Baptistery were decorated in impressive enough detail to earn the name Gates-of-Paradise from none other than Michelangelo. She stopped in the piazza by the baptistery to look back at the entrance to the Cathedral. She surveyed the slowly swelling number of tourists. But there was still no sign of the priests, Mei-Li thought. *I might not even be at the right church.*

As Mei-Li waited and watched, a tall Asian man walked past her and toward the Cathedral entrance. She didn't see his face as he passed, but he was tall and athletically built, suggesting he took care of himself in the gym. He kept his hair short, but wore a couple of days stubble on his jaw. He's handsome, she smiled, enjoying the distraction. It wasn't as though there weren't thousands of Asian tourists in Florence. *But he doesn't look like a tourist.* Tourists wear strange, multi-pocketed vests and carry cameras, she thought. And tourists wander slowly, wearing expressions like babies, as though everything they see is a surprise to them. But this man knew where he was going. He also wore a long black leather jacket, which was a little too well dressed for your average tourist. Mei-Li watched him as he walked away from her and toward the Cathedral. Just before the entrance, the Asian man stopped and looked back toward the piazza before disappearing inside. Is that San Lee?

"Sir!" Mei-Li barked into her mouth piece, trying to maintain composure.

"Any sign of the priests?" demanded Agent Tao Ma.

"No. But, I may have just seen San Lee."

"Are you sure?" Tao sounded as though he was unsettled by the news. "What's he doing in Florence?

"I can't be sure Sir. But someone looking like him just entered Florence Cathedral."

Finding San Lee wasn't as good as finding the two priests with the bronze rat's head sculpture, thought Tao. *But he could definitely help us fill in a few blanks.* "Where are you?" asked Tao.

"I'm at the west end of the Cathedral, between the entrance and the baptistery."

"Don't move on him until I get there," ordered Tao. "Maintain surveillance, but keep an inconspicuous distance. Just get close enough to confirm his identification."

"Understood." Mei-Li began walking excitedly toward the same Cathedral entrance that the tall Asian man had used a minute earlier.

"I'm just leaving the Basilica of the Holy Cross." Tao was now breathing heavily. It was clear to her that he was now running. "I should be there in less than ten minutes." Tao hung up abruptly.

Mei-Li began weaving between the tourists on the steps of the Cathedral and toward the entrance. She was nervous that the delay caused by calling her boss might have meant that she would lose track of the tall Asian man inside the Cathedral. But stepping into the dark interior of the Cathedral it was only a moment before she spotted her quarry again. The tall Asian man was slowly walking up the right hand edge of the Cathedral toward the altar. But it was very hard to make a positive identification, because the aisles at the edges of the Cathedral were so much darker than the center aisle, and periodically he would also disappear from view behind a column. But I'm almost ninety percent sure it's San Lee, she thought. To keep a safe distance, Mei-Li walked down the center aisle and sat down in one of the pews pretending to rest.

Now he looks like a tourist, thought Mei-Li. She watched the tall Asian man admire each sculpture and every painting in the Cathedral. *No, it's more than being a tourist.* Tourists wander about, rarely reading anything that might actually give them some insight into what they are looking at. Tourists focus instead on which photo opportunity was most likely to impress their friends on Facebook. But, this man was closely examining every artwork, and diligently reading every inscription in the Cathedral. *It's as though he's searching for something.*

Patiently, Mei-Li waited for the tall Asian man to walk

out from the shadowy aisle on the right-hand edge of the Cathedral and into the brighter space under the Cathedral's dome. The Asian man turned and looked up into the underside of the Cathedral's famous dome, giving Mei-Li a clear look at his face. It's definitely him, she thought excitedly. *It's San Lee.*

"Sir?" Mei-Li didn't wait for Tao's response. "I have made a positive identification. It's definitely San Lee."

"Excellent work! Where can I find you?"

Mei-Li looked around for a landmark of some kind. She spotted a large painting on the wall to her left. "I'm halfway down the church on the left hand side of the center aisle. I'm in front of the painting of Dante."

Mei-Li watched San staring at the painting of heaven and hell on the inside of the Cathedral's dome. As she did, a slightly built young lady, with long black hair, wearing jeans and a biker's jacket walked up to San and began talking to him. But it wasn't until the lady turned around, revealing her pale skin and exaggerated Eurasian features, that Mei-Li recognized her too. It's the lady from the church in Rome, thought Mei-Li. *The lady who was tortured!*

Mei-Li sat bolt upright, fumbling her mouthpiece in a rush to bring it close to her lips. "Tao?" she whispered, in her excitement forgetting all of the normal formalities.

"Yes?"

"It's not just San Lee. San is meeting..."

But Tao heard nothing further from Mei-Li, just a dull crunching noise, and then the crackle of static. The line had gone dead.

CHAPTER 47

San Lee and Su-Lin both hurried toward the nearest exit of Florence Cathedral, both excited by the prospect of perhaps having finally understood the second date that Doctor Chan had left them. They took the small wooden door in the left transept, which led out into the street on the north side of Florence Cathedral. It was a little warmer than when they had entered the Cathedral and significantly busier in the street. On the north side of the Cathedral the street passed only a couple of yards from the Cathedral's external wall. Furthermore, the street was busy with not only increased foot traffic, but cars too, because it was about as close as vehicle traffic could easily get to the old city. San and Su-Lin turned sharply left after leaving the Cathedral, skirting the north edge of the Piazza del Duomo.

They didn't have far to go to get to the Basilica di San Lorenzo because it was less than half a mile from Florence Cathedral. In a stunning demonstration of Florence's wealth and power during the Renaissance, the Basilica di San Lorenzo, which was almost as large and grandiose as Florence Cathedral, was not only built very close to Florence Cathedral but it was built at approximately the same time.

However, unlike Florence Cathedral, which had a wide public space in front of it, San and Su-Lin approached the Basilica di San Lorenzo through a bustling, open-air market selling hats, leather goods, and souvenirs. Walking up a short but broad flight of steps to the entrance, Su-Lin could see that the Cathedral and the Basilica were also built to a similar design. Both were topped with a large terracotta dome and the facades of both churches were penetrated by three doors and a large alcove above the central door. But instead of being clad in marble like Florence Cathedral, the Basilica had been left with a modest, bare stone exterior. Similarly, whereas the doors of Florence Cathedral had been made from bronze, those of the Basilica were made more modestly of wood.

As Su-Lin stepped through the leftmost wooden door and into the Basilica, a shiver ran down her spine. The interior looked frighteningly familiar. The two lines of thin columns, but most particularly the square patterned ceiling reminded her of the Basilica di Santa Maria Maggiore in Rome, and the ordeal she had endured there.

San could sense Su-Lin's unease. "Are you feeling alright?"

Su-Lin involuntarily winced and rubbed her broken arm. "It's nothing." She forced herself to smile, and tried a joke to relax herself. "I'm having trouble telling these churches apart."

"They do blend together after a while," agreed San. "But you might have noticed from the names on all the tombs." San waved vaguely in the direction of some of the Basilica's funeral monuments, as he walked down the center aisle. "This Basilica was the local church of the Medici family."

Su-Lin was heartened by the change of topic. "The Medici family virtually ran Florence when the *Jinyi Wei* arrived with the Chinese embassy to Pope Eugenesis IV. The Medicis ran Europe's largest bank, they were the Dukes of Florence, they were bankers to the Holy See, and could count several Popes among their family."

"And in my own field," enthused San. "It's pretty difficult to study the providence of any artwork from the Italian Renaissance without running across the Medici family name. They commissioned or bought a vast proportion of renaissance art. Or built the buildings they're now housed in."

"I see you're a fan."

"Artists have always needed rich patrons."

"And so have art buyers." Su-Lin grinned cheekily.

"This Basilica is a perfect example." San smiled politely, ignoring Su-Lin's jibe. "The Medicis financed the building of this Basilica and commissioned the artists to decorate it." San pointed at the pulpit as an example. "And they didn't just commission any artists. It was built by Brunelleschi - the architect that built Florence Cathedral's dome, Donatello designed the pulpits, and Michelangelo built the Library."

"And who painted the night sky in the Old Sacristy?"

"Oddly enough, we aren't entirely sure," conceded San. "But, as you'll see, they knew an awful lot about astronomy."

Su-Lin raised a surprised eyebrow. She had not considered the possibility that the painting of the night sky in the Old Sacristy might be more closely related to her own field of expertise – cartography and navigation, than San's expertise in art history.

"The financial accounts relating to the Basilica's construction suggest that Leon Battista Alberti was being paid for the painting." San shrugged dissatisfied with his own explanation. "But Alberti was neither an artist, nor an astronomer. He was an architect."

"So if he painted it himself, he would have needed help?" asked Su-Lin.

"Yes. But on the other hand, Alberti could have certainly afforded help. He had access to considerable resources. He was a member of one of Italy's noble families, a hereditary member of the Roman Curia, and a Papal notary."

Again Su-Lin flinched at the mention of the Roman Curia, remembering what two of its members had done to her the night before.

"I'm sorry Su-Lin. That was insensitive of me."

"No San it's OK. In fact it might explain how Alberti executed the painting. As a papal notary, he would have come to Florence with Pope Eugenesis IV." Su-Lin looked at San, expecting he would understand the implications immediately.

"So he would have attended the mass celebrating the reunification of the church?"

"Possibly." Su-Lin smiled. "More importantly, if Alberti was in Florence at that time, in all likelihood he would have met the Florentine astronomer Pablo Toscanelli, if not the Chinese embassy itself."

"Toscanelli was the guy who was conducting astronomical experiments in Florence Cathedral to confirm the validity of the Chinese technology?"

"The same." Su-Lin nodded.

"So Alberti could have learned how to paint the Old Sacristy's night sky in one of two ways. He could have learnt the technique from Toscanelli who learned it from the Chinese embassy, or he could have learned it from the Chinese directly."

Su-Lin was pleased that another piece of the puzzle seemed to fall into place. "The connection between Alberti and the Chinese embassy would also explain why Doctor Chan might have been interested in the Old Sacristy as a potential hiding place for the *Proditio.*"

San pointed to the far left hand corner of the Basilica. "So let's see what we can find in the Old Sacristy."

CHAPTER 48

Inquisitor Jerome led the Prefect across the Piazza della Signoria, up a short stone staircase, and through the entrance of the Palazzo Vecchio. Jerome noticed that the Prefect walked more comfortably and quickly that he had when they first met him at the airport. Maybe he has recovered from the flight, he thought. *Or maybe he was looking forward to this.*

The cube-shaped, Palazzo Vecchio was built in the fifteenth century as Florence's town hall. It was solidly built, made of rough-hewn stone with little external adornment except for the nine coats of arms of the Florentine republic which were displayed above the third floor windows. As the crenellated battlements suggested, the Palace could also protect the city's magistrates in times of civil strife.

But the first arcaded courtyard that Jerome and the Prefect now crossed was more finely decorated than the exterior of the Palace. The quiet courtyard was open to the sky and surrounded by finely carved columns. A red porphyry fountain in the center of the courtyard caught Jerome's eye. Made of the same stone as Constantia's sarcophagus in the Vatican Museum, he thought it was hard to imagine, that all the ancient world's red porphyry sculpture came from a single quarry in the Egyptian desert.

"This way Your Eminence." Jerome gently guided the Prefect across the courtyard to its eastern edge. The Prefect's black-suited body guard followed a couple of yards behind them.

"*Quare adduxistis eum?*" Jerome, asked in Latin, so as to avoid being overheard. He disapproved of the Prefect's use of bodyguards from outside the order and he wanted to know why the Prefect insisted on bringing him along.

"Don't fuss Jerome. You and Brother Michael are far more valuably employed on the more complicated assignments."

Jerome knew that he was being flattered, but couldn't also help but feel that his territory was being encroached upon.

After entering the Palace's interior, they began to climb a wide, grandiose staircase to the Salone dei Cinquecento – The Hall of the Five Hundred. The hall was designed to host Florence's governing body, the Grand Council, of which, as its name suggested there were five hundred members. It was an enormous room. Almost as large as an indoor swimming pool, thought Jerome, as they walked up to its entrance. *It's also probably the place where Pope Eugenesis IV had received the Chinese embassy and signed the Proditio.*

Jerome waited for a moment at the entrance to the Salon, because the Prefect was starting to lag behind. The enormous room was decorated with paintings of Florence's military victories over its neighbors. But not so famous as the paintings they replaced, he thought. Michelangelo's Battle of Cascina originally decorated one of the walls, but was destroyed by later building work. Leonardo da Vinci's even more famous Battle of Anghiari melted from the walls when the artist inadvisably tried to accelerate the drying process.

Once the Prefect caught up with Jerome, they continued

on to another narrower staircase that led into the Palace's clock tower. At the base of the staircase, the Prefect paused for breath, sweat having already broken out on his forehead. Jerome waited respectfully for the Prefect to recover and indicate he was ready to carry on. The Prefect eyed the staircase warily. He was unenthused by the prospect of a long and far steeper climb. But he licked his lips at the prospect of what was to come once the climb was finished.

"Your Eminence, it was most fortunate that we were able to secure the use of the Palazzo Vecchio." Jerome was trying to break the uncomfortable silence, although he was genuinely impressed with the Prefect's connections.

"The Catholic Church has sold the Medicis the papacy on more than one occasion in the past," snapped the Prefect. "The least they could do is lend us the use of their own home."

"Not to mention the banking business we have given them over the years."

But the Prefect was paying him no attention, tutting irritably. "Was it really necessary to use the tower Jerome?"

"We were concerned about the noise Your Eminence." Jerome spoke in a hushed voice. "We don't want to attract any unwanted attention."

"You are probably right," conceded the Prefect. "Guard?" The Prefect turned to his bodyguard. "Wait here won't you? We won't be too long." The bodyguard nodded and assumed his position at the bottom of the stairs that led into the tower. The Prefect patted the bodyguard's shoulder gently.

Jerome's face twisted in disgust.

After a few deep breaths, the Prefect began the slow climb up into the Palazzo Vecchio's clock tower. The clock tower of the Palazzo Vecchio was even older than the palace in which it was now incorporated. At about three hundred feet tall it was also the only other building in

Florence to compete with Florence Cathedral in terms of height. A fact that is seemingly taking its toll on the Prefect's temper, thought Jerome. *But at least he has someone other than me to vent his anger on.*

Jerome was relieved to finally get the top of the stairs. The Prefect had stopped to rest many times on the way up, and Jerome had worried that it would have been an ignoble end if the Prefect had expired on the staircase. *And God knows how we would have carried him out.* On the small landing at the top of the stairs, Jerome could see that the heavy wooden cell door was still securely shut. Brother Michael, who had been guarding the cell, knelt hastily as Jerome and the Prefect approached. But the Prefect, although wheezing shallowly, shook his hand impatiently, gesturing for Michael to stand up and get out of the way.

The Prefect nearly ran the last couple of steps to the cell door. He lunged forward and grabbed the iron bars of the cell door's window with both his hands. He drew his sweat covered face close to the window, straining greedily to examine the cell's contents. A satisfied smile spread slowly across the Prefect's thin dry lips.

CHAPTER 49

Agent Tao Ma sprinted toward the entrance to Florence Cathedral. He shoved tourists out of his way in a rush to get to San Lee. Tao only slowed as he entered the Cathedral not wanting to draw attention to himself should San be close to the Cathedral's entrance. He looked desperately around the Cathedral. But it was difficult for him to focus immediately. Not only was it darker inside the Cathedral, but Tao was still breathing heavily after running half a mile from the Basilica di Santa Croce.

It was hard not to be impressed with the enormity of the Cathedral, admitted Tao. He took a couple of steps into the Cathedral across the elaborate marble floor. The floor by the entrance was decorated with an octagonal, maze like pattern, with three letters written, "OPA," at its center. Tao had no idea what it meant. He looked up and above the entrance to what looked like a clock. But it was covered with indecipherable symbols that also meant nothing to Tao. Before he had joined the Ministry, he had never had the money, or the interest to travel abroad. And it was at moments like this that Tao felt his lack of familiarity put him at a significant disadvantage.

Tao scanned the milling tourists for San Lee. He was pleased to see that a fair number of the tourists were Chinese, despite that it would make finding San that much more difficult. It was a symptom of China's growing wealth and power, he thought proudly. Although his first priority was the recovery of the bronze rat's head sculpture, which they had last seen in the possession of the two priests, San might be able to tell them who the priests were and what they wanted with the sculpture. *But where is Agent Mei-Li, let alone San?*

After a minute or two of searching the Cathedral, Tao was thoroughly frustrated. He could not find Mei-Li or San anywhere. As large as the Cathedral was, it was ultimately one large room, with few corners in which people could hide. He had even tried standing still in the center aisle under the dome, reasoning that if San or Mei-Li were moving about, he need only wait for a minute and they would eventually wander into his field of vision. *But after five minutes there was still nothing.*

Tao switched on his mouth piece again. "Agent Mei-Li? Are you there?" Tao demanded, thinking what punishment would be appropriate for Mei-Li having left her post without warning. But again there was no reply. Tao could still only hear a low crackling static.

"Where had Mei-Li said she was sitting?" Tao thought for a moment and then remembered that Mei-Li had said something about the left side of the Cathedral. Tao walked across to the left most aisle. She had also said she was sitting in front of an artwork, a painting of Dante, thought Tao. *Or was it a painting by Dante?*

The first art work Tao came to was a large fresco on the left hand external wall of the Cathedral. The painting looked to be a gray horse and rider. But as he got closer he realized that it was a painting of a gray marble statue of a white horse. The plaque by the painting told Tao that it was a, "Funerary monument to Sir John Hawkwood, by Paolo

Uccelo."

"Didn't have enough money to buy a real sculpture," he sneered.

A young tour guide, standing to the side of the mural, gestured enthusiastically to a confused looking tour group. "This fresco is a splendid example of Uccello's personal expression, the composition more symbolic than natural..."

"Looks like a man on a horse to me," thought Tao. And the closer he looked, the more convinced he was that the artist had made a mess of the perspective.

A little further on, Tao saw another fresco. At first glance he thought the painting was identical to the first. It was only after stepping backwards, and comparing the two, that the differences became obvious. "Another man on a horse," he announced sarcastically, rolling his eyes. Although this horse is a little whiter than the first, he conceded. "And the plaque's different." Tao smiled, pleased with his own joke. The plaque next to the painting identified it as, "a Funerary monument to Niccolò da Tolentino by Andrea del Castagno."

The third artwork that Tao came to on the left hand side of the Cathedral was far more striking. High on the wall surrounded by a stone frame was a complicated painting of demons on the left, angels sitting in a castle in the center, and what looked to Tao to be the city of Florence pictured on the right. But the focus of the painting was a red robed priest holding an open book. Tao searched for the accompanying plaque.

"Dante and the Divine Comedy by Domenico di Michelino," Tao read aloud.

Tao span on his heel, and strode away from the painting, toward the center of the Cathedral. This is the painting Mei-Li mentioned, thought Tao. *So she would have been sitting somewhere around here.*

But there was no one sitting in the area, and certainly no sign of Mei-Li. Tao walked between two of the pews that ran perpendicular to the painting, searching for some sign of where Mei-Li may have been.

Tao had reached the end of the pew closest to the center aisle, when there on the floor, almost concealed by the pew, he noticed a small piece of broken, black plastic. He bent down to pick it up. It was Mei-Li's mangled ear piece. It had been smashed to pieces. A thin black wire led away from the ear piece and under the pew to Tao's right. He had to kneel down to pull out the mobile device to which the ear piece was attached. It too had been crushed underfoot.

"Mei-Li would never have left this behind, let alone destroyed it herself," thought Tao, standing up. "Mei-Li has been taken." *But by whom?*

CHAPTER 50

San led Su-Lin down to the Old Sacristy which was a small chapel in the far left hand corner of the Basilica of San Lorenzo. The chapel got its name because not only was it one of the oldest parts of the church, but it had to be differentiated from the New Sacristy, which was designed by Michelangelo, and faced the Old Sacristy in the opposite transept.

The Old Sacristy was a simple square room, about twenty feet on each side, with a modest white altar at the far end, opposite the door. The floor was covered with an unattractive red granite and the white walls were decorated with small, simple murals. To the right of the door was a wooden hip high cabinet that ran along two walls and to the left of the door ran a similar dark wood bench.

It appeared to Su-Lin that there were two tombs in the chapel. There was one tomb in the center of the room under a large white marble table. The second tomb was built into a metal grill that made up the wall to the left of the door separating the Old Sacristy from the adjacent chapel. Su-Lin was initially surprised by how small the Old Sacristy was. If the *Proditio* was hidden somewhere inside the Old Sacristy, it was certainly a lot less daunting a task to find it, than having to search the cavernous interior of Florence Cathedral.

San was staring at the domed cupola in the center of the ceiling. The inside of the small dome was divided into twelve segments by six black lines. Around the cupola, ochre colored Biblical scenes had been painted in the four corners of the ceiling. But the distance made it hard for Su-Lin to make out what the images were of.

"The structure was designed by Brunelleschi," explained San. "The same guy who finished the dome on top of Florence Cathedral."

"He clearly had something for domes." Su-Lin felt frustrated that she couldn't see the painting that they had come here to find. "Where is the painting of the night sky?"

San didn't move. He simply pointed to the ceiling over the altar. Above the altar was a smaller dome. Since the chapel didn't have any windows, the dome over the altar would have been shadowy, even if hadn't also been painted a dark blue - the color of the night sky. Su-Lin squinted, struggling to see any painting at all.

"This is the date from Doctor Chan's ephemeris table." San smiled. "The sixth of July, 1439 wasn't just the date at which Pope Eugenesis IV held a mass to celebrate the unification of the church." He shook his finger at the inside of the smaller dome over the altar as if to underscore the point. "The sixth of July, 1439 was the subject of this painting!"

Su-Lin tried to share San's enthusiasm and stared for a long moment at the dark mural. As her eyes adjusted, she could make out that stars, constellations and the moon were painted on the inside of the dome. But the mural looked to her to be a fairly stylized depiction of a night sky. It even had a poorly proportioned dog painted on the roof to represent the constellation Canis Major.

Su-Lin did not know what to make of it. "What is it?"

"It's a painting of stars," said San simply. This earned an exasperated groan from Su-Lin. "More precisely, it's a painting of the stars exactly as they were on July the sixth, 1439."

"Exactly as they were?" Su-Lin asked, with the emphasis on the word exactly. "Are you saying that this painting is a star map?"

"Yes." San nodded. "It's an astronomically precise map of the position of the stars on July the sixth 1439. It has been checked against modern, astronomical software and it's an impressively accurate representation."

"This would certainly have been of more interest to Doctor Chan the cartographer and navigator, than the Cathedral used to celebrate the unification of the Churches."

San crossed his arms as he leant back, examining the mural. "But even more interesting is that the mural was painted long after the sixth of July, 1439."

But it was not obvious to Su-Lin as to why this was interesting at all.

San could see Su-Lin's next question emerging and hastened to add, "In 1439 Europeans had no way of estimating the position of stars at a given point in time."

But Su-Lin was not impressed. "Maybe they just observed the stars at night on that day and took notes?" she suggested. "They could have then painted it later using their notes."

"That would be a possible explanation, except for the painting's second most notable feature. This is a painting of the position of stars as they would have been on July the sixth, 1439 at noon, in the middle of the day."

"What?" Su-Lin shook her head. "But the stars aren't visible in the middle of the day?"

"So the question remains, how did Europeans manage to paint such a painting? Because they hadn't yet discovered some fairly elementary astronomical facts, like the earth revolves around the sun."

It took only a moment for Su-Lin to provide the explanation. "They used the same Chinese astronomical technology that led Europeans to colonize the Americas," she gushed excitedly. "The Pope's notary Alberti either worked with the astronomer Toscanelli who he met in Florence or from material presented by the Chinese embassy to Pope Eugenesis IV for who Alberti worked."

"It would seem likely," agreed San. "The painting could have been composed using an ephemeris table like the piece of paper that Doctor Chan used to give us this location."

"So where is the *Proditio?*"

CHAPTER 51

The Prefect smiled greedily as he peered at the young Agent Mei-Li through the bars of the cell in the Palazzo Vecchio. She wore blue jeans, a black collared shirt and sneakers. But her hands had been bound with rope behind her back and then tied to the back of a solid wooden chair. Her legs had been similarly bound to the legs of the chair. A thick piece of gray electrical tape had been placed across her mouth, securing a white cloth gag. The chair Mei-Li had been tied to sat in the middle of a small, windowless room. The bare stone walls were slightly damp, giving the air an unhealthily dank smell.

Seemingly satisfied with what he saw, the Prefect moved back from the door. "Where did you find her Jerome?" he asked in Latin.

"One of our allies spotted her in Florence Cathedral this morning," said Jerome. "Brother Michael went and collected her."

The Prefect turned to Brother Michael. "I hope you didn't begin the investigation prematurely Michael?" The Prefect chuckled to himself.

Michael flinched and his eyes widened. He did not know

what to say when addressed by the Prefect directly. So Michael decided to say nothing and instead hurried to get the large, iron key to let the Prefect into the cell.

"Was she alone?"

"Yes, Your Eminence." Jerome nodded. "We have not heard any news of either of her two colleagues."

The Prefect turned back to Michael, pointing at the door. "Let us begin."

Stooping low, Michael unlocked the cell door. He pushed it open and stepped inside. After he entered, he stood to one side of the door and held it open for the Prefect.

The Prefect used a handkerchief to wipe the sweat from his brow. He paused briefly with his eyes closed and hands together in prayer, before stepping into the cell after Michael.

Mei-Li's eyes followed the Prefect as he entered the room. She squirmed briefly in her chair, making another futile effort to pull her hands free.

But the Prefect halted when he saw Mei-Li struggling. He stood a few feet in front of her and held out his hands in an open welcoming gesture. "There is nothing to fear my child." The Prefect smiled. "Did you know that the great Cosimo de Medici was once held in this very cell."

Mei-Li stared back at the Prefect. She neither comprehended what she was being told, nor why she was being told it.

The Prefect watched Mei-Li closely. But he could see no sign of recognition or understanding in her eyes. "Once he was freed, Cosimo went on to finance the Italian Renaissance. He commissioned many of the Renaissance's most famous works of art. He paid for the dome on top of Florence's Cathedral, and he paid to move his Holiness' Pope Eugenesis IV's ecumenical council of 1439 to Florence from Ferrara." The Prefect tried to smile warmly. "So there is still hope my child. You too could achieve great things after leaving this cell… after helping us with our inquiries."

The Prefect gestured for Michael to come forward and remove his black velvet cloak. The scarlet robes of a cardinal that he wore below his cloak fitted his barrel shaped torso tightly. While his chest now extended below toward his stomach, the Prefect would have been a powerful man in his youth.

As Michael took the Prefect's cloak, Mei-Li's eyes flicked fearfully from the Prefect to Michael and back again.

The Prefect noticed Mei-Li's apparently heightened anxiety. "I'm sorry," said the Prefect in a soft voice, indicating to Michael. "Does Brother Michael bother you? He can be unnecessarily rough sometimes." The Prefect nodded agreeably, as though Mei-Li had responded in the affirmative. "Rest assured he won't be bothering us again." The Prefect turned to Michael who had been standing at the back of the cell, waiting to assist the Prefect. "Please, leave us Michael." The Prefect waved toward the door dismissively.

Michael froze for a second. He was worried that the Prefect's order, although certainly an order, might place the Prefect in danger. Michael looked to Jerome for approval.

"Go on," repeated the Prefect even more firmly. "And close the door."

Michael bowed, and then obeyed.

The Prefect watched Michael go, waiting until he had locked the cell door again from the outside. "See," he said happily. "No one will disturb us now."

The Prefect approached Mei-Li. He bent at the waist, with his hands on his thighs, so that their eyes met at the same level. The Prefect reached out slowly toward her face.

But Mei-Li panicked, wrenching her neck away from his approach.

"Shush, shush, my pretty little *Jinyi Wei*," mewled the Prefect, withdrawing his hand. "What kind of monster do you think I am?" He presented his hands to Mei-Li, palms open, demonstrating that he held nothing. "I'm not going to hurt you. In fact, I would very much like to remove this gag." The Prefect's smile faded to a neutral firmness. "Is that OK with you?"

Mei-Li did not know what to make of the Perfect and did not react immediately. But after considering the question for a few seconds, she nodded firmly.

The Prefect reached for the cloth that Michael had taped into Mei-Li's mouth.

Her body tensed at the increased proximity of the Prefect. She shivered nervously, her eyes and the muscles in her neck flinching from the Prefect's touch.

The Prefect did his best to remove the tape gently. Once the tape was removed, he gripped the gag between his thumb and forefinger. But before removing the gag, he stopped and looked directly into Mei-Li's eyes. "For me to remove this gag, I need you to cooperate," he whispered. "Most importantly, I need you to cooperate very quietly." The Prefect looked warmly at Mei-Li. "Can you do that for me? Can you be very quiet?"

Again, Mei-Li nodded.

CHAPTER 52

Su-Lin stood with her hands on her hips exasperated by how little there was in the Basilica di San Lorenzo's Old Sacristy. There would be more hope of finding the *Proditio*, she thought, if there was actually somewhere to have possibly hidden it.

"Where does Doctor Chan expect us to look?" complained an exasperated Su-Lin. "He can't be suggesting that the *Proditio* is hidden in one of these tombs?"

Su-Lin had initially thought that there were only two tombs in the Old Sacristy. But after a closer inspection of the inscriptions, it became clear that there were two people buried in each sarcophagus. All four people buried in the Old Sacristy were members of the Medici family. Giovanni di Bicci de' Medici and his wife Piccarda Bueri were interred in a white stone sarcophagus, in the center of the room. It was an odd design thought Su-Lin, because a rectangular piece of white marble, decorated with a bronze disc, had been placed above the sarcophagus but not on it. It looked to her as though a dining table, with a bronze Lazy Susan in its center, had been placed over the tomb in order to conceal it.

Despite humble origins in Florence, Giovanni di Bicci de' Medici rose to found the Medici Bank and marked the beginning of the Medici Dynasty. His son Cosimo and grandson Lorenzo used the family fortune made in banking, to finance many of the renaissance's greatest artistic and architectural achievements. They patronized artists like Botticelli, Michelangelo and Leonardo da Vinci. They financed the construction of the Laurentian library, the Basilica di San Lorenzo and finished the dome on top of Florence Cathedral.

Two of their grandchildren, Giovanni and Piero de' Medici were buried in a sarcophagus that was set in the wall of the Old Sacristy, to the left of the door. This second sarcophagus was mounted in a bronze grill that separated the Old Sacristy from the adjacent chapel. It was significantly more elaborate than the grave of their grandparents. The sarcophagus was made of red and green porphyry. It sat on a white marble plinth, and was decorated with sweeping bronze floral patterns at both ends of the sarcophagus. The floral decorations at each end of the coffin, flowed into bronze claws forming the coffin's legs.

"I hope not." San jokingly tapped on the underside of one of the sarcophagus lids. "I can't imagine that they'd let us casually remove the lids of these sarcophagi to take a peak. But even if the *Proditio* was hidden within one of these sarcophagi…" San switched to a more serious tone. "…how would Doctor Chan have ever discovered its location?"

"Was there anything in the cabinets?" Su-Lin pointed at the low hip high cabinets that lined two of the Sacristy's four walls.

"No. They were probably once designed to store the priests' vestments." San frowned. "But now they're empty." San was at a loss as to what more he could say to Su-Lin. He had to concede, that while Doctor Chan's date had led them to the Old Sacristy, the chapel was a small simple room in which there was no obvious place in which to hide anything.

"And there's nothing further you can read into that painting of the night sky?" asked Su-Lin hopefully.

San shook his head. "Do you think that Doctor Chan considered the painting was proof enough by itself?"

"A star map painted more accurately than any European technology of the day would allow is certainly evidence consistent with pre-Columbian maps of the Americas," agreed Su-Lin.

"Its conspicuous accuracy is certainly poorly addressed by modern scholarship." But San spoke without much conviction, doubting that it was what Doctor Chan was referring to.

"But the ceiling of the Old Sacristy can hardly be considered new." Su-Lin's frustration was blossoming into anger. "And Doctor Chan wouldn't have considered it a discovery either."

"More obviously, if Doctor Chan's proof was simply the ceiling of the Old Sacristy," San gestured at Su-Lin, "it wouldn't explain the Inquisition's interest in either Doctor Chan or yourself."

"Inquisitor Jerome and Brother Michael made it very clear that Doctor Chan's proof was a treaty between Imperial China and the Catholic Church, signed by Eugenesis IV and the Emperor Xuan De." Su-Lin folded her arms and scowled at nothing in particular, frustrated to have reached an impasse."They even had a name for it - the *Proditio.* There's got to be more to it than this painting."

San approached Su-Lin. He touched her shoulder warmly, hoping to mitigate her anxiety. Su-Lin forced a smile, and pointed at some of the tomb's details that she had noticed earlier. "The turtles look cute." At each corner of Giovanni and Piero de' Medici's sarcophagus was a small bronze turtle that held the white marble plinth off the floor on which the sarcophagus rested.

After two stressful days, the moment of levity gave San a moment to look at Su-Lin. She is very pretty, he thought. But Su-Lin caught him staring and he fumbled to break the awkward silence that ensued. "It reminds me of that Chinese legend." San clicked his fingers, trying to access a memory. "The one that describes the earth being held up on the back of a turtle."

"Coincidentally enough, that turtle legend is a myth that the Chinese share with Native Americans."

But San had hardly heard what Su-Lin at said. He had tilted his head, and was staring intently.

Su-Lin couldn't figure out whether San was staring at the turtles, or at the far end of the sarcophagus. But the sudden change in San's mood suggested to her that he might have found something.

"I think I've seen this before," murmured San.

CHAPTER 53

The Prefect smiled at Agent Mei-Li satisfied that she would cooperate quietly if he removed the gag from her mouth. He reached for the white cloth that Brother Michael had stuffed into her mouth.

Mei-Li's eyes tracked the Prefect nervously. She could feel the Prefect's fetid breath on her face. She could smell the sweat running down the side of his face. And while all her instincts screamed at her to pull away from the Prefect, she wanted the gag out of her mouth.

The Prefect gripped the gag between his thumb and forefinger, and pulled it lose. But before he could even ask the question that was forming in his mind, Mei-Li began screaming. She screamed at the top of her lungs in a flurry of confused Italian and Mandarin.

"Enough!" The Prefect's nostrils flared and his eyes narrowed as he grimaced with displeasure. He grabbed Mei-Li by her lower jaw pushing her head backwards. He squeezed, forcing her mouth open, before violently stuffing the gag back into her mouth. The gag cut short her cries for help. A barely audible groan was all that she could muster.

But Mei-Li would not give up. Her face reddened as she

strained to scream despite the gag. She threw her weight from side to side, rocking the chair she was tied to, like a child throwing tantrum.

The Prefect snatched Mei-Li by the scruff of her shirt, twisting it in his fist as he lifted her off the ground. "I said enough!" he yelled into her face. But she continued to defy him. The Prefect dropped Mei-Li and as the chair to which she was tied hit the floor, he tore at the shirt he had clenched in his fist. The buttons of Mei-Li's shirt exploded outwards as the Prefect wrenched away a large hand full of cloth. Her shirt fell uselessly from her shoulders, to hang from her wrists bound to the chair behind her back.

Mei-Li's chest was laid naked except for the black, lycra sports top under her shirt. Her tanned, well-muscled shoulders hunched over reflexively as she tried to conceal her nakedness.

"Don't be ridiculous," sneered the Prefect, now red in the face. "I can assure you, that you are not to my taste."

Mei-Li's smothered screams turned to sobs at the humiliation. Tears ran down her cheeks and dripped from her chin. Her chest heaved with the effort, but only a dull gasp could be heard, and only by those within her cell.

The Prefect stepped back and studied Mei-Li. He wore a slightly disappointed twist to his lips. "I thought we had an understanding?" he said dispassionately. "I had hoped we could make this a civil conversation." He sighed, and with his hands on his hips he stared at Mei-Li, considering his alternatives. "You leave me no choice, my child."

The Prefect removed his gold cardinal's ring and placed it carefully on the small wooden table by the door of the cell. "The Congregation for the Doctrine of Faith has been charged by his Holy Father and through the apostolic succession, by God himself, to defend the integrity of the faith and examine all false doctrines." Now free of the ring, he clenched his fists, forcing life back into arthritic fingers. "We have defended the faith from you *Jinyi Wei* for centuries." He closed his eyes, rolled his shoulders once and exhaled. "And I assure you that I will not flinch from seeing God's work done." The Prefect reached under the right shoulder cape of his cassock with his left hand, and reached under the left shoulder cape with his right hand. With his arms crossed across his chest he slowly retrieved the objects he needed.

When Mei-Li could see what the Prefect had retrieved from inside his robes, her eyes widened. She moaned in disbelief and began frantically shaking her head. Tears pooled in her eyes, and she shrank into the chair, simpering weakly.

In his left hand the Prefect held a blade that was not much more than an inch wide at the base, and slowly tapered over the eight inches of its length. It had no cross guard, and instead she could see that the blade terminated in a splintered wooden handle. It was as though a spear point had been snapped from its shaft. In his right hand, the Prefect bore a shorter but heavier bladed dagger which bent evilly, at about thirty degrees, midway along its length.

The Prefect stood very still, the veins in his forehead bulging rhythmically. "Do you like deadlines?" he asked.

There was no response from the terrified Mei-Li.

"I do." The Prefect nodded faintly. "I confess that I am an impatient man. But nothing focuses the mind on achievement, like an imminent and irrevocable deadline." He tilted his chin slightly, thinking to himself for a moment. "Optimal stress, the management consultants would call it." The Prefect stared intently at Agent Mei-Li, "Don't you agree?"

Mei-Li couldn't tear her attention away from the Prefect's two blades, to notice the increasingly empty look his eyes had taken.

"No?" asked the Prefect quietly. His lips had thinned. His face was hard and expressionless.

Without waiting for a response, the Prefect lunged at

Mei-Li, with surprising speed. The prefect drove the narrow blade of the spear point into her abdomen. It entered her exposed belly just below the lower edge of her ribcage. It pierced the skin, but angled upwards, exiting between two of Mei-Li's ribs, fracturing them both and skewering her to the wooden chair.

Mei-Li's eyes bulged as the surprise arrived faster than the pain. But then her eyes winced and her face quickly paled. She cried in agony, before her head lolled limply, and her chin fell against her chest.

The Prefect exhaled heavily as though relieved of a burden. He squinted at his workmanship until blood started to ooze from the wound. The blood seeped from the wound, ran down the blade still embedded in the chair and dripped from its shattered shaft. The Prefect studied the color of the blood carefully. He reached out with his empty hand and tested the blood's consistency between his thumb and forefinger. For a moment the Prefect feigned surprise. "The blade has punctured your liver. Blood is now pooling in your abdominal cavity." He nodded knowingly. "If you do not get medical attention in the next thirty minutes, you will die." The Prefect let Mei-Li absorb this new information for a moment. "So I suggest you try to keep this conversation concise."

The Prefect moved the knife to his left hand and lifted Mei-Li's head by her sweat drenched hair. Her eyes were glazed but the Prefect saw little risk of her falling into unconsciousness. Or not yet anyway. "I'm going to remove the gag. Let's see if we can't be a little bit more cooperative this time."

Mei-Li wrenched her head away, refusing to meet the Prefect's gaze. She twisted her torso, trying desperately to shake the blade from the wound. Pain shuddered through her body when she moved. But, the blade was embedded deep in the chair and could not be dislodged.

"No, no, no my pretty *Jinyi Wei*," said the Prefect with

concerned eyes. "Leave the blade where it is. You'll only do more damage to yourself fidgeting like that."

As Mei-Li's mind fled from the pain, she felt light headed and the Prefect's voice seemed more distant than before. She gave up struggling and the Prefect took the opportunity to pluck the cloth again from her mouth. Mei-Li gagged involuntarily as the cloth came free. Drool and blood ran from the corners of her mouth before she spat to clear her throat. But she remained silent, and the Prefect's smile spread.

"That wasn't so hard, was it?" The Prefect took half a step away from Mei-Li and straightened his back. "So my little *Jinyi Wei*," he crooned. "Where is the *Proditio?*"

Mei-Li's face winced as she tried to focus on her anger, and fend off the dizziness she suffered from her injury. "Like I told him," she screeched, gesturing with her head toward the door by which Michael had left, "I have no idea, what…"

But the Prefect did not wait for Mei-Li to finish. With the blade in his right hand, he swept up and across from his left hip. The single stroke bit into Mei-Li's right shoulder, parting the skin across her scapula, before digging deeper into the right side of her chin, and separating the fleshy part of her cheek in a vertical line up her face. The blade finally exited at the height of her cheek bone. Blood flew in a wide arc, spattering the ceiling above Mei-Li.

Mei-Li reeled backwards. At first she winced as though nicked by a very sharp razor. Then warm blood welled out of her shoulder and ran across her breast. The metallic taste of her own blood spilled into her mouth from the gash through her cheek. She screamed long and freely.

"Let's try that question again," suggested the Prefect.

CHAPTER 54

Su-Lin stared at San. "Where have you seen this before?" Although she was still unsure as to which part of Giovanni and Piero de' Medici's sarcophagus that San was referring to.

"I'm not sure." San walked to the end of the sarcophagus mounted in the wall of the Basilica di San Lorenzo's Old Sacristy. He reached out to touch the bronze floral pattern that decorated the end of the sarcophagus. The bronze had darkened with age, except for the most exposed surfaces on the corner, which had been kept polished by the hands of thousands of similarly curious tourists.

"That's not entirely helpful," muttered Su-Lin, venting her frustration.

"Sorry." San ran his hand through his hair, searching his memory.

"Are you familiar with the style?"

"Not really." San's eyes narrowed. "There's not much of a collector's market in antique sarcophagi."

"Particularly those still in use."

San was too preoccupied to laugh. "Who sculpted this?"

Su-Lin shrugged automatically, since it was far from her field of expertise. But she looked about for an explanatory plaque. "It says here, that it was sculpted by Andrea del Verrocchio?"

It meant nothing to her, but faint recognition flickered across San's face. "Verrocchio was a Florentine painter and sculpture," said San. "He was one of the many Renaissance artists patronized by the Medici's." His cheeks flushed a little. "Obviously I guess, since he sculpted one of the Medici sarcophagi."

"Has he painted anything I might know?"

"Probably not." San had a wry smile on his face. "And I'm not being condescending. Only one painting has been reliably attributed to Verrocchio."

"So what brought him to your attention?"

"He's slighter better known for his sculptures, several of which decorate the churches and palaces of Florence. But he is much more famous for one of the apprentices who worked in his workshop." San gave Su-Lin a questioning glance. "You may have heard the story?"

Su-Lin shook her head.

"According to Verrocchio's contemporary Vasari, a fellow Florentine artist and architect, Verrocchio was so embarrassed that his apprentice was a more talented painter than he was, that Verrocchio gave up painting completely." San smiled at Su-Lin, raising an eyebrow, inviting her to hazard a guess as to whom Verrocchio's famous apprentice was.

But Su-Lin pouted and shook her head again.

"Verrocchio's famous apprentice was none other than Leonardo da Vinci."

"Oh? That famous copier of Chinese drawings."

But San did not respond to Su-Lin's provocation. San's forehead wrinkled as though considering a thought that had just struck him. "And that's where I may have seen this tomb before." San grinned at Su-Lin. "Leonardo Da Vinci used Verrocchio's sculpture. This tomb..." He stabbed at Giovanni and Piero de' Medici's tomb with his forefinger for emphasis, "...as inspiration for an element in one of his paintings."

"Which painting?" Su-Lin fidgeted eagerly.

"The Annunciation."

While San's knowledge of art history was deeper than Su-Lin's, The Annunciation was one of the few paintings executed by the most famous artist of the Renaissance. Su-Lin searched her memory and conjured a rough image of the painting in her mind. "It's an altar piece I seem to remember," said Su-Lin hesitantly.

"Yes. It's a painting of the biblical tale of the archangel Gabriel announcing to the Virgin Mary that she will bear a child – Jesus, the Son of God." San started gesticulating excitedly. "It's about so big." His arms stretched about as wide as they could go. "An angel kneels on the left side of the scene – that's Gabriel. He's holding a white lily – both a symbol of Mary's virginity and a symbol of Florence. Mary sits on the right, reading from a book. The book sits on a white marble table."

"But how does this relate to Giovanni and Piero de' Medici's sarcophagus?"

"In the painting, the decoration on the table at which the Virgin Mary sits, looks exactly like the decoration on the end of this sarcophagus," exclaimed San. "Leonardo da Vinci used his master Verrocchio's sculpture of this sarcophagus, as inspiration for the table in his painting of the Annunciation."

"So the first date which Doctor Chan left us has led us to Florence, and the second date that Doctor Chan left us with has led us to Leonardo Da Vinci's painting of The Annunciation." Su-Lin's enthusiasm was palpable. "But where is it?"

"It's hanging in the Uffizi," declared San. "The Uffizi Gallery here in Florence."

CHAPTER 55

The Prefect stormed out of the cell in the Palazzo Vecchio. His eyes flashed threateningly at Jerome and Brother Michael. "That was utterly pointless," he spat angrily through clenched teeth. The Prefect was breathing hard from his exertions. His scarlet robes were soaked with sweat and his hands were stained with blood. Once outside the cell, he paced restlessly backwards and forwards, using up the residual adrenaline still raging through his system.

Michael approached the Prefect hesitantly. He offered him a wet towel. The Prefect stopped pacing abruptly and snatched the towel from Michael. He wiped his sweat and Agent Mei-Li's blood away from his face and forehead.

"The *Jinyi Wei* demonstrated remarkable endurance," said Jerome, trying his best to sound sympathetic. Although Jerome was quietly pleased that the Prefect had been no more successful questioning the *Jinyi Wei*, than he had been questioning Doctor Chan.

The Prefect ignored Jerome's comment, unsure as to whether Jerome was being sarcastic. He turned his back to Jerome, and clicked his fingers, indicating that he required his cloak.

"Perhaps the language difficulties were always going to be insurmountable?" suggested Jerome, as he lifted the cloak on to the Prefect's back. After the Prefect shrugged the cloak up and onto his shoulders, he looked over at Jerome to check for any sign of disrespect. But Jerome's face was inscrutable and there was no obvious excuse for the Prefect to vent his anger.

"Her lies were most consistent Jerome," said the Prefect. He turned back to face Jerome. "She claimed to be an attache assigned to the Chinese consulate in Rome." The Prefect spoke with a level tone, but raised an eyebrow suspiciously.

Having donned the Prefect in his cloak, Jerome stepped back, avoiding eye contact. "But most improbable Your Eminence."

"She said she was searching for a bronze sculpture." The Prefect's eyes narrowed accusingly. "She said she was searching for you, Jerome."

"Yes," agreed Jerome. "No doubt hoping we would lead her to the *Proditio.*"

"It would be most embarrassing if she really was a Chinese spy." The Prefect thrust a pale, chubby finger into Jerome's chest. "It would be most embarrassing for you, Jerome."

"But it's very difficult for us to confirm, since the Holy See maintains no diplomatic relations with the People's Republic of China," Jerome lowered his eyes in deference.

"That's an awfully convenient excuse," growled the Prefect. "Awfully convenient for you Jerome."

"She also rescued her co-conspirator in Rome," countered Jerome pleadingly. "She rescued another member of the *Jinyi Wei.*"

The Prefect grunted, nodding begrudgingly.

"Not only that," continued Jerome. "But she rescued a *Jinyi Wei* who admitted to us during our inquiries that she was searching for the *Proditio* in Florence." He finally managed to force some confidence into his voice. "Which means...," Jerome pointed at the cell. "...this *Jinyi Wei* was lying to you."

For a moment the Prefect just stared at Jerome. "Well I suppose we can work with that assumption inquisitor. Relations between the Holy See and China could hardly be any worse."

"Yes, Your Eminence." Jerome grinned, relieved that the conversation was coming to an end.

But the Prefect snapped at Jerome's impertinence, his face red with anger. "The only way that this could get any worse Jerome," yelled the Prefect, "is if you fail to find the *Proditio* before the *Jinyi Wei* do." He stepped toward Jerome waving a finger threateningly, saliva spraying from his mouth. "The Chinese Government might not be able to make much political capital out of losing an agent somewhere in Florence. But if the *Jinyi Wei* were to find the *Proditio* and reveal its contents to the world, it would shake the Church to its foundations."

Jerome, remained silent, cursing himself for his indiscretion.

"If the world discovered that their Church betrayed the apostolic succession from Christ, it would erode the people's faith in the Church and undermine the authority of our Holy Father." The Prefect shook his head. "We cannot allow it."

"Yes, Your Eminence. We face no more serious threat than this." Jerome searched for something with which to mitigate the Prefect's anger. "Do you think perhaps, that the *Jinyi Wei* were recruited as an instrument of the Chinese government?"

"Such speculations are a distraction Jerome." The Prefect waved the suggestion away. "We need only to find the *Proditio* and destroy it." His eyes flicked back toward the cell.

But Jerome anticipated the Prefect's concerns. "Please

don’t worry yourself, Your Eminence. Michael will take care of it,” he assured. “He is most thorough.”

The Prefect nodded a begrudging assent. “Just don't let it wash up in tomorrow's newspapers.” He took a second towel from Michael and dried his face. After cleaning himself, the Prefect used the soiled towel to wipe off the gore that remained on each of his two blades.

Michael had been watching the Prefect and stepped forward quickly, offering to clean the Prefect’s knives for him. But the Prefect snatched the knives away, glowering at Michael. He tossed Michael the used towel and replaced his knives in the folds of his cassock. With nothing further to say to Jerome, the Prefect headed toward the stairs that descended from the Palazzo Vecchio's clock tower.

Jerome watched the Prefect leave, preparing a mental list of the tasks he would give to Michael now that the Prefect had finished the interview.

But before disappearing from view, the Prefect turned back and pointed at Jerome. “You said there were three *Jinyi Wei*?” he asked rhetorically. “Bring me another.”

CHAPTER 56

"Lead the way," encouraged San, as they pushed open the heavy wooden door of the Basilica di San Lorenzo and set off in search of the Uffizi Gallery and Leonardo da Vinci's painting of the Annunciation.

"It's basically back the way we came." Su-Lin considered for a moment the fastest route to the gallery. "The Uffizi Gallery isn't far from where we spent last night."

They headed back down the short flight of steps that led from the Basilica and through the busy street market which occupied the square in front of it. The Uffizi Gallery was little more than half a mile in a straight line. But Su-Lin had no option other than to lead them on a twisting path through Florence's narrow streets.

"What do you think the painting will tell us about the location of the *Proditio?*" she asked. Although excited to be one step closer to understanding the second date that Doctor Chan had left them, she knew that The Annunciation was one of the most famous paintings of the Renaissance. It was difficult to believe that Doctor Chan could have seen something in the artwork that had not been previously studied in great detail.

"I'm not sure," admitted San. "I'd have to concede that it's only a visual similarity that connects Giovanni and Piero dei Medici's sarcophagus and Leonardo da Vinci's painting of The Annunciation."

While Su-Lin had seen the painting before, she was no expert, and could not recall any visual similarities. She had no choice but to trust San in this regard. "When we see the painting, we can confirm the similarities." But her somber mood told San, that she wasn't entirely convinced by the connection.

Eventually Su-Lin led them out into a wide, sunlit space - the Piazza della Signoria - the largest Piazza in the old part of Florence. They emerged from the residential area on the north edge of the square. From where they stood, the Piazza sloped down and away from them toward the Arno river. The square was dominated by the imposing stone facade of the Palazzo Vecchio on the east edge of the Piazza to their left. Opposite the Palace, on the western edge of the Piazza, were a row of cafes that in warmer months would be brimming with tourists.

"We're almost there." San smiled, shielding his eyes from the sun and pointing to an alley that led from the Piazza. Between them and the avenue to which they were headed, there was a line of sculptures that sat in front of the Palazzo Vecchio. Immediately in front of them stood a bronze sculpture of Cosimo the First, Grand Duke of Tuscany. Beyond that, there was the so called, Fountain of Neptune, and a copy of Michelangelo's famous statue David.

As they wound their way among the statues, they passed what San could only describe as a mythologically themed outdoor sculpture museum housed in a large stone verandah facing the Palazzo. "It's an odd-looking building," observed San.

"The Loggia dei Lanci was a canopy to keep the nobility dry during public ceremonies," explained Su-Lin. "But soon after the *Jinyi Wei* arrived in Florence, the Loggia was used to house Cosimo's feared German mercenaries."

After passing between the Palazzo and the Loggia, San and Su-Lin could finally see their destination - the Uffizi Gallery. The gallery was laid out in a narrow, but elongated U-shape. The open end of the U-shaped building faced north and connected to the Piazza della Signoria from which they walked. The closed end of the U-shaped gallery sat on the banks of the Arno River, further down the hill. The archway on the ground floor of the closed end, meant that the two long sides of the Uffizi Gallery formed an alley thorough which pedestrian traffic moved from the Piazza to the river.

The Uffizi, which in Italian meant simply offices, were built by Cosimo the first as offices for the magistrates of Florence. But ever since the sixteenth century the Uffizi had also displayed art works. At first it was just the Medici's family collection which was hung in the Uffizi. But after the Medici Dynasty ended, it was negotiated that the artworks remain in Florence. This made the Uffizi one of the oldest art galleries in the western world.

"We're now on your turf," smiled Su-Lin, knowing that while she had led them to the gallery, it would be San who would be more familiar with the gallery's interior, let alone the art.

San pointed to the building's left wing. "The gallery entrance is just up here."

San and Su-Lin walked to the ground floor entrance under the covered arcade that decorated the left wing of the gallery. At the small booth immediately past the door, San paid for two tickets, before they started up a wide, winding staircase. There were temporary exhibits on the second floor. But San ignored them and kept climbing to the third floor and the permanent collection.

"No lift?" complained Su-Lin, jokingly.

"Unfortunately, the Arno River floods periodically," said

San between breaths. "So they have to keep everything on the upper floors."

"It's a bit like Venice," said Su-Lin. "Where none of the locals live on the ground floor anymore."

"I suppose so." San nodded. "One flood in 1966 washed away the Arno embankment, killed dozens of people in Florence and ruined countless works of art."

At the top of the stairs on the third floor landing, San paused for breath. There was a small stall selling post cards and exhibition catalogues. "Let's grab a map," suggested San. "I'm not sure in which room The Annunciation is hung."

Su-Lin picked up a couple of the museum's complimentary maps and passed one to San.

Turning left from the landing and into the galley's main corridor, Su-Lin was struck by how impressively long and straight the gallery's corridor was. It ran down the entire length of the building, about the length of a football field Su-Lin reckoned, before turning right at the banks of the Arno River. From there it completed the U-shape by returning up the right wing of the Uffizi Gallery. San noticed her admiring the near perfect illustration of perspective and a vanishing point that the gallery's hall provided. "The gallery was designed by Vasari," said San. "You remember?"

"He's the artist who told the story about Leonardo da Vinci's talent having had a demoralizing effect on his master."

San grinned. "The same."

The right hand side of the corridor was lined with large windows, allowing natural light to spill across the geometrically patterned black and white granite floor. Each window was separated from the next by a white marble statue. The gallery's paintings were hung in what had once been the individual Uffizi or offices of Florence's administrators - small rooms off to the left of the main corridor.

After only a couple of steps down the corridor, Su-Lin stopped to consult her map. "It says The Annunciation is in here, room three."

San popped his head in to check. "No. This is the Sienese room." He pouted, apologetically. "It's the wrong Annunciation." San didn't want to sound like an art snob. "Easy mistake to make, there's three or four paintings in this gallery called the Annunciation. This one's by Martini."

Su-Lin rolled her eyes. "It's all Madonna and Child this, or Adoration of the whatever." She made a wearied expression. "The Renaissance artists do wash over you after a while."

San's mouth open and closed a couple of times, but nothing came out. Instinctively he felt defensive, as though his profession had just been impugned. But he didn't completely disagree either. "It's not my favorite period. I can see it is a bit repetitive. But, I guess it's what the buyers wanted at the time."

"It's not just repetitive," Su-Lin said shrilly. "It's downright depressing. How many paintings of people being nailed to pieces of wood can you look at in one day before it puts you off your lunch?"

San laughed.

After leading them more than halfway down the corridor San stopped. "This is it." He checked the map again. "This is room fifteen, the Leonardo da Vinci room."

They entered a small rectangular room that was much darker than the corridor that had led them to it. No doubt kept that way in order to preserve the precious paintings, San thought. But, like many old art galleries, the age of the gallery and therefore the correspondingly large collections meant that the artworks were crowded into what limited space was available in the historic buildings in which they were housed.

Although the room was called the Leonardo room, only

two and a half of the dozen artworks in the room were painted by Leonardo da Vinci. Su-Lin smiled, imagining that the other artists, if they had been alive today, might feel slightly aggrieved by the room having been named after Leonardo alone.

San spotted the first of the two Leonardo da Vinci paintings hung in the Uffizi. The Adoration of the Magi was an eight foot wide square painting of the biblical nativity scene - the baby Jesus and his mother Mary surrounded by old men, kneeling and offering gifts. But the Adoration of the Magi was hardly a painting, thought San walking toward it, and hardly by Leonardo Da Vinci either. Most of the canvas was covered by only a fading pencil sketch. And like many paintings that Leonardo da Vinci had started, it was never finished and research had shown that all of the paint was added later by an unknown artist.

It took San another moment or two of scanning the room before he located Leonardo's painting of The Annunciation. San took two steps toward where the painting should have hung and stopped. He stared at a faint outline where dust had collected around the painting's frame. He turned to Su-Lin. "It's gone," exclaimed San desperately. "The painting has gone."

CHAPTER 57

Brother Michael ran into the first courtyard of the Palazzo Vecchio, panting heavily, his eyes searching for Jerome and the Prefect. But they were nowhere to be seen, so he carried on into the Palace's interior.

Whereas the first courtyard was decorated with murals and elegantly carved columns designed to welcome dignitaries to the Palace, the second courtyard was unadorned. It had been the entry to the Palace's stables, and while the second courtyard like the first, was also open to the sky, it was filled with a dense forest of thick, square sandstone columns which held up Vasari's grand staircase and the vast Salone dei Cinquecento to which the staircase led. So the small portion of natural light that actually managed to filter down past the columns and the staircase, cast deep shadows on the floor.

Michael spotted the Prefect and Jerome standing in one of the shadows cast by the staircase. Judging by the Prefect's vigorous gesticulations it looked to be an animated discussion, if not a heated argument.

"I will stay as long as it takes to find the *Proditio* and destroy it," growled the Prefect, wagging his finger at

Jerome. Neither of them paid any attention to Michael as he approached.

Michael hesitated for a moment before disturbing his superiors. "I'm sorry, Your Eminence." He bowed, struggling to bring his breathing under control. "And you, Your Excellency." He bowed again toward Jerome.

The Prefect couldn't keep the look of disgust from his face, at Michael's presumptuousness for interrupting them. But he waited to hear what Michael had to say for himself.

"The *Jinyi Wei*," gushed Michael in between breaths. "We've found them."

"Where Michael?" Jerome involuntarily took a step forward. "Where?"

"They're here!" Brother Michael pointed south, as best as he could reckon it. "We've spotted them on the Uffizi Gallery security cameras."

"But that's right next door!" gasped the Prefect, surprised by the *Jinyi Wei's* sudden proximity.

"Who have you seen?" demanded Jerome.

"I saw the girl who we questioned in Rome."

"Is she alone?" asked the Prefect, wetting his lips. "You said 'them'"

"No, Your Eminence." Michael shook his head. "She's with another one of those heathens." He thought for a second. "A *Jinyi Wei*, by the looks of him." Michael thought back to the gunfight in the Basilica in Rome. "But I didn't recognize him. I don't think we've seen him before"

"You said that two of them attacked you in Rome," interjected the Prefect, turning to Jerome. "One of which I examined earlier." The Prefect smiled briefly. "This must be the other one!"

"Why are they in the Uffizi?" Jerome turned back to Michael. "What are they doing Michael?"

"I am not sure, Your Excellency," admitted Michael. "They appear to be looking at the paintings." His brow furrowed. Jerome always managed to ask a difficult question, he thought. "They look like tourists," suggested Michael. "But I didn't watch them for long. I came here as soon as I saw them."

"Why the Uffizi?" wondered Jerome aloud, turning to the Prefect. "Is there anything connecting the Uffizi to the *Proditio*?"

The Prefect shrugged.

While Jerome could not imagine what connection might explain the *Jinyi Wei's* interest in the Uffizi, he was determined to take advantage of their good fortune. "Follow them Michael and…."

"No!" interrupted the Prefect firmly. "Bring one, but preferably both of them to me Michael." The Prefect's eyes were distant, as though he was already planning as to what he would do, once the *Jinyi Wei* were within his grasp.

"Yes, Your Eminence," mumbled Michael, acknowledging his new orders.

"But Your Eminence," whined Jerome, alarmed by the Prefect's suggestion. "We should follow the *Jinyi Wei.* They might lead us to the *Proditio.*"

"Doing nothing risks everything Jerome," snapped the Prefect. "Your passivity has so far gotten us nowhere."

"But neither did your..." Jerome halted mid-sentence suddenly aware that he was not only interrupting the Prefect but criticizing his methods. "…But neither of our inquiries were successful."

The Prefect's nose flared and his eyes blazed. "How dare you contradict me!" he yelled, frothing at the mouth.

"My humble apologies, Your Eminence," groveled Jerome. He bowed his head apologetically, annoyed with himself for breeching protocol and contradicting a superior. "I forgot myself, Your Eminence."

Michael swallowed hard, knowing that he was likely to suffer a similar rebuke for joining the conversation. "Excuse me, Your Excellency, but taking the prisoners into custody might attract some attention to us." Michael wore a worried expression. "They are unlikely to come willingly."

"Brother Michael has made a good point, Your Eminence," added Jerome. "It is the middle of the day. The piazza between the Palace and the Uffizi will be full of tourists.

"Have you lost your nerve as well as your skill Jerome?" screamed the Prefect. The purple veins in his forehead were beating so hard they looked as though they might shake themselves loose. "And if you've lost both of these faculties, then try using your head!"

Both Jerome and Brother Michael remained silent, not knowing what the Prefect had in mind.

"Think Jerome!" urged the Prefect, waving his hand as though giving up on his subordinates. "We don't have to drag the *Jinyi Wei* back here through the piazza. We can bring them back to the Palace in secret..." The Prefect studied Jerome and Michael's face in turn, hoping that his prompting might have provoked an understanding of his plan. "...If we use the Vasari corridor."

CHAPTER 58

Su-Lin clutched at San's arm in frustration, staring at the wall of the Uffizi Gallery where Leonardo da Vinci's painting of The Annunciation should have been hanging. She feigned a head butt into San's shoulder and squeezed her finger nails into his forearm. Apart from a thin line of dust outlining where the painting's frame used to be, a small sign had been placed in what would have been the center of the painting. The sign read, "This exhibit has been temporarily removed for academic research and restoration."

Su-Lin slowly shook her head, unable to conceal her disappointment. Doctor Chan's second date had led them to the painting, thought Su-Lin, only for the museum to have removed it before they got here.

"It might still be here," San suggested quietly.

"Really?" Su-Lin's mood improved, hopefully.

"If it's only a minor restoration, the work may be being conducted here at the gallery."

"In that case…" She began scanning the room. "We need to speak to someone from the museum."

Su-Lin was the first to spot one of the museum's

attendants. In one of the corners of the room, sat a middle-aged attendant vigilantly studying the museum's visitors. Her humorless expression made her perfectly suited to scolding tourists who encroached on the museum's artworks or ejecting those who thoughtlessly used flash photography. Su-Lin approached the attendant and politely asked what had happened to Leonardo's painting of the Annunciation.

Su-Lin walked back to San with a half-smile. "She didn't know where the painting had been taken, but she suggested we check with the laboratories downstairs."

Following the gallery attendant's directions, Su-Lin led them out into the main corridor and back toward the staircase that they had climbed from the museum's entrance. "She said that the museum's offices and laboratories are on the second floor, under the main gallery." So once they had retraced their steps to the second floor, instead of continuing down the stairs to the entrance, they looked around for the museum's laboratories.

"There's a sign." San pointed to a gray metal plate bolted to the wall with text followed by arrows pointing either left or right. "But you'll have to help translate it."

Su-Lin stepped over and read the sign. "It says the laboratories are over there." Su-Lin pointed to her right.

They both turned around to see an inconspicuous set of gray double doors to the side of the stairs which had earlier led them up to the main gallery. There was a red circle painted around some Italian text and a red line across the circle and text. San didn't have to read Italian to understand that the door was clearly marked, "No admittance, staff only." A black security card reader was mounted on the wall to the right of the doors. On it, a small LED emitted an ominously red glow.

"It's locked." San sighed. "And it's probably alarmed."

But Su-Lin wasn't listening. She had spotted a man in his early thirties, dressed in a white lab coat heading toward the door. The man wore loose khaki slacks and a black Nine Inch Nails T-shirt under his lab coat. He hadn't shaved in a couple of days and his black rimmed glasses had slipped awkwardly forward on his nose. He wasn't necessarily unattractive, she thought, just very poorly maintained.

The lab technician carried a couple of folders under one arm and a brown, paper bag with red and yellow stripes in his other hand. He's eating McDonalds, grimaced Su-Lin, repulsed by the idea. And eating McDonalds in Italy, she thought, which somehow made it even worse. When the lab technician got to the gray double doors he pinned the brown, paper bag to his chest with his chin as he searched in his pockets for his security pass.

Su-Lin waited until the lab technician had found his security pass, before stepping toward him quickly. "Let me help you with that," said Su-Lin in Italian, smiling sweetly, and taking the brown paper bag from under his chin.

"Thanks." The lab technician was somewhat surprised, but now free to swipe the card and open the gray double doors. As he waved his card the LED on the card reader turned from red to green and the door opened with a satisfying click.

"I'm Su-Lin from Nanjing University," she said, as the lab technician pushed open the double doors. "And this is my colleague San Lee," she continued, but this time in English. Su-Lin gestured to San, who now followed a few steps behind.

"Hello," mumbled the lab technician nervously, struggling to switch to English as comfortably as Su-Lin had. His brow furrowed and his eyes flicked from Su-Lin to San and back.

But it was discomfort rather than suspicion thought Su-Lin. It was as though he was trying to place my name.

"We've been working at the Library of St. Marks in Venice," explained Su-Lin confidently, flashing her security pass from the Doge's Palace, as they pushed passed the double doors and into the corridor beyond. "We've come about Leonardo's painting of the Annunciation." Su-Lin put on a confident and expectant look, hoping the lab technician would take up the conversation.

"I'm Frederico," said the lab technician shaking Su-Lin's hand, "Frederico Visconti, one of the Gallery's lab technicians."

I seem to be making him nervous, thought Su-Lin. Or maybe conversation isn't part of his job description. "We were wondering about the progress of the current research," she probed again.

"Do you work with Doctor Chan?" asked the lab technician tentatively, seemingly reluctant to make eye contact with Su-Lin.

Su-Lin glanced at San, surprised that the lab technician knew Doctor Chan. "Yes, we do. I'm one of Doctor Chan's PhD students."

"Oh, I see," answered the lab technician, nodding furiously. He stopped at the second door on the left hand side of the corridor. "Well I must apologize for the delay. Please come in."

"Delay?" mouthed San at Su-Lin, when the lab technician had turned his back to enter the room. Su-Lin raised her eye brows and shrugged, agreeing with San that she had no idea what delay the lab technician had referred to.

The lab technician punched a code into the key pad on the right hand side of the door. He waited a moment, before hearing a click, and then pushed the door open. San could hear the faint hiss of air being released from inside the room. Climate control, thought San, to protect the paintings in the laboratory.

The laboratory was a long, windowless room that disappeared into darkness to Su-Lin's left. The lab technician crossed to a computer laden desk opposite the door in the only part of the room which was properly lit. The room looked and smelt almost painfully clean, in stark contrast to the disheveled appearance of the lab technician.

"Please take a seat," said the lab technician, indicating to the two office chairs between the door and his desk. The lab technician set down his folders, and then clearly flustered, tried to remove some of the papers and the remains of yesterday's dinner, from the desk between himself and Su-Lin and San. "I'm sorry, we don't get many visitors down here."

"Not at all." Su-Lin smiled easily. "Thank you for your time." She pulled her chair up as close to the lab technician as possible and leant an elbow on his desk. "Doctor Chan asked us to stop by while we were in Florence and get an update."

"Well as I said earlier, I must apologize." The lab technician's face reddened a shade. "Doctor Chan had requested that these scans be taken months ago. But The Annunciation is one of the gallery's most popular pieces, and the curators don't like having it taken off display."

Su-Lin's jaw fell slack for a second. She had not been aware that Doctor Chan had requested to have Leonardo's Annunciation scanned at all.

"So the Annunciation," asked Su-Lin nervously, "is it still here?"

"Of course!" The administrator chuckled. "The painting is so valuable, and so expensive to insure, there's no way the gallery would ever let the piece out of its sight." The lab technician warmed to the common interest they had in art. "Come, would you like to take a look?"

CHAPTER 59

The Prefect led Jerome and Brother Michael up the Palazzo Vecchio's main staircase to the third floor. He smiled smugly, knowing that they were travelling at his pace for a change, because neither Jerome nor Michael knew of the Vasari Corridor, much less where it was. Once on the third floor, the Prefect traced a counter clockwise path around one of the light wells that penetrated the Palace to the second courtyard.

The third and highest floor of the Palace was once the personnel office of the Grand Duke. It had been used by the Florentine Republic's most senior administrators, the most famous of which was the diplomat and political philosopher Niccolo Machiavelli.

The Prefect grimaced as they passed Machiavelli's statue. "Heretic," he muttered, before turning to Jerome. "After our Dominican brother Savonarola was wrongfully executed, this pagan was elected to be Secretary to the Chancellery." He waved at Machiaelli's statue disdainfully. "Savonarola had labored hard to rid Florence of licentious art, homosexuals, and other objects of sin."

"In the original bonfire of the vanities," added Jerome.

"But, once Savonarola was so tragically killed, the city lost its moral compass, and Machiavelli was free to write that filth The Prince."

"His writings were in gross theological error," agreed Jerome.

"We should have burnt him at the stake." The Prefect raised himself to his full height and bellowed, "the *index librorum prohibitorum* should never have been abolished!"

Jerome nodded firmly. "The list of banned publications had protected the faithful for hundreds of years."

The Prefect shook his head. "The list should never have been taken from under the Congregation's purview." He held Jerome firmly by the shoulder. "But I'm afraid Jerome." The Prefect frowned mournfully. "It was before my time."

At the end of a corridor that had threaded its way between the two light wells that lit the Palace's first and second courtyards, the Prefect halted. "This is the oldest part of the Palace," he said, respectfully. "They're called the apartments of Toledo Eleonora, although they were built three hundred years before her residence."

At the end of the corridor was a small rectangular room. Its walls had been painted in, what Jerome considered to be, a hideous green color. The ceiling was painted in odd floral and animal designs. The air felt still and smelt stale, despite the large windows in the south wall, suggesting to Jerome that the room was rarely used.

"This is it," announced the Prefect, pointing across the room to a doorway. "This leads to the Vasari Corridor." The brown painted double door was framed in a heavy stone. It bore two latches. One latch fixed the left door to the floor, and the other latch was padlocked sealing the two doors together. The heavy padlock was covered in a thick layer of dust and cobwebs.

It struck Jerome as odd to be on the third floor and yet be looking at a door in an external wall of the Palace. But

Jerome could see through the window on the left side of the door, that a short bridge or elevated corridor spanned the narrow street below.

The Vasari corridor was an elevated passage way built by Cosimo the first to link his office - the Palazzo Vecchio, to his home – the Palazzo Pitti. This was not immediately impressive until Jerome considered that the Palazzo Pitti was almost a mile from where he now stood, and on the other side of a large river – the Arno.

"The corridor crosses over to the Uffizi Gallery on the opposite side of the street," explained the Prefect. "After passing through the Uffizi, it turns right at the Arno River, following the river downstream until it can cross the Arno at the Ponte Vecchio. It then continues uphill to the Palazzo Pitti."

The corridor had been designed to enable the Florentine monarch to move between the center of government and his home, without risking any contact with the public. At the time, the public were a threat to be avoided because Cosimo had usurped the Florentine republic and installed himself as a king.

"May I, Your Eminence?" asked Michael politely, pointing at the door.

The Prefect gestured his assent.

Michael edged himself past the Prefect and approached the heavy wooden door sealing the Palazzo Vecchio end of the Vasari corridor. He first lifted the padlock securing the latch holding the two doors closed. He had intended to measure its weight and durability. But instead, Michael noticed that the padlock did not hold the latch perfectly flat against the door. He then crouched down to lift the latch at the bottom of the left hand door holding it in position on the floor. The lower latch slid open easily. Standing back up, Michael leant on both doors. Although the doors were heavy and well fitted, without the lower latch they moved slightly, enlarging the gap between the remaining latch and the surface of the doors.

Michael glanced back at Jerome, questioningly.

Jerome nodded his encouragement.

Michael reached into his jacket pocket for the dull metal club that he had used the day before during the investigation in Rome. He took a step backwards and then leant forward against the doors with his shoulder. The doors groaned under Michael's weight, and although the doors did not give way, he managed to insert his metal rod behind the latch. Then placing both hands on the top of the rod above the padlock he pulled and rocked backwards trying to tear the latch away from the door. He then leant forward again, into the doors, trying to force them open. He repeated the process in a rhythmic rocking motion. The metal rod bit into the wooden door below the latch and Michael's weight slowly bent the latch away from the door. It took Michael only a couple of swings before the bolts on the left hand side of the latch gave way, clattering to the ground. While the padlock remained in place, the latch hung limply to one side, no longer attached to the left hand door. Michael had to catch himself so as not to tumble into the corridor beyond.

After regaining his balance, Michael covered his mouth and nose as a plume of dust washed into the air from the movement of the opening door. The short corridor from the Palace to the Uffizi Gallery was inaccessible to the public and the thick coat of dust suggested it was seldom used for formal occasions either.

The Prefect pointed at the door that they could now see at the end of the short elevated corridor leading to the building on the opposite side of the street. "That door leads to the Uffizi Gallery." The Prefect turned to Michael. "From that door to the Arno River, the Vasari Corridor has been integrated into the Uffizi's portrait gallery. Once you have the *Jinyi Wei*, bring them back to us through this corridor."

Michael bowed an acknowledgement before bending his head low to enter the Vasari Corridor. He had his orders, and while he no longer worried how he would get back to the Palace, Michael wondered how exactly he would be able to snatch the *Jinyi Wei* from the middle of a crowded art gallery.

CHAPTER 60

The lab technician stood up from behind his desk in the Uffizi Gallery's laboratories and gestured for San and Su-Lin to follow him. He stepped outside the small pool of light that illuminated his desk, before they heard the tell-tale clicking sound of the lab technician switching on the lights.

As the lights grew brighter, both San and Su-Lin were surprised by how large the laboratory was. Immediately to the left of the lab technician's desk were two work stations, each set up with a stool in front of a large wooden easel. An extraction fan was positioned above each easel, as well as a desk of drawers filled with brushes, swabs and other cleaning tools. At each work station an overhead camera was mounted from the ceiling, like a dentist's X-ray machine. Behind each of the two work stations was a spotlessly clean white table where photographic enlargements of some of the gallery's paintings had been spread out for further study.

The lights didn't flicker on like a fluorescent tube might. Instead, the lights slowly rose in intensity, but to only a gloomy yellow glow. LED lamps, San thought, impressed with the extent to which the gallery went to protect its paintings.

The lab technician led them beyond the two workstations to the far end of the room where an even larger aluminum framed easel was positioned. The easel had been rotated ninety degrees by the automated metal arm to which it was attached, and held a painting in a horizontal position like a table top. What looked to San like a large camera, mounted to the ceiling, had been lowered close to the surface of the painting.

The lab technician picked up a device that looked like a television remote control and punched a series of buttons. San and Su-Lin could hear the faint whirring sound of electric motors and the camera above the aluminum easel moved up and away from the painting. After the camera was safety out of the way, another touch of the lab technician's remote control and the easel began rotating up and toward a normal, vertical position.

“Here it is,” announced the lab technician proudly.

San and Su-Lin gasped audibly as Leonardo da Vinci's painting of the Annunciation rolled slowly into view.

The first thing that struck Su-Lin was that seeing the painting for the first time was an experience completely unlike the disappointment of first seeing the Mona Lisa and realizing just how small a painting it was. *The Annunciation was huge!* It was almost nine feet wide, Su-Lin estimated. The painting showed the Angel Gabriel on the left kneeling before the Virgin Mary seated on the right. The angel presented Mary with a lily, while Mary read from a book. The vivid blues of the Virgin Mary's dress contrasted sharply with her pale porcelain skin and the vibrant rich red of the Angel Gabriel's robes.

“It’s magnificent,” gushed San.

Su-Lin didn't mock San at all. She was too busy absorbing the beauty of the painting, almost forgetting why they were here and what they were looking for.

San, pointed at the white marble table in the painting

that sat in the center between Mary and the Angel Gabriel. The book that Mary was reading from rested on the table. "See the similarity between the floral detail on the table and the design on the end of Giovanni and Piero de Medici's sarcophagus."

Su-Lin nodded enthusiastically. "This is definitely the connection Doctor Chan wanted us to see."

The lab technician smiled, pleased that San and Su-Lin shared his enthusiasm for the painting. "Initially we had thought that Doctor Chan was merely seeking to separate the contribution to the painting by Leonardo from the contribution made by his master Verrochio, using the latest high resolution technologies."

"Verrochio used lead based paint," enthused San, by way of explanation for Su-Lin. "But Leonardo did not, which means that the two artists' contribution to the painting can be studied separately by using x-rays."

"That's how it was studied in the past. But, since then, the technology has moved on," continued the lab technician. "We can now use spectroscopy to understand a painting's chemical constituents, or optical tomography to see the different layers of a painting."

"With tomographic techniques we can see the pencil sketch that lies under the paint. Or we can see the parts of a painting that were later painted over," added San. "It helps determine a painting's authenticity or identifies contributions made by a second artist."

"We had been waiting for Doctor Chan to give us feedback on the first set of images before proceeding." The lab technician looked expectantly at Su-Lin. "But that was a couple of weeks ago and we haven't heard anything since."

Su-Lin cast her eyes downward. "Doctor Chan's work has been..." She bit her lip, as a lump rose in her throat. Memories of Doctor Chan and the sadness of his murder flooded back. Su-Lin did not know what to tell the lab technician. "His work has been unexpectedly interrupted.

I'm afraid that…," she whispered.

But before Su-Lin could explain further, the lab technician carried on. "But after examining the first batch of images that Doctor Chan had ordered, it was obvious that we should be applying the full battery of tomographic testing." The lab technician struggled to hide his excitement.

"You found something in the scans?" asked San.

The lab technician smiled. "Doctor Chan didn't tell you?"

He walked back to the large table behind the second of the two workstations and turned on an overhead light. He opened one of the thin wide drawers built into the table and fished out a large A2 envelope. The envelope was marked, "Doctor Chan – The Annunciation." After unwinding the string that sealed the envelope, the lab technician took out a sheaf of photographic quality paper.

"We started by taking five hundred mega pixel images across a range of spectra." The lab technician laid the images out on the table, one by one. "Visible spectrum of course, but also UV and infrared." The first couple of images that the lab technician showed them were in vibrant color, but most of the images were shades of gray. "The Annunciation has been examined before and we were not surprised to confirm the earlier observations."

"Like the extension of the angels' wings by a later artist?" interjected San.

"Yes exactly." The lab technician pulled out two gray scale images showing a close up from The Annunciation, of only the Angel Gabriel's wings. "Different pigments, under different layers of varnish, created with different brush strokes, will reflect light differently, even if they are superficially the same color to the naked eye." The technician pointed at the obvious differences in the two images. "We've used mathematical transformations to enhance the images. But you can clearly see that a different artist, using a different paint, and different techniques, has extended the Angel Gabriel's wings at a later date."

"Interesting," said Su-Lin impatiently. "But doesn't this only confirm, albeit in much greater detail, what we already knew? Didn't you suggest earlier that you may have found something new?"

The lab technician nodded. "Most of the time we are examining the topmost layer of paint and the varnish for the purposes of cleaning an old painting without damaging the layer of paint. Or we might be detecting forgeries by examining the layers of varnish over the signature. The deepest we would ever typically go is to search for the underdrawing, the pencil sketch on the canvas, on which a painting was based." The lab technician, paused to look at San and Su-Lin in turn, as though he expected his enthusiasm to be contagious. "Doctor Chan's genius," gushed the lab technician, "his breakthrough, was to look instead at the surface on to which the paint had been applied."

The elevated pitch and pace of the lab technician's voice made it clear to both San and Su-Lin that something had been discovered.

"But what did you find?" Su-Lin asked in an increasingly excited tone.

"We'd always thought that The Annunciation had been simply painted on a wood panel. If I was to turn the painting over it would be obvious to anyone that it had been painted on wood. It was a common technique, especially for altar pieces." The technician hastily pulled another image from the manila folder. "But following Doctor Chan's request, between the wood and the paint, we found a single layer of paper."

"Paper?" San furrowed his brow, folded his arms, and looked questioningly at Su-Lin.

"Initially, we thought it might have been a study by the artist, or perhaps the sketch on which the painting was based. But then we found text written on the paper buried under the paint."

"Text?" urged San. "You found a document under the painting?"

"And not just a Latin document." The lab technician enjoyed the anticipation growing in San and Su-Lin's faces. "We found an Asian script too." The lab technician pointed at one of the gray scale images of The Annunciation. There, deep under the layers of paint, magnified and enhanced, San and Su-Lin could see clear columns of fifteenth century style Chinese characters.

"It's the *Proditio*," gasped Su-Lin. Her eyes moistened, overwhelmed to have found Doctor Chan's proof. "The treaty signed by Eugenesis IV and the Ming Emperor Xuan De is hidden in the layers of Leonardo's painting of The Annunciation." Su-Lin began to sob.

"We could not read the Chinese, so we don't know what it says," The lab technician looked a little worried, not sure how he had managed to upset Su-Lin. "But we thought Doctor Chan might like to translate it himself."

San put a reassuring arm around Su-Lin's shoulders. "We've found it Su-Lin. We've found the *Proditio*, just as Doctor Chan had wanted us to." He squeezed her shoulders warmly. "And we've found it just where Doctor Chan's clues had suggested it would be found."

Su-Lin threw her arms up around San's neck and sobbed with a bitter happiness. "Thank you San," whispered Su-Lin. "I couldn't have done this without you."

Su-Lin clung there for a moment enjoying the warmth of San's chest almost as much as the thrill of finally understanding Doctor Chan's two mysterious dates. Her breathing slowly calmed, and she looked up from San's shoulders. But, Su-Lin's cheek inadvertently brushed softly against San's lips. She froze and buried her face again in San's shoulder again. She was acutely aware of her racing heart and determined not to meet San's gaze.

CHAPTER 61

San could feel his face reddening, embarrassed by how much he enjoyed the sudden intimacy of Su-Lin's embrace. He tried to look down to see her face and read her expression. But Su-Lin hugged him tightly and her head was buried under his chin. Before San could think of a way of breaking the awkward silence, the laboratory door swung open violently and slammed against the wall with a loud bang.

Both San and Su-Lin jumped at the noise. They turned to see a solidly built Chinese man in a dusty gray suit and trench coat charge into the room, brandishing a pistol. He looked about the room manically, sweat shining on his forehead. "Where's Agent Mei-Li?" shouted the Chinese man in Mandarin. He leveled the gun at San and strode toward him purposefully.

Su-Lin screamed, the lab technician ducked behind a desk and San froze, having nowhere to run from the gun pointed at his chest. Recognition flashed in San's mind. It was the Chinese man that he had seen last night in Rome – the Chinese man from the gun fight in the Basilica. *What the hell is he doing here?*

"Tell me!" Agent Tao Ma demanded, yelling even louder than before. He stopped only a couple of steps from San. Hearing no satisfactory response, Tao pointed his gun at Su-Lin instead. "What have you done with her?" he screamed in almost incoherent anger.

San lifted his hands in a submissive gesture. "Sorry, who?" he asked, hoping to placate the intruder. Not taking his eyes from the pistol, San took half a step to the side, interposing himself between Su-Lin and the gunman.

Tao gritted his teeth, unimpressed with San's answer. He took another two steps forward, drew back his pistol and swung upwards, striking San viscously in the jaw with the butt of his pistol.

"San!" wailed Su-Lin.

San's head whipped backwards and to the side. Pain flashed inside his head. The room went blurry and his knees buckled. San groped for the table to his left as he fell, just managing to retain his footing. He shook his head trying to clear his vision.

But Tao was not yet finished. He stepped forward and struck San with a more precisely aimed blow to the forehead.

Pain flashed again through San's skull, and this time the blackness took him. He lost his balance and tumbled into the table, before dragging the images of The Annunciation with him as he crashed to the floor.

Tao stood intimidatingly over San's limp body. "Was it you traitor?" he spat, pumping his fist angrily in the air toward San.

But San was barely conscious. He lay on his side, clumsily dabbing at the stream of blood that poured from his nose and over his top lip.

"Did you sell her out?" Tao was still furious. "Just like you sold the bronze rat's head sculpture?"

San's head swam with blurred images. Everything sounded so distant, he thought, as though muffled by pillows. But thankfully the pain was dulled too. San clutched at the ground groggily, wondering where all this blood had come from. *Why is it so difficult to sit up?*

Tao lost patience with San and turned his attention back toward Su-Lin. "You!" grunted Tao. "You're coming with me."

Su-Lin's eyes flicked from San's bloodied face, to the lab technician cowering behind the table, and to the doorway beyond Tao. But there was only one exit and no way she could get away while Tao had his gun trained on her. She slowly raised her hands in submission.

"Here. Now!" yelled Tao, shaking his pistol, indicating to Su-Lin that she should approach.

Su-Lin stepped forward.

"Turn around," barked Tao, as he removed hand cuffs from his jacket pocket with his free hand. "Get on your knees."

Su-Lin obeyed. She turned around to face the large easel at the far end of the room and slowly knelt with her back toward Tao. "San?" she whispered. But although he lay only a couple of feet away, he was too concussed to respond.

"Hands behind your back!"

She bit her lip at the pain as she twisted her fractured left arm behind her back. But while it hurt, she knew it would hurt far worse if Tao was to do it himself.

Su-Lin felt handcuffs being slapped over her right wrist and then her left. Tao then tested they were securely fastened by shaking the handcuffs violently. Su-Lin's eyes watered as pain shot through her fractured left arm.

Tao grabbed Su-Lin by the collar of her shirt. But as he buried the muzzle of his gun in the small of her back, Su-Lin could hear footsteps approaching from the corridor. Tao leant forward to Su-Lin's ear and whispered quietly, but assuredly. "Don't think for a minute I won't shoot you."

Su-Lin heard Tao grunt at he strained to lift her to her feet by the scruff of her neck. As she was hauled off her knees and into the air, she could hear the footsteps accelerating across the room. Then Su-Lin fell. As the floor rushed up toward her, she realized that Tao had dropped her. But why?

With her arms handcuffed behind her back Su-Lin could not break her own fall. She yelped as she slammed into the ground. She hit the ground awkwardly on one knee, toppled over, and slumped forward heavily on to her right shoulder. She could not understand why Tao had let her go. Su-Lin rolled on to her back to see what was going on.

An enormous bald-headed young man in a white suit and black shirt had grabbed Tao from behind. Su-Lin's eyes widened and her stomach turned. It was Brother Michael, one of the two priests who had tortured her the previous evening in Rome. Michael had hold of Tao's pistol wielding right arm by the wrist. He was desperately trying to keep Tao's pistol pointed in a safe direction while wrapping his other arm under Tao's chin, with what looked like the intention of tearing Tao's head from his shoulders. Tao's face slowly turned red as he fought for breath. He scrabbled with his left hand, trying desperately to force his chin down between Brother Michael's forearm and his windpipe.

But the muscular Michael was patient. He slowly straightened his back lifting Tao from his feet. Tao's legs flailed helplessly in the air. Drool oozed from Tao's lips. His face turned from red to beetroot. Tao could feel the fog of unconsciousness approaching and he knew he had the energy left for only one last effort. Instead of struggling with his chin to protect his throat from Michael's forearm, which slowly but irresistibly restricted the oxygen to his brain, he arched his back violently. Tao jerked his head backwards and kicked his feet up between Michael's legs.

Although Tao's feet grazed harmlessly off the inside of Michael's thigh without doing any damage, the back of Tao's skull crashed into Michael's nose with sickening force. There was the sickly sound of cracking cartilage and a wet deluge of blood. It stunned Michael for a moment and although he didn't lose his grip on Tao, he wobbled backwards, then overcompensated, before toppling over on top of Tao.

Su-Lin shrieked as Tao and Michael fell toward her. She rolled out of the way to avoid being crushed beneath them.

As Michael crashed to the ground on top of Tao, he lost his grip on Tao's pistol arm. But Tao was pinned to the floor face down and unable to aim at Michael with any confidence. As the two wrestled on the floor between one of the workstations and the table, Su-Lin pushed herself away from them with her feet.

Michael slowly worked himself astride Tao's prone body, and while pinning Tao's head to the floor with a meaty hand, he methodically sought to bring Tao's pistol under control. Each time Michael grabbed Tao's pistol arm he tried thrashing it against the floor in an attempt to knock the pistol from his grip. And each time Tao escaped Michael's grasp he tried to aim the pistol over his shoulder and toward Michael.

A sharp crack exploded from the gun as the two men struggled with the pistol.

Su-Lin threw herself flat on the floor, her eyes pinched tightly closed.

A second and third round burst from the pistol, aimed in no particular direction.

When Su-Lin finally opened her eyes, she could see three large holes had been torn in the chest of drawers under the table next to where she lay. Behind the table lay the crumpled body of the lab technician in a quickly expanding pool of his own blood. His mouth hung open, his eyes were wide with shock, and two fleshy red holes punctured his otherwise pristine, white lab coat. He did not move.

Su-Lin recoiled, but she did not yet spare a tear for the lab technician, with panic urging her to run and avoid sharing a similar fate. Lying on to her side, she drew her knees up and close to her chest, so that she could roll herself over into a kneeling position. Once upright, Su-Lin turned to watch Brother Michael holding Tao's pistol arm with both hands and pounding it into the floor in an endeavor to dislodge the gun. The front of his neat white suit had been stained red from the blood that ran freely from his nose.

Su-Lin pushed herself from her knees to her feet and sprinted toward the door. She ran clumsily, because with her arms still handcuffed behind her back, it was not easy to keep her balance. But as she passed the white suited giant, Michael released Tao and instead lunged at Su-Lin with one arm, snatching at her ankles. It was enough to cause Su-Lin to trip. Pain ripped through her fractured forearm as she fell heavily on her left shoulder. Still lying on the floor, she began screaming, "Gun, gun! He's got a gun!"

But preventing Su-Lin's escape had meant that Michael now had only one hand with which to control Tao. And although Tao was still unable to move because Michael's knee in his back had him pinned to the floor, he simply bent his pistol arm at the elbow, and began firing blindly behind him.

The first bullet scared Michael as it passed harmlessly overhead, and he instinctively leant backwards and out of harm's way. But this allowed Tao to fire again. The second bullet punched a hole through Michael's right shoulder. He arched his back and groaned as though the wind had been kicked out of him. The third bullet tore flesh and a fine red mist from Michael's neck. He released Tao completely and fell backwards, panic in his eyes. He lay on the floor, scrabbling with both hands to stem the blood gushing from his torn carotid artery. Michael thrashed on the ground, until his resistance slowed, and then finally stopped.

Tao staggered back to his feet. He had a series of bruises down the left hand side of his face. His shirt was soaked with sweat and covered with grime from the floor. He tested his jaw. There was blood, but it was not broken. Tao straightened his torn jacket and walked over to Su-Lin, paying Michael only a casual glance. She was lying face down on the floor, still screaming a warning to the rest of the Gallery. Tao gripped her by her upper arm. "Get up now!" growled Tao, hauling her roughly to her feet. "You're still coming with me."

CHAPTER 62

San felt a dull throbbing in his head and a wet metallic taste in his mouth. He heard a woman screaming. But it sounds so far away, he thought. He tried opening his eyes. But the world was out of focus and his stomach churned. So he closed his eyes again and instead tried to focus on standing up.

San forced himself up on to his hands and knees. But he could feel with his hands that the floor was slick. He opened his eyes again, wondering what it was. Dark red streaks and an occasional drip had been sprayed across a mess of gray photographs. It's blood, thought San. *But why is it there?* He rubbed his jaw thoughtfully. His jaw was slick too. *And it hurts like hell.* San groaned. *Is it my blood?*

The loud cracking of gun fire dragged San's consciousness back out of the fog. He pushed himself up on to one knee. But while his vision of the laboratory around him sharpened, so did the pain in his temple and jaw. He winced, and then spat the blood out which had gathered in his mouth. When San heard the scrabbling of feet against the gray linoleum floor his head snapped around in time to see Agent Tao Ma disappearing into the corridor dragging Su-Lin, kicking and screaming, behind him.

"Su-Lin!" San tried to yell, but the pain in his jaw made it fall away in a whisper. He tried to force himself up and onto his feet, but the sudden change in altitude was dizzying and he leant on the table to steady himself.

The pain pounding in his forehead was suddenly compounded as the Uffizi Gallery's alarm began blaring throughout the gallery. Museum staff started running past the laboratory door yelling incoherently in Italian. San dabbed at his forehead. A large lump had appeared on his forehead where he had been pistol whipped. An angry gash on his jaw was weeping a steady stream of blood. *But nothing too serious.*

San surveyed the room. The commotion had swept photographs all over the floor. Brother Michael lay on his back in the middle of the floor with a ragged hole in the side of his throat. His once white jacket was stained a dark red. The lab technician had fallen in a crumpled heap behind the table against which San had steadied himself. They were both very still, completely silent, and clearly dead. San gagged, confronted by the guilt that in some small way, their interruption of the lab technician's day, had led to his untimely death.

San shook his head clear and was about to run to the door and after Su-Lin. But he turned back, knowing that she'd never forgive him for leaving the *Proditio* behind. San knelt down again, and quickly assembled the collection of photographs of The Annunciation that had fallen on the floor. He returned them to the lab technician's manila envelope. Once confident he had all of the images that the laboratory had taken on behalf of Doctor Chan, he folded the yellow envelope under his arm. Stepping over Michael's corpse, San took one deep breath before stepping into the confusion of the corridor leading from the laboratory.

Staff and tourists ran for the fire escapes, looking

furtively over their shoulders. Many of them looked confused as much as scared thought San, not sure of either, what they were running from, or why the gallery's alarm had been tripped.

San had not seen in which direction Tao had taken Su-Lin. But the staff and tourists were overwhelmingly running in one direction and San guessed that was most likely toward the nearest exit. Tao would have wanted to leave the building having just murdered two men and so San decided to join the throng rather than fight against it.

San was swept along with the crowd that one way or another emptied itself into the street in front of the Uffizi Gallery. Once outside, the crowd of tourists milled about listlessly, trying to reconnect with friends lost in the panic, or hoping to get a glimpse of the Asian man with a gun from whom they were all running.

San looked up and down the alley that ran through the middle of the Uffizi. Neither Tao nor Su-Lin were anywhere to be seen. But it was difficult to be sure, because the crowd outside the gallery made it impossible to see more than ten feet in any direction. Tao would not have wanted to stick around, thought San. *And neither should I.*

San didn't want to be confused for that Asian man with the gun that had forced the evacuation, and his bloodied face had already attracted more than one suspicious look. So he walked quickly downhill toward the Arno river. When San reached the river he turned left and headed uphill to the next bridge. He could hear Police sirens somewhere behind him, bearing down on the Uffizi Gallery.

It wasn't until San had crossed the Ponte Alle Grazie, a modern brick bridge, to the south side of the Arno that he allowed himself to rest. He dropped into a chair outside one of the many open air restaurants that lined the streets. Florence on the south bank of the Arno was newer, the streets wider, and without the tourist attractions of the old town, the streets were also far less crowded. San ordered a bottle of water to clean his wounds and a glass of wine to settle his nerves.

San took out the manila folder he had stuffed into his coat and placed it on the table. He didn't dare open it. Once translated, the document would show that the Chinese embassy from the Ming Emperor Xuan De to Pope Eugenesis IV had enabled the European discovery of the New World and sparked the Renaissance. But San was in no mood for celebrating, because it had cost two men their lives today. *And hundreds more throughout the centuries had died to conceal its truth.*

Furthermore, while San had found the *Proditio*, he had lost Su-Lin.

San was pretty sure that he recognized the Chinese man who had dragged Su-Lin from the Uffizi Gallery. It was the same Chinese man who had exchanged fire with the two priests in the Basilica last night in Rome. The accent with which he had spoken Mandarin suggested he was from Northern China. *Beijing most likely.*

The Chinese man had said he had been searching for something, remembered San, an Agent Mei-Li. Whoever she is? If he's searching for an agent and wielding a gun, he's most likely a government type. Police, army or secret service, guessed San. If he's from the Chinese government, he could be based out of the embassy. He may have even taken Su-Lin into custody, worried San. *And there's no hope of getting her out of there.*

"But why did he think that we might know something about Agent Mei-Li's whereabouts?" San leant back in his chair and considered his options. *What might he want in exchange for Su-Lin?* The Chinese man didn't show any interest in the *Proditio* he thought. But he did mention the bronze rat's head sculpture. *Unfortunately, I don't have that either.*

CHAPTER 63

The Prefect and Inquisitor Jerome waited for Brother Michael to return to the Palazzo Vecchio through the Vasari corridor. Jerome paced the room, slowly beating an echoing rhythm into the floor with his cane. Conversely, the Prefect sat quietly on a wooden chair, resting his hands on his knees and staring at the door that separated the Uffizi Gallery and the short bridge to the Palace.

One muffled explosion broke the silence. Jerome halted, lifted his head, and the rhythm of his pacing was lost. Then a second later another pair of explosions echoed from somewhere inside the Uffizi Gallery. They were unmistakably gun shots, thought Jerome. *But why are they being fired at all?*

Jerome felt the Prefect's eyes upon him. "I'm sure that was necessary," he reassured confidently. "Brother Michael is one of our best."

The Prefect did not respond, but sat bolt upright, focusing all his attention on what he could hear. But there was no further sound to tell them what might be happening inside the Uffizi gallery. "He should have been back by now," said the Prefect evenly, despite the concern etched into his forehead. "Whether or not that was necessary."

"I'll give him a call," declared Jerome, pulling his cellphone out from his jacket pocket. But before he had dialed Michael's number, they heard another three muffled explosions from inside the Uffizi Gallery.

"I'm sure Michael is taking all necessary steps," reiterated Jerome. But this time his voice shook nervously.

"Who the hell is he shooting at?" roared the Prefect, staring daggers at Jerome.

But Jerome had no better idea than the Prefect.

Less than a minute later, the Uffizi Gallery's alarm began to ring.

"Fire?" suggested Jerome weakly.

The Prefect grated his teeth. Not only was the alarm loud but its high pitch seemed to pierce to the very center of the Prefect's skull. He covered his ears with his hands and moved to the window in time to see people pouring from the Uffizi Gallery's exits. "Get someone down there Jerome!" yelled the Prefect, pointing at the crowd growing in the street below.

But Jerome could also hear sirens in the distance. "We can't go in there now." He looked helplessly at the Prefect. "Not with the Police on their way."

"This is another unmitigated disaster!" The Prefect took a step toward Jerome jabbing his finger into Jerome's chest. "You have disappointed the Church for the last time."

But Jerome's cellphone rang loudly, interrupting the Prefect's tirade. Jerome snatched up his phone. He checked the number, hoping it was Michael. But he did not recognize it. He looked to the Prefect for permission to answer the phone. "It could be Michael."

"You don't recognize the number?" snapped the Prefect tersely.

Jerome shook his head. "He could be using a landline."

The Prefect waved angrily, urging Jerome to get on with it.

Jerome nodded and put the phone to his ear.

"Your Excellency, this is the Holy Office. You have an outside call. May we connect you?"

"Not now," growled Jerome, glad to have someone onto whom to deflect the Prefect's anger.

"But, Your Excellency, they said it was an emergency." The operator paused nervously. "They said it was about a shooting."

Jerome motioned frantically for the Prefect to come closer. He switched his cellphone to speaker and held it out in the palm of his hand. When the Prefect was standing close enough to hear, Jerome continued. "Yes, please connect me now."

They both waited. "Hello?" asked Jerome nervously. There was no response. But they could both hear someone breathing on the other end of the line. "Who is this?"

"Brother Michael is dead," said a male voice, in an awkward and Asian-accented Italian.

Jerome's jaw went slack and his eyes widened in shock. A lump rose in his throat. He could not believe it. But he had no idea what to say.

"Who is this?" demanded the Prefect. "What do you know about Brother Michael?"

"I shot him in the Uffizi Gallery laboratories."

"I'll kill you!" exploded Jerome furiously. "I'll break every bone in your..."

But the Prefect lashed out with his hand, grabbing Jerome under the jaw, forcing his neck backwards and squeezing his trachea. "Silence," he whispered in a threatening tone.

Jerome gagged in surprise, struggling to draw breath. But he dared not use force to free himself from the Prefect's grasp.

The Prefect held Jerome by the throat, staring into his eyes until he was convinced that Jerome would control himself. Once satisfied, the Prefect shoved him away, leaving him coughing and spluttering.

"What do you want?" continued the Prefect.

"I want Agent Mei-Li..." demanded the voice.

"We don't have Agent Mei-Li," whispered Jerome to the Prefect. "Mei-Li is...

The Prefect muted the cellphone's microphone. "Shut up," urged the Prefect through clenched teeth. "This man, whoever he is, thinks we have agent Mei-Li, and for the moment, that's all that counts!"

"...and I want the bronze rat's head sculpture," continued the voice calmly.

The Prefect turned the cellphone's microphone back on. "I'm afraid I don't know what you're talking about?" The Prefect didn't expect that playing dumb would fool the caller, but if he could lengthen the conversation, he might lure the voice into revealing something that they could use.

But the voice ignored him. "I have the *Jinyi Wei.*" The voice waited for Jerome and the Prefect to absorb this new piece of information. "I have the girl that Brother Michael was sent to collect," the voice added, to avoid any shadow of a doubt. "I will exchange the *Jinyi Wei*, for Agent Mei-Li and the bronze rat's head sculpture."

The Prefect covered the microphone with his hand and gave Jerome a querying look.

Although the Prefect looked keen to accept the mysterious caller's offer, Jerome was worried. "We have no idea who this is?" whined Jerome. "Nor whether anything he tells us is true."

"But if we get Doctor Chan's whore, she could lead us to the *Proditio.*"

Jerome scratched at his beard nervously. But seeing no more direct course of action to recovering the *Proditio*, he nodded once at the Prefect.

"How do we do this?" asked the Prefect. He intentionally used a resentful tone, so that the caller might believe they were desperate enough to accept an inadequate exchange.

"Meet me on the Ponte Vecchio at midnight. And unless you want this to escalate into a major diplomatic incident, come alone. No local Police, and no colleagues. You bring help, and you'll never hear from me or the *Jinyi Wei* again."

"Wait!" yelled the Prefect. But the line was dead.

CHAPTER 64

Agent Tao Ma stared out of the Chinese consulate's conference room window. Just a few hours earlier, he had been discussing the search for the bronze rat's head sculpture with Agent Mei-Li and their superiors in Beijing. But now, it was San Lee's companion who sat across from him on the other side of the table. Tao stood up and paced nervously. Su-Lin sat quietly, handcuffed to the radiator to the left of the door.

Tao rubbed his sore neck. The pain from the bruising on Tao's arms, neck and back was distracting enough, but adrenalin still coursed through his veins, clashing loudly with the nausea of knowing what he had done. "I have killed two men today," he remembered guiltily. One was justifiably self-defense, Tao thought. *But the other...* He shivered involuntarily. "That might be enough to end my career," he mumbled. *Quite apart from having lost Mei-Li.*

Furthermore, Tao did not know what to make of this woman. Su-Lin seemed to be not only lucid, but highly intelligent. And while her story was incredible, it seemed internally consistent to Tao. Su-Lin had claimed to be a member of the *Jinyi Wei*, an organization which was searching for a treaty agreed upon by the Ming Emperor Xuan De and Pope Eugenesis IV in the fifteenth century. A treaty she claimed had been suppressed by the Church for over five hundred years. Such a claim would normally identify her as a conspiracy nut at best, and a raving loony at worst. But Tao had seen her mercilessly tortured by representatives of the Catholic Church for information regarding the location of this treaty. *And that makes her story entirely more credible.*

And her motives, considered Tao, to preserve the history and achievements of the Chinese people, in the face of foreigners determined to steal or belittle them. It's admirably patriotic, he thought. *Something I sympathize with completely.*

Conversely, Tao was not convinced at all by Su-Lin's claim that she knew nothing about Mei-Li's disappearance. But there is little more I can do to get to the bottom of it, growled Tao, not with the limited variety of investigative techniques that the ministry permits in foreign postings. By her own admission, Su-Lin had visited Florence Cathedral that morning, at about the same time that Mei-Li had disappeared. Coincidental to say the least, thought Tao. *She must have had something to do with it.*

Su-Lin had also worked for Doctor Chan, the previous owner of the bronze rat's head sculpture. Moreover, Tao had seen her boarding a train from Venice to Rome with San Lee, the man who had killed Doctor Chan and stolen the sculpture in the first place. Yet she claimed that San did not have, nor ever had, the bronze sculpture in his possession. Tao's face wrinkled in confusion. But Mei-Li had followed San to the Basilica in Rome where the sculpture was to be sold, he thought. Instead, Su-Lin claimed that it was the Catholic priests who had killed Doctor Chan and taken the sculpture, not San. *But why would they do that?*

Tao couldn't make sense of it at all. Were his superiors

in Beijing right and the Church had wanted the bronze sculpture for political reasons? But if so, once they had it, why did they continue torturing Su-Lin? *And none of this explains Mei-Li's sudden disappearance.* Tao, wondering if it was the pain from his injuries that clouded his thinking, forced himself to focus on his original objective, and the only course of action which might save his career. *I have to find the bronze rat's head sculpture.*

Tao's train of thought was interrupted by one of the consular staff knocking hesitantly on the meeting room door.

"Agent Tao Ma?" a voice called out warily, without opening the door. "Sir? You have a call from the Chinese embassy in Rome. It's on line three."

The consulate in Florence was clearly not used to hosting attaches like himself, Tao thought. They had been tiptoeing around him since he arrived. And the situation had only deteriorated when badly bruised himself, he had dragged a handcuffed prisoner through the office.

"Got it," yelled Tao, before awkwardly adding, "thanks." Such pleasantries weren't normally required in the Ministry's discourse, sneered Tao. *Bloody civilians.*

Tao picked up the handset of the phone sitting in the middle of the dark wood conference table and punched the button for line three. "Agent Tao Ma," he said brusquely. But for a moment there was silence. "Who is this?"

"We have Agent Mei-Li and the bronze rat's head sculpture," stated an emotionless voice in a strangely accented mandarin Chinese.

"Who are you?" Tao demanded with renewed intensity. He cursed silently, realizing that the consulate was less well equipped than what he was used to, and had no way of tracing incoming telephone calls.

The dry voice ignored Tao's question. "We want the girl."

"What girl?" Tao did, not want to reveal any

information unless the caller signaled that he already knew it.

"The girl you took from the Uffizi Gallery," growled the voice angrily. "The *Jinyi Wei* in your custody."

Tao was stunned. He wasn't sure whether he was more surprised that the caller knew he had captured Su-Lin, or more surprised that they too believed her to be a member of the *Jinyi Wei.* It had to be a colleague of the priest he had killed in the gallery, he thought. Maybe it's the older priest from the Basilica last night. *They're the only ones who would believe she's a member of the Jinyi Wei.*

The voice on the phone continued methodically. "We'll give you Agent Mei-Li and the bronze rat's head sculpture, in exchange for Su-Lin."

Tao's heart skipped a beat. The possibility of being able to recover Mei-Li and the bronze sculpture was irresistible. *And I might still be able to rescue my career.* "If you bring Mei-Li and the bronze sculpture to the consulate, we can exchange it…"

"No," interrupted the voice. "Meet me on the Ponte Vecchio at midnight." The voice then added, "and unless you want the local Police getting involved, come alone."

"I have a question," blurted Tao. "Why do you think she's a...?" But the line was dead.

CHAPTER 65

San Lee fidgeted nervously. He checked his watch. It was almost midnight. He looked out across the Ponte Vecchio from his position in the hotel's roof top bar on the north bank of the Arno. But no one had arrived yet. *And I'm still not sure that anyone will.*

During the day the pedestrian-only Ponte Vecchio would be bustling with tourists, taking photos looking down the Arno River, or shopping at the jewelry stores which lined either side of the bridge. But this late at night, the shops were all boarded up, the tourists asleep in their hotels, and the street lights dimmed to a soft orange glow.

The Ponte Vecchio was a three arch, stone bridge, almost a hundred yards in length, and for centuries it had been the primary crossing of the Arno River. It was built in the fourteenth century after two earlier bridges had been washed away by the periodic flooding of the river. Nowadays, both sides of the bridge were lined by goldsmiths and souvenir sellers. But originally the bridge had been populated by butchers until the nobility crossing the bridge began objecting to the smell. The shops on either side of the Ponte Vecchio had an odd effect, thought San.

The shops concealed the fact that one was on a bridge, because from street level it was impossible to see the river for most of the length of the Ponte Vecchio. It was only in the very center of the bridge that was free of shops and you could walk to the edge of the Ponte Vecchio and look up and down the river.

San was one of the last patrons left in the roof top bar. While the bar wasn't scheduled to close until midnight, the barman had been giving San a dirty look for quite some time. The bar was located in the rooftop terrace of a small family run hotel. In happier times it would have reminded San of the hotels he had stayed at in Marrakech or Istanbul. There were wicker lounges and chairs scattered about the terrace among planter pots of untamed vines that grew up and over the edge of the roof. In summer, umbrellas would have replaced the gas heaters that were now placed strategically around the bar. San had chosen the gas heater closest to the bridge under which to sit. He played with his drink absently, having decided shortly after it had arrived, that it was probably best to keep a clear head.

From his position, he could look down to the intersection at the closer north end of the bridge. And while it was some distance, he could also make out what was happening in the small piazza at the far end of the bridge and everything in between. So where are they? thought San. He hoped that both parties would take the bait that he had offered them. But he was not yet sure how he would free Su-Lin if they did.

As nervous as San was about how the night might proceed, he was somewhat relieved when a large, black sedan pulled up at the far end of the Ponte Vecchio. That's one out of two, he thought. The car paused, its engine still running. The driver seemed to be assessing the situation. San watched apprehensively until the driver turned the car engine off and opened the door. The driver got out of the car slowly as though he was encumbered. Or perhaps he's just old, wondered San. He was dressed in a long black hooded cape, in the style of a Dominican priest. Although it was dark and quite a distance, he thought the priest was wearing scarlet robes under his cape. San wondered if it was one of the priests from the Basilica in Rome, but he was too far away to be sure. The priest waited by the passenger door, watching for any activity on the bridge.

It wasn't long before a second car appeared, this time at the north end of the bridge, closest to San. A metallic gray, four wheel drive, with dark tinted windows, dawdled past the end of the bridge before parking in a motorcycle bay. The driver's door opened first and a stocky Asian man jumped out. His hair had been shaved short and he wore a black trench coat and a determined snarl. San recognized him immediately as Agent Tao Ma, the Chinese man who had abducted Su-Lin from the Uffizi Gallery that morning.

"That's both of them." San exhaled in relief, pleased that both of his bluffs had worked.

Tao opened the rear passenger door of the four wheel drive, reached in and pulled a black haired young lady from the car. Her hands were tied behind her back with a white plastic cord and she stumbled out of the vehicle. It was Su-Lin! While San's nerves jangled with the uncertainties of the imminent meeting, he was happy just to see her alive.

San leapt up, hurriedly dropped some money for the drink and a generous tip next to his unfinished wine glass before grabbing his jacket and rushing downstairs. The roof top bar was only on the fourth floor, so instead of waiting for the lift, San ran down the fire escape to the hotel lobby. The night watchmen didn't even look up from his portable television, as San passed through the hotel's narrow lobby and out into the street.

San arrived in the street in time to see Tao and Su-Lin crossing the road to the Ponte Vecchio. Tao held Su-Lin tightly by the upper arm, marching her forward a half pace in front of him. Su-Lin winced each time Tao shoved her forward, as pain shot through her fractured left arm. San waited until they had climbed part way up the gentle slope toward the center of the bridge, before crossing the road behind them.

San stopped at the first shop on the Ponte Vecchio, crouched, and poked his head round the corner. Beyond Su-Lin and Tao, San could see the old priest opening the rear passenger door of his car. From the car he fetched a brown leather bag about the size of a bowling ball. That would be the bronze rat's head sculpture, San guessed. The priest then muttered a few words that San could not make out at this distance. From the back seat of the car, a small-framed figure in blue jeans, sneakers and a brown bomber jacket stepped out. The small figure's hands were bound with rope and a black cloth bag had been placed over their head. *That must be Agent Mei-Li.*

With the cloth bag over her head, Mei-Li could not see where she was going. The priest gripped her by the shoulder and snarled, "Move," pushing her forward along the bridge. As Tao and the priest, each with their respective prisoners, approached the center of the bridge, San crept along in the shadows of the right hand row of shops. He kept a safe distance behind Tao and Su-Lin, making sure not to be noticed.

When Tao and the priest reached the open square in the center of the bridge they were no more than forty feet apart.

"That's close enough!" yelled the elderly priest. Everyone halted where they were.

"Who are you?" shouted Tao.

"You can call me, Your Eminence." The Prefect sneered. "Send over the *Jinyi Wei.*"

"Not until you show me the bronze rat's head sculpture," barked Tao.

The Prefect considered Tao's demand for a moment before putting the brown, leather bag on the ground. He unzipped the bag and took out a sculpture about the size of a football. Its bronze finish shimmered in the limited moon light that penetrated the otherwise overcast sky. The Prefect held the bronze sculpture up and turned it left and then right, to show Tao that it was real.

Tao nodded once.

The Prefect then shoved the bronze sculpture roughly into Mei-Li's bound hands. "Hold this," he ordered.

"OK, now start Mei-Li walking toward me," demanded Tao.

The Prefect shoved Mei-Li forward a step. But he still held her by the shoulder, preventing her from moving forward. "And you send over the *Jinyi Wei*."

Tao pushed Su-Lin forward a step and she stumbled, reluctant to be any closer to the Prefect than she needed to be. But instead of ordering her forward, Tao took a step to the side and drew his pistol pointing it at the base of Su-Lin's skull.

San froze, gripped with panic.

"No tricks. Or I'll execute your precious *Jinyi Wei*." Tao cocked his pistol to underscore his seriousness. "Now send over Mei-Li."

But if Tao was surprised by the Prefect's reaction, he didn't show it.

"A perfectly reasonable position," smiled the Prefect, drawing his own pistol from under his cloak and pointing it at Mei-Li. "I wouldn't want it any other way."

CHAPTER 66

Su-Lin's cheeks were streaked with tears as she quietly walked toward the Prefect across the center of the Ponte Vecchio. But her jaw was set and with gritted teeth she stared daggers at the Prefect. She was not crying, thought San, these were tears of frustration and anger.

Agent Mei-Li shuffled forward in the opposite direction to Su-Lin and in the general direction of Agent Tao Ma. But she made slow progress. She walked with a slight limp and the bag over her head prevented her from seeing where she was going. Her hands were bound in front of her with rope, clutching the bronze rat's head sculpture.

To San, it seemed to take an age for Su-Lin and Mei-Li to pass each other in the center of the bridge. Tao and the Prefect both kept their guns trained on each other's hostage, to ensure neither of them reneged on the exchange.

San crept forward past another of the shops before hiding again, as close as he dared to the center of the bridge, some twenty paces behind Tao.

"Come my pretty *Jinyi Wei*." The Prefect leered at Su-Lin as she approached. "Jerome has told me so much about you." The Prefect's eyes flickered from Su-Lin to Mei-Li and back.

Su-Lin halted in front of the Prefect, staring at him defiantly.

"Come closer," the Prefect cooed suggestively. But when Su-Lin seemingly refused, the Prefect stepped forward and grabbed Su-Lin by the shoulder. Su-Lin grunted in surprise, but could do little with her hands still tied behind her back. He spun her around to face Tao, his gun still trained on Mei-Li. The Prefect wrapped his forearm around Su-Lin's neck, drawing her into his chest like a human shield.

Su-Lin could feel the steady rise and fall of the Prefect's chest. She could feel his humid breath on the back of her neck. She shivered as his lips brushed against her ear.

"We can watch this together," whispered the Prefect.

Su-Lin could almost hear the Prefect smiling.

"This way, this way," urged Tao, impatiently.

Mei-Li responded by adjusting course, heading toward the sound of Tao's voice.

Tao holstered his pistol. "Now give it to me," he barked greedily, snatching the bronze rat's head sculpture that Mei-Li had been carrying. Tao felt a wave of exhilaration wash over him. Not only had he completed his mission and returned the sculpture to the Chinese people, but the specter of failure had been lifted from his shoulders. Tao turned the sculpture over in his hands feeling its weight and admiring its design. He couldn't help but smile childishly.

While Tao was focused on the bronze rat's head sculpture, San watched Mei-Li step past Tao. But to San's surprise, the rope which a moment ago had bound her wrists slipped to the ground effortlessly. With her hands free, Mei-Li reached up to remove the black cloth bag which had covered her head. She pulled the bag away in one swift motion. It was not Mei-Li.

Once the black felt bag had been removed, San saw a

gray bearded man, with a weathered, angular face. It was Inquisitor Jerome. But instead of his white suit and black shirt, he wore Mei-Li's bomber jacket and jeans.

Tao turned to share the satisfaction of having recovered the bronze sculpture with his colleague. But instead, Tao's eyes widened and his mouth fell open, because it was not Mei-Li that he saw, but Inquisitor Jerome drawing a knife.

"This is for Brother Michael," screamed Jerome, plunging the knife toward Tao's chest. "Heathen!"

Tao jumped aside from the lunging Jerome, throwing his arms up and away from the path of the knife. Jerome's knife missed its mark, but skidded across Tao's ribs, leaving an ugly tear in his suit, and a thin line of red along the center of the tear. Grimacing in frustration at having missed his target, Jerome reversed his grip on the knife, holding it as he would an ice pick. He stepped right and slashed at Agent Tao's stomach, and again Tao leapt back and away from the blade's deadly trajectory.

But having seen Tao's defensive pattern after the first strike, Jerome knew what to expect. He was already following Tao as he retreated again in the same way, from the second blow.

As Jerome closed, Tao began to panic, knowing that Jerome was now dangerously close, and he had not yet had time to draw his own weapon. He instinctively threw the bronze rat's head sculpture at Jerome. It was a weak throw because Tao could only use his left hand. The sculpture glanced off Jerome's left shoulder, making a dull ringing sound as it bounced along the cobbled street, rolling to rest in the gutter. It hadn't hurt Jerome, but he flinched, halting his advance. That precious second gave Tao enough time to draw his gun.

Jerome roared, angry at his own hesitation. He knew that with Tao now armed, he was committed. The safest place for Jerome was to be so close to Tao that he wouldn't be able to use his pistol, without risking a fatal injury from

Jerome's blade. He had little choice but to continue pressing the attack.

As Tao brought the gun to bear, Jerome slashed at Tao's pistol arm with the knife before setting his right shoulder and charging at Tao. Jerome's knife sliced across the top of Tao's wrist, cutting deeply, through the skin and into the tendon and muscle. It only loosened Tao's grip on the pistol for a moment, but it was enough to cause Tao to fire wide of Jerome. The bullet ricocheted harmlessly off the road and shattered one of the jewelry shop windows. Jerome then barreled into Tao, pushing him off balance. Pain ripped through Tao's damaged wrist as he landed heavily on his back. He dropped the pistol and it skittered away.

Jerome fell on top of Tao and for a moment they both scrabbled on the ground. Tao desperately searched for his pistol, while Jerome sought to get on top of Tao and press his knife down toward Tao's chest. Tao could see his pistol agonizingly close, but he had no time to reach it, having instead to defend himself, wrapping his hands around Jerome's knife arm.

Although Tao was by far the stronger man, he was now on his back, and had to fight both Jerome and gravity to prevent Jerome's knife skewering him to the road. Tao grunted with the effort, his face reddening.

Jerome knew he needed only to be patient. His knees were positioned on either side of Tao's hips providing Jerome balance and preventing Tao from wriggling away. Jerome then had only to lean forward against the knife and wait for Tao to tire. He leant over the blade, his face only a foot from Tao's.

"Are there any last confessions you would like to make?" Jerome smiled, as Tao's arms began to shake with the effort needed to resist him.

But Tao did not respond to Jerome's taunts.

"It's just as well, you are long beyond forgiveness now." Jerome shook his head. "For the wages of sin is death."

The gash across Tao's wrist bled steadily, and just as steadily Jerome's blade descended toward Tao's chest. Sweat was pouring from Tao's forehead. He gritted his teeth and shook the sweat free that had pooled in his eyes.

"I am an avenger to execute upon him that doth evil," Jerome said coldly his eyes empty and without sympathy. "Brother Michael was a man of God. And you heathen, have done God evil."

Tao knew he had to get to his pistol, but first he had to find it. He emitted a hoarse cry and arched his back as far and as violently as he could. While he failed to throw Jerome to the side, he bent his head backwards desperately searching for where his pistol had come to rest. Twisting his head to the left he could see it no more than two feet above his head and easily within his reach. But both of his hands were fully occupied keeping Jerome's knife away from his chest.

"Your death rattle," snorted Jerome, laughing with glee at the prospect of his imminent victory.

Agent Tao could feel his strength being sapped slowly away and Jerome's blade inching irresistibly toward his chest. He looked again at the gun lying tantalizingly above his head. I'll get one chance at this, thought Tao, taking a final breath.

Tao arched his back once more. Jerome, thought that he was merely trying to throw him off again. But Agent Tao dropped one hand from Jerome's wrist, reached back, and grabbed for the pistol. With his other hand he pushed down on Jerome's knife hand and to the left. Tao felt his fingertips scrape across the grip of the pistol, but he couldn't grab hold of it. His remaining wounded hand was not strong enough by itself to keep Jerome's knife away. But Tao was prepared for the inevitable injury he must suffer and sought only to deflect it into a non-vital organ. Jerome grimaced in annoyance as his knife veered away from the intended target, and instead plunged toward the flesh below Tao's rib cage.

Tao dropped Jerome's wrist altogether and twisted his body to make the last couple of inches to reach his pistol. With his wounded arm he could only draw his elbow into his stomach to protect himself as best he could.

Jerome smiled gleefully as Tao's fingers slipped from his wrist and the blade slid easily and deeply into Tao's stomach.

Tao squeezed his eyes tightly and groaned as the strength of the blow forced air from his lungs. But now he had the pistol.

Jerome drew back the knife, poised to strike once again.

San heard an explosive crack. Jerome's head whipped backwards as blood, flesh and chips of skull blew across the street toward San. Jerome froze in mid-air, still straddling Tao. Jerome's back was arched and his arms bent backwards as though in surprise.

Tao's gun had dug a gruesome hole in the place where Jerome's left eye socket had been, the bullet exiting somewhere behind his ear. Tao kicked Jerome away. A fine mess of blood and gray matter cushioned Jerome's skull as it cracked wetly against the street. Tao scrambled backwards, as Jerome's lifeless body, crumpled at his feet.

Breathing heavily, Tao clutched at a pain in his chest. He looked down. To his horror, from between his third and fourth rib, protruded the hilt of Jerome's knife. Tao stared at the knife in disbelief. Blood bubbled out of his mouth and over his chin. He reflexively pulled the knife out and threw it away in disgust. But removing the knife only increased the speed with which the blood flowed from the wound. Tao held his hand over the inch wide hole in his chest, but it did not staunch the blood. For a moment, he looked up and down the street, with desperate pleading eyes. But there was no help to be found, and the urgency slowly faded from his face. He fell gently on to his back, his life running out and over the cobbles.

CHAPTER 67

"Jerome?" asked the Prefect tentatively, almost in a whisper, as though he was scared what answer he might get. He knew that Jerome had been shot, but he was not yet sure as to the extent of his injuries. "Get up Jerome!" urged the Prefect. But the Prefect's voice shook betraying his nervousness. The Prefect took two steps toward Jerome before he could see the sodden wreck that was now the left side of Jerome's face. The Prefect's lip curled in disgust and then quivered for a second in sadness. But, there was nothing the Prefect could do for Jerome. He was clearly dead.

The Prefect turned away from Jerome. "We're leaving."

Su-Lin gurgled as the Prefect dragged her around and headed toward the car, keeping her neck locked in the crook of his forearm. With her hands tied behind her back she could do little but follow him meekly.

San saw the Prefect and Su-Lin were about to leave. *It's now or never*. San ran from his hiding place in the shadows between two of the shops screaming, "Wait!"

"San?" Su-Lin's eyes widened in surprise.

"Who are you?" demanded the Prefect, hurriedly

pointing his gun at San.

San stopped advancing and raised his hands in an unthreatening gesture. "I'm the guy with something you want."

The Prefect's brow furrowed, confused by the interruption.

San put his hand inside his jacket.

"Easy there," warned the Prefect with a grim face, unnerved by San's move toward his pocket.

To avoid any confusion, San pulled back his jacket to show he had no concealed weapon. Instead he pulled from his pocket, a large manila envelope. He held it up, showing it to the Prefect.

But the Prefect stood motionless, no less confused.

"No!" shouted Su-Lin. She had immediately grasped what San intended to do. She began struggling with renewed energy, screaming at the top of her lungs, "Don't do it San!"

"Shut up!" snapped the Prefect, his interest piqued as much by Su-Lin's resistance as the appearance of this strange Asian man. The Prefect shook Su-Lin like a rag doll until she ceased her resistance.

San stared at Su-Lin. He was startled by her reaction. He had thought she would be relieved. San had hoped she would be happy to see him.

"I'm listening." The Prefect pulled San's attention back to him, inviting him to explain.

"I have the *Proditio*," said San bluntly.

The Prefect froze. His eyes narrowed as he studied San, still not knowing what to make of him.

"No San," implored Su-Lin. "Please don't do it."

But the Prefect squeezed his forearm around her throat, cutting her off. "Where did you find it?"

"Doctor Chan left us its location before he died." San looked accusingly at the Prefect. "Before you killed him."

There was only two other people who could make sense

of what this man had just said, thought the Prefect, and both of them have died today. It was enough to convince the Prefect that San knew what he was talking about. "And what do you want?"

"I want the girl." San tried his best to nod confidently toward Su-Lin. "Release the girl, and I will give you the *Proditio*."

The Prefect smiled inwardly, surprised that this disaster might end happily after all. "A fair exchange."

But Su-Lin looked wretched, her face torn between helpless and hopeless. "They'll destroy it San," she said quietly, as tears ran down her cheeks. "The truth will be lost forever."

"I said shut up," snarled the Prefect, shaking Su-Lin even more violently by the neck. He turned to San. "I can't just let the girl go, and hope you give me the *Proditio*," continued the Prefect. "Come closer and we'll make the exchange."

San didn't trust the Prefect. This was one of the animals that had tortured Su-Lin, he thought. But while San had the *Proditio*, he knew that he had leverage. San edged his way toward the center of the bridge.

"That's quite close enough," said the Prefect. "Now put the *Proditio* on the ground and step away."

San put the envelope down by the side of the road.

"Now go on." The Prefect shook his pistol, indicating to San that he should back up.

San took a couple of steps backward, and each step was matched by the Prefect approaching the envelope. But San stopped after only a couple of paces.

"What are you doing?" demanded the Prefect anxiously. He punched his gun in the air toward San's threateningly.

"I'm going no further," said San firmly. "Now let the girl go."

The Prefect kept walking until only a couple of steps from the manila envelope. The Prefect's eyes flicked from

San to the envelope. With no further use of Su-Lin, and with the option of using his firearm if something went badly wrong, the Prefect threw Su-Lin forward.

With her arms still tied behind her back, Su-Lin had no way of balancing. She shrieked and stumbled to her knees. She looked despairingly up at San through disheveled hair. Su-Lin silently shook her head at San, tears rolling down her cheeks.

The prefect holstered his pistol, knelt on one knee, and snatched up the envelope. He stood again, to open the envelope and examine its contents. He pulled out one of the photos and a victorious grin spread slowly across his face. There, deep under the layers of paint of Leonardo's painting of The Annunciation, the Prefect read an unmistakably Renaissance Latin text. The *Proditio* was finally his.

"Why San?" asked a forlorn Su-Lin.

San met Su-Lin's gaze. "You're more important than the *Proditio*."

"No I'm not San." Su-Lin said quietly and coldly, slowly shaking her head. "No I'm not."

"You are to me," whispered San, begging Su-Lin to understand.

San thought he could see the faintest of smiles on Su-Lin's lips, as she forced herself up and off her knees, to stand again. But Su-Lin turned away from San and toward the Prefect. She suddenly launched herself at the Prefect, covering the three steps that separated them with surprising speed. The Prefect, so engrossed in the photos of the *Proditio*, barely looked up before Su-Lin charged into him. With her shoulder set low, she charged into the Prefect's chest with all the force she could muster. The Prefect stumbled backwards, grunting in surprise, and dropping the envelope. Driving with her legs, Su-Lin shoved the Prefect back against the railing on the side of the bridge. They hung there for a moment, balanced precariously, before toppling over the edge.

San heard the Prefect scream as they fell, and then the sound of a loud splash. He ran to the Ponte Vecchio's railing and looked over to the river below. But Su-Lin and the Prefect were gone, swallowed by the black, swirling torrent of the Arno river.

EPILOGUE

The Florentine Police Inspector, put down his pen and rocked back in his office chair. He flicked through some of the notes he had taken previously.

San Lee sat patiently, on the other side of a simple bare wooden desk.

He couldn't imagine that Italian Policemen were incredibly well paid. But the inspector wore a finely tailored gray suit, an open necked pink shirt, and a carefully considered two days of stubble across his jaw.

"We still struggle to understand motive," said the Inspector, gesturing extravagantly to underline his frustration. "We have a nameless Chinese man stabbed to death in the middle of the Ponte Vecchio. But, there is no record of him having entered the country and no embassy has claimed him as their own."

San shrugged, sympathetically. He had spent most of the last week, since the incident on the Ponte Vecchio, filling out reports and answering questions. But after having been interviewed by half a dozen different branches of the Italian government, he kept his answers as short and consistent as possible to avoid the process dragging on any longer than it needed to.

"We also have an Italian priest wearing women's clothing." The Inspector rolled his eyes and shook his head. "And half of his skull is missing." The inspector ran his hand through his hair. "Did you see or hear anything on the bridge that might explain what precipitated their disagreement?"

San did not want to appear dismissive of the inspector's question. He waited for a moment, pretending to comb through old memories, before answering simply and firmly, "No."

San had hidden the bronze rat's head sculpture and the photos of the *Proditio* in his hotel room. He had decided almost immediately that he would mention neither of them to the Police. San reasoned that to describe what they were, what they meant, and why they constituted a motive for murder would raise far more questions than it answered. Besides, I still need the bronze sculpture to repay my father's debts, he thought. *And Su-Lin would have never forgiven me if I surrendered the Proditio.*

The Police Inspector nodded, clenching his jaw in frustration. He waited for a couple of seconds to see whether San would volunteer anything new. But when it was clear that San had nothing to add, the Inspector concluded, "Then I think we are done."

With the investigation effectively over for San, the Inspector smiled. "I know this can't have been the easiest week for you." The Inspector stood up and straightened his jacket. "But I would like to express the Italian people's gratitude for the help you have given us in completing our investigation."

"I only wish I could do more," muttered San, quietly and with little conviction.

"I know your trip to Italy has probably been far more eventful than you would have liked." The Inspector walked around the desk and leant on its front edge. "And far longer," he added. "But if there is anything we can do for you, please let us know." The Police Inspector had intended his offer to be a meaningless pleasantry.

"There is one thing." San sought direct eye contact with the detective. "I have a question."

"Please." Although the Inspector was surprised, he gestured for San to continue.

"Did you ever find the body of the girl."

The inspector pressed his fingers together thoughtfully, making sure that when answering such delicate questions he did not accidentally make an embarrassing error of translation. "Later, we recovered the body of another priest. He had been washed several miles downstream." He pursed his lips in distaste. "After several days..." The Inspector shook his head. "Needless to say, it was not pretty. It has been difficult to make an identification." Finally, the inspector put on a solemn expression. "But no. I am afraid we did not find any girl."

San struggled to maintain his composure. "Well thank you Inspector." San stood, and offered his hand to the Inspector.

The Inspector shook his hand firmly.

San maintained a wearied expression until he left the Police Station. But stepping outside into the brisk evening air, and as the last of the sun faded below the horizon, San took a deep breath and allowed himself to smile broadly. *Su-Lin might still be alive!*

www.ingramcontent.com/pod-product-compliance
Lightning Source LLC
Chambersburg PA
CBHW062108170626
46813CB00002B/368

* 9 7 8 9 8 8 1 6 7 0 9 2 2 *